Salmon River Magic

Nez Perce Coven Chronicles

By Lorretta Smith

Star Sapphire Press
Darby, Mt
2019

First edition
First printing 2019
Book design by Lorretta Smith Cover art by Lorretta Smith
Author photo by Renee Knowles

Library of Congress Cataloging in Publication Data Smith,
Lorretta 1972-
Salmon River Magic/ Nez Perce Coven Chronicles / Lorret-
ta Smith -- 1st ed.
ISBN: 978-0-578-21739-0 Library of Congress Control
Number: 2019902017
Star Sapphire Printing / Star Sapphire Press
629 Bridge Lane
Darby, Mt 59829
Printed in the United States of America

Born and raised all over the Northwest, Lorretta makes her home in Darby, Montana where she lives with her two pugs, Lollah Loo and Corona Cerveza, and her Maine Coon Cat, Clyde. They live in the tiny house she built herself on the banks of the Bitterroot River. When she isn't writing, Lorretta enjoys camping, hiking, rafting and kayaking.

Lorretta is divorced with one child, twenty year old son, Cory, who is the love of her life, partner in adventures and comic relief in life. She earned a Bachelors degree from Eastern New Mexico University in Psychology and Sociology. Prior to her writing career, Lorretta worked as a social worker.

Photo by Renee Knowles

Dedication

To my favoritest Uncle, John Jarvis, for his guidance throughout the years and providing me a safety net when needed. Thank you, and Johnny Pail Face for the inspiration for the Morning Salutation.

Thank you, Ronda Lang, Yoga Instructor extraordinaire, for the moves for the Morning Salutation!

And to my father, Mike, for teaching me how to enjoy life.

1

FACING THE RISING sun, I knelt. Child's pose to Mother Earth. *Kiss the Earth. Thank you, Mother, for the water we drink, the scents of the wild, the ground we walk on, the air we breathe, the beauty we see.*

Push up into down dog, walk hands back to feet, inhale deeply, roll up, arms extended at sides, circle arms above, exhale as arms drop into prayer pose. *Thank you, Father Sky, for the sun that rises, the moon that sets, the stars that guide us, the rain that falls from your clouds. Thank you for feeding Mother Earth with your sun and rain.*

I honor my Mother and Father by treating both with great respect. I treat my fellow humans with love and kindness. I continue to learn, exude patience and understanding each day as I walk through life.

Let me keep this day so when I am called I may come to you, Father, with clean hands and straight eyes. When my life fades as the fading sunset, my spirit may come to you without shame. Let my body feed you, Mother Earth, as I continue as a small part in the cycle of life.

Create water and let it rain on Mother Earth. Breathing deeply, I filled my lungs with sweet, clean air. Something interrupted my peace. I tried to ignore the call. I felt the pull building. I arrived in Lewiston less than twenty-four hours ago. Scoping out the lay of the land, I procrastinated introducing myself to the Were Pride, being the new cat in town. I longed to breathe freely prior to subjecting myself to the rule of a new Clan.

Uhhh. Again, I felt the tug of magic. Negativity pulled energy and attempted to deposit residue into the earth. The earth rejected it vehemently. I couldn't find the origination of the magic without communing with nature, literally.

I stood in an ideal spot for communing, a city park. Sighing, I surveyed the trees, looking for the oldest, tallest one. A pine tree reaching higher into the sky than the rest offered my best choice. Placing my right hand on the rough bark, I slipped out of my sandals and ground my bare feet into the lush grass, squishing my toes into the dirt. I closed my eyes, breathing the scent of the Clearwater River deep into my lungs, and pulled energy through the pine tree, up from the ground, into my center. I held it while my mind traveled through astral space, searching for the source.

I felt the ugliness before I found it. Since I didn't know where I teleported to, my mind sought out a pine tree near the origin. With my right hand on the bark and my bare feet buried in grass, I opened my eyes, facing a street of nondescript houses, guarded by a row of cottonwood trees. Magic radiated from a yellow house across the street and several houses away from where I materialized.

A police car parked in front of the house with a cherry red Ford Excursion behind it. A few men stood conversing in front of the house. Two of the men wore uniforms and the others, street clothes. None of them radiated the magic I sensed.

Ambient Wiccan energy flowed from magical talismans adorned by two of the plainclothes men. The source lay within the house. They lacked the abilities to deal with what lay inside.

Unsure of their intentions, I closed my eyes and looked at them again. The two uniforms and one of the plainclothes men radiated lawfulness, a lavender aura. The other two men sported similar auras, lavender with touches of emeralds, the older man with more emeralds. Inquisitiveness. Interesting. The intentions of the men appeared honorable. Breathing deeply, I walked across the street. None of the men noticed me.

They walked towards the front door, with the uniforms leading. An officer knocked, announcing "Nez Perce County Sheriff! Dwayne Reynolds!" He knocked again, receiving no response.

The plainclothes officer stated, "Break the door down!"

"Wait!" I called out, startling them. "The door is warded. Unauthorized entry triggers it." I stooped down, grabbing a handful of grass and dirt. I walked between them and up to the door. As I studied the ward, I explained the mechanics behind it.

"The porch light serves as a ward of intrusion. Breaching the house sets it off. I can't tell for sure what happens, but based on the magic radiating from inside, I think it probably sucks. Electricity from the light powers the ward." I rubbed grass and dirt between my thumb, pointer and middle finger, closed my eyes and touched the fixture, short circuiting the spell. I unlocked the dead bolt and opened the door.

"Who the fuck are you?" asked the plainclothes cop, gaping at me. He wore his badge clipped to the belt loop of his navy blue trousers. A red tie adorned his neck and a blazer concealed a shoulder holster on his left. His right hand moved to the gun.

"My name is Shyenne. Someone performed dark magic here and none of you possess the skills to adequately protect yourselves. You and you," pointing to the emerald aura men, "might stand a chance, depend- ing on your protection talismans, but I doubt it. What are you trying to accomplish?"

Reminding me of Dick Tracy, the older emerald aura guy stated, "We intend to arrest Dwayne Reynolds." He wore no badge or gun. I pushed the door wider, revealing a short, unlit hallway, opening into a larger room. Coats lined the wall on the right hand side, behind the door. "Does the hallway appear safe?" asked Dick Tracy.

After scanning the entry, I nodded. "Yes. I don't see anything."

One of the uniforms yelled into the house, "Nez Perce County Sheriffs. We are entering the house! Any and all persons inside identify yourself!"

I moved to the front of the group, stopping them. Using some of the dirt I picked up outside, I created a ball and fed energy into it, creating a bubble. I set the bubble to encompass them. This provided protection from most magics. We moved through the hall and into the great room.

A bottle of water sat on the coffee table. Dumping the contents into into my hand, it formed as if it held in a glass. I moved towards the closed door at the south end of the room. A rage of magic built behind the door, heat accumulated into a ball. The intention behind the spell was to kill us. A lesser emotion of excitement radiated from the casting. The door would open into the room and swing to my right.

Using the water, I formed a bunch of thin, long, sharp icicles. I stood with my back against the wall and carefully turned the doorknob. A man with long brown stringy hair rushed out, cupping a fireball. He raised it in his right hand, winding his arm back to pitch it towards the men. Half of my icicles flew into the witch and the other half pierced the fireball, popping it.

3

A mass of wet ash bounced off the protection bubble. The mage dropped like a sack of potatoes.

The uniforms jumped him, cuffing his wrists behind his back, with zip ties. Plainclothes guy read him his rights. The situation appeared under control.

Scanning the room, I noticed books shelved on a side wall. One caught my eye. It oozed black, oily yuckiness. Books typically didn't generate auras. I'd never met a book with an aura. Otherwise occupied with the suspect, the men secured, searched and identified him. I touched the binding and "moved" the book to my backpack.

Dick Tracy turned his attention from Dwayne, to me. "Would you mind doing a walk-through with us to ensure no other traps exist?"

"Sure," my curiosity piqued. Not every day I found an evil book.

To the left, an open archway led to the kitchen. The sink overflowed with dishes. Precarious stacks of mail and empty fast food containers littered the table. The garbage stunk like rotting fruit. Flies buzzed above. One major drawback to being a Were cat? Heightened smell. I didn't see any magical auras lurking about. The kitchen led to a laundry room and outside exit. As with the kitchen, the laundry room stunk. Piles of clothing reeked of sweat and soil. Nothing here. Oddly, no ward protected the back door. In the great room, officers escorted Dwayne to the patrol car.

I entered the doorway he attacked from, leading into a hallway with one door to the left and two doors on the right. Opening the first door revealed a bathroom making the kitchen look and smell sterile. No magic, so I quickly closed it. The next one led to a spare room. An old patchwork quilt lay on the bed. A layer of dust coated the surfaces but otherwise tidy. The door to the left opened into his bedroom. It appeared cleaner than expected. His bed was a tangle of gray cotton sheets and a brown bedspread. Dirty clothes spilled out of a laundry basket. A dresser stood against the wall with a change jar on top, his wallet and a watch. An open window looked out into a small backyard, pale yellow curtain waving in a slight breeze. I did a quick scan and noted a magical aura around Dwayne's wallet. A find spell, in case he lost it.

Witches keep a spot dedicated to magic. Remnants of past works would be visible to me. I looked around the room, then walked back into the hall. I measured the spare room and bathroom versus the master bed- room. I walked back and gazed at the wall bordering the great room.

"Do you sense something?" Behind me, Dick gazed at the wall.

"A room may be concealed behind this wall." A couple pictures depicting mountain scenes hung on the paneling. Wear marks brushed the muddy brown carpet. Taking the pictures off the wall revealed a wire hook. I pulled it and a door swung open.

I felt the remnants of magic emanate from within. I didn't see any wards so I entered into complete darkness. Pulling a pine cone petal from the pocket of my cutoffs, I whispered, *luz del sol.* The petal provided illumination into a windowless, long, narrow room.

I groaned inwardly. I hate small, windowless rooms. A bookshelf full of books stood against the long wall. Quickly scanning the bindings, nothing noteworthy appeared, just magic school texts or books found at a local grocery store.

Adjacent to the wall hung a large painting covering the entire surface. The painting disturbed me. It depicted a goat man standing in Hell, with demonic beings kneeling. The style of the painting was akin to kindergarteners on a pixie stick sugar high. The shit I get myself in to.

I sighed, entering, sidekick followed. Artificial light suddenly lit up the room. Sidekick located a light switch. This room appeared sterile, compared to the rest of the house. To ensure no contamination during casting, witches require a clean area.

In the center of the room, lay an altar. Half burnt black candles stood at each corner, with warm wax dripping down the sides onto a black velvet cloth. An open spell book lay on top.

I glanced at the page. A spell for personal wealth written in the style of Dr. Seuss. Rolling my eyes, I flipped through the book, curious if the spells improved. I laughed out loud when I reached one for washing dishes. "Wishes for the fishes to come off the dishes. Wow. After seeing the kitchen, I'm guessing this is a work in progress," shaking my head. "What are you arresting him for? Crimes against poetry? Illegal use of a metaphor? Maintaining a toxic waste site?"

Sidekick laughed. "Actually, purchasing illegal spell components without a license."

To ensure magic doesn't run rampant or spells aren't cast by witches unable to control them, it's illegal to purchase dangerous spell components without a license. Some components are illegal depending on what it is and how it's obtained.

I laughed. "This guy can't wash his dishes, let alone cast a real spell. "What did he try to obtain?"

"Pituitary gland from a Were creature." Sidekick replied, reading the bindings of the books in the bookcase.

Pituitary gland? From a Were? Not a typical component. Spells in- volving healing or morphing utilized the organ. But a Were? Either way, those type of spells lay well beyond his abilities. For that matter, a fireball and protection ward were too difficult, given his skills. Why would he purchase dangerous spell components?

I groaned again. "He's obtaining spell components for someone else. Someone who doesn't want anyone to know." I shook my head and walked out of the room, into the bedroom then out to the great room. I strolled out the front door to a pine tree and 'ported to the farthest spot along the Snake River I had explored since leaving home.

2

I RAN UPRIVER, allowing the smells to invade my senses, my paws sinking in the mud. I searched for the intersection of the Snake and the Salmon Rivers. The scents of the wild, the wet, sailed with the wind. Cars, people, signs of civilization disappeared as I bounded along the muddy bank, following a worn game trail. The mixture of scents relayed how many critters, and my people of old, used the trail over years, decades, centuries. I inhaled the scent of the Salmon River. It smelled different than the Snake or the Clearwater. The Snake reeked of people and industry. The Clearwater, of wildness, pine trees with a hint of cedar. The Salmon, it emanated wildlife, fish, gold and gems. My excitement grew as I loped towards the convergence. Though, not as powerful as Lewiston, where the three rivers combined, the magical energy coursed stronger for me. Water and earth mixed, strengthening my power.

My paws pounded against the old trail. I thought of those who passed before me. The Nez Perce Indians traversed it for fishing, hunting, transportation back and forth, following the seasons. A major part of their cul- ture included the Salmon and Steelhead fish returning to their "birthing" site to spawn annually.

Bison proved of great importance to the tribes, as well. They relied on the meat, and more. The hides were used for teepees, clothing, blankets, and moccasins. Each season, traveling hundreds of miles, warriors from the tribes hunted migrating bison across what is now Montana, Idaho, and Wyoming.

Scents faded as time tried to wash away the tribes, slower than that of the white man. My heart ached for the tribes lost in the white man's need to control what Mother Nature created.

From my mother, I'm the product of Native People, the Nez

Perce, and the Hopi. I grew up with history of both. While their histories differ, the white man persecuted them the same.

Suddenly, I reached it. The convergence. The power! The earthiness of the Salmon and the strength of the Snake. I filled my lungs with the scents. I sucked magics from the earth into my claws, my paws, up my haunches, along my spine, into my center, mixing water and earth magics into a tornado.

I raced up the Salmon River. I didn't run too far before I saw a channel entering into the Salmon. It created an island between the Salmon and the convergence of the two rivers. The current appeared strong here. *Probably shouldn't try to swim across.* I thought to myself. *I'd end up half way back to Lewiston.*

I 'ported to the island, facing the bank I just ran up. I loped counter- clockwise around the land isle. The first point was where the Salmon entered into the Snake. I ran along the bank of the Snake, heading upriver. I loped for a little while before I reached the point where a channel of the Snake cut through, creating an island between the two.

I loped along the shore of the island following the channel of the Snake to the Salmon. Half way across, I noticed a sign on the other side of the channel. Surprisingly, it was a real estate sign. For sale. Somehow, I missed the run down log cabin nestled back in the trees. Cabin wasn't an accurate description. More like a guest lodge. It stood several stories high with lots of windows, many broken or boarded up. Some logs appeared half rotted.

I gazed at the large, U shaped building. Leaping into the river, the current flowed easily and I swam to the other side. I shook water out of my fur as I walked up to the sign. A water proof box held brochures describing the property. I chuffed my laughter. Not too many people hung around to read a brochure, here.

I changed from kitty to person and took one out of the box. It read: Hells Canyon Hotel. Historic stopping point for boat traffic headed down the Salmon and Snake Rivers to Lewiston. Ten bedrooms, a formal dining room, a breakfast nook, patios for each room overlooking the rivers, great room, bar, library, kitchen, all wood heat on one hundred acres. It listed the price. Money meant nothing to me. Literally. I held cat form for a good part of my formative years and didn't grasp the concept of numbers.

I opened a portal and took out a pair of shorts, t-shirt and sandals. *Might as well grab my phone.* I snapped a picture of the sign. I dressed quickly, stuffing the cell in my back pocket.

I walked to the rickety front porch. Boards covered the first floor doors and windows. But not the second. Using kitty strength, I leapt to the patio above me. The floorboards felt soft and kind of rotted, but held my weight, if I placed my feet, gingerly.

The patio door was locked, but a cracked window lay beside the door knob. Using my elbow, I broke the pane out and reached in to unlock it. The door swung open and I entered a nice size room, dominated by a queen bed with an old patchwork quilt and two plump feather pillows. The floor proved far more stable inside. A log end table stood next to the bed with an oil lamp on it. Opening two slider doors revealed a closet.

Exiting a pine door led to a hallway lined with windows displaying the wildness out back. Pine trees punctuated rock cliff outcroppings with multiple caverns. Perfect kitty dens!

Taking a left in the hall, the number six marked the next door. I revealed a beige room similar to the last. Door number eight lay at the end of the hallway. Wow!

It opened into the Salmon River! Windows covered the wall overlooking the water as it tumbled towards the Snake River. A stone fireplace was off to the left. Conflicting views of the rivers and the forest out back provided all the decoration. Larger than the other rooms, more of a suite, I saw a bathroom off to the left and a walk-in closet to the right. A large bed made of logs faced the convergence of the rivers in a sun filled nook. Boards obstructed part of the view from the windows. But I saw the potential of this room, this house, this haven.

The rest of the upstairs included more bedrooms with another suite at the far end. The view fell onto the Snake River and the island between the two rivers. It had a spectacular view, but not like the view from the first suite. A gentle winding staircase reached to the first floor. A small dining nook and a formal dining area led into a kitchen. The hardwood floors desperately needed cleaning and care. The kitchen was empty of appliances, but a bar and counter top made of long cut beetle kill blue pine added all the character. The kitchen boasted views of the Snake and the island. As with the rest of the building, many of the windows were boarded up or broken out.

Back through the dining areas, I found the great room, with panoramic views, if the windows weren't boarded. Above, lay a mezzanine floor. The great room revealed a hall with doors to the left and right. The right led to a library and sitting room with views of the back. The room to the left was completely empty. At the end of the hall, I discovered a large open room the same size and views as the suite I fell in love with.

In the backyard, I changed back to a kitty. Leaping from rock to rock I reached the windy top, gazing at the rivers. I leapt down to one of the caverns where I could see over the lodge but found shelter from the wind. I curled up and slept.

3

UHHH. I PROCRASTINATED long enough. I needed to present myself to the Were Tiger Pride. But before I did, I made cosmetic changes to my appearance. My burnt copper hair with platinum highlights I bled to a strawberry blond. My emerald eyes changed to forest agate. I added padding to my slender form. I hoped the Pride would ignore me if I ap- peared dull.

I dressed in a pair of gray slacks and a black knit top. A little warm for early summer in Lewiston, but I wanted to appear dowdy. As much as I hate wearing shoes, I put on a pair of gray flats. I readied a protection bubble spell, just in case. I cast it in a petal off a pine cone and placed it in my pocket. I couldn't enter with weapons. They would search me. Between earth and water, I can almost always find spell components in case of an emergency. I didn't want to openly use magic. The less the Pride knew about me, the safer I would be. Sighing deeply, I 'ported half a block from the front gate.

The Pride Home set back at the end of a cul de sac, in the Heights above Clarkston. Lewiston lay on the Idaho side of the convergence and Clarkston was across the rivers in Washington. A couple other houses lined the street before the home. From the smell, I noted Weres resided there. A stone wall as tall as me encompassed the house, disappearing into pine trees.

A wolf in human form sat in a small building guarding the entrance. I casually walked up to the gate. "I am Shyenne. I belong to no Pride. I present myself to the Leader of the Asotin Were Pride." Protocol dic- tated Weres must notify the clan, when entering another Were's territory. Lewiston and Clarkston belonged to the Asotin Were Pride.

The guard, clad in black denim jeans and a black silk button down shirt, scrutinized me. His eyes said he found me unim-

11

pressive. Perfect. Just the look I hoped for. He picked up his cell and informed someone of my presence.

"Alright." He ended the call, triggering the gate to open enough for me to enter. "Follow the road to the main entrance and wait at the door."

I nodded, entering. The circular driveway enclosed a water fountain. I walked up to the front door, noticing a camera pointed at the entrance. After a few moments, the door opened, revealing a tall man with brown hair and brown cat eyes. "Enter," he said in a deep voice. Like the guard, he sported all black. He obviously worked out. His muscles had muscles.

I walked into a foyer. A door opened to the right and left. Straight ahead, the foyer led to a hallway. Muscles said in a deep voice, "Up against the wall. You must be searched prior to meeting with the Pride."

I acquiesced. His strong muscular hands slid up my right leg, scraping my crotch and down my left. He slipped his hands along my right arm and then my left, performing a very thorough search. Satisfied I harbored no weapons, he led me down the left hall, passed several doors into an open room.

Quite a few people milled about. Everyone was a Were of some sort. I carefully scanned the room, searching for the Pride Leader. No one jumped out at me as a magic user and I didn't want to alert anyone I was a witch. I spotted him, Kyle McCormack. He stood against a fireplace mantle, holding a crystal glass with scotch and ice. I hate the smell of scotch. My grandfather drank scotch.

I approached him. "I am Shyenne. I belong to no Pride. I present myself to the Leader of the Asotin Were Pride," I said, standing tall. Not wanting to draw attention to myself, I didn't want to seem like a victim, either. Victims don't last long.

"Why don't you belong to a Pride?" A Scottish accent hinted in his tone. "I was born as a bobcat. My Pride considered me an aberration. My father died recently. Without him, I am no longer welcome," I provided the abbreviated version.

He raised an eyebrow at my admission and scrutinized me closer. Prejudice still ran rampant within Were communities. "Are you educated?" I heard the skepticism in his voice.

"My Pride felt an education was wasted upon me. I couldn't maintain human form until adolescence."

"There is no place for you here. You aren't breedable, uneducated, no skills." Kyle drank his scotch, dismissing me.

"I want her."

A female laughed. "Malachi, why in the world do you want her?" The derision in her voice would have been insulting, if I hadn't been used to it.

I turned to the man. He wore a talisman of protection. I glanced at his aura, gulping my response. His aura appeared similar but unlike anything I ever saw. Oddly, it was reminiscent of Dick Tracy from the wannabe witch house earlier. Lavender, emeralds, with spikes of sapphires. My brother, Bane, was the only person I knew with sapphires. Bane oozed sapphires, Malachi sported spikes. Bane told me my aura glittered with them. I could see others auras, but not mine.

"Malachi, she's ugly, uneducated. You don't want to risk children with her. We need to send her away." Kyle declared.

"That favor you owe me, Kyle. I'm cashing it in now." Malachi said, stepping forward. How had I not noticed him? Malachi was tall, several inches taller than me. His long, black, wavy hair fell past his shoulders. He wore a pair of leather pants clinging to his legs, hugging his hips. His olive t-shirt emphasized his pectoral muscles and biceps. His hazel eyes almost melted me. Yum.

I opened a mind link to him. Even though his outward appearance seemed calm and nonchalant, he was anxious. He needed to protect me? I didn't get that. Nobody protected me.

I glanced at Kyle. He appeared shocked, then smiled. "The debt is free and clear, for her?" He asked incredulously.

"Yep." Man of few words, after my own heart. In his mind, he thought, *Ahhh, Dad. Call me now.* I pushed his plea forward.

"Okay!" Kyle swept his arm from me to Malachi. "She's yours!" Just then, Malachi's phone started playing, *The Leader of the Band*.

"Oh, that's my Dad. Hang on. Hey, Dad. I'm in middle of something. Dinner? Okay. Where and when? That works. See ya soon." I felt his sense of relief as he ended the call.

"Shyenne, you're with me. I hate to grab the girl and run, but I need to catch my father. He's trying to recruit me," Malachi explained with a devil- ish smile, meeting me part way across the room. He put his left hand to my back and none too gently, pushed me towards the hallway.

Just get the hell out of here. I heard Malachi think.

I couldn't agree more. I replied as we exited the room.

Did you just talk to me? Malachi thought.

I did.

Malachi opened one of the closed doors in the hallway. It led to a carport. Malachi pointed to a blue sports car and said, "This one's mine. Get in." He pulled the key out of his pocket. It beeped twice and the doors unlocked.

Being claustrophobic, I really hate vehicles. I swallowed hard. I needed to leave with Malachi and was curious as to his reaction towards me. And his aura. Okay, and his body.

Malachi started the car, pulled out of the carport and into the driveway. He drove slowly to the gate as it slid open, waving at the guard. Once we passed, he shifted and increased speed exponentially. Again, I swallowed down my stomach. Breathing a sigh of relief, "Drop the disguise. I want to see what you really look like." I looked at him for a moment, then let my features return to normal. He glanced at me. His mouth fell open, the car swerved and I squeaked. He quickly righted the vehicle.

"I possess enough innate magic to see your disguise and your abilities.

Lying to the Pride is very bad. What are you?" He demanded.

"I stated the truth, but omitted I'm a witch. My father was a Were bobcat and my mother was a witch. I try not to mention it as it tends to make introduction time even more uncomfortable. Why did you stand up for me?" I braced myself against the dash as he merged with traffic. Vehicles surrounded us. I inhaled deeply, trying to steady my nerves.

"I see auras. You have the most beautiful aura. When I saw it, I knew I had to help you." Malachi answered, weaving around cars.

"You're aura is pretty cool too." His intentions seemed protective? No one ever tried to protect me, other than Bane.

"I'll tell you about yours if you tell me about mine." Malachi said in a deep, teasing voice.

"Deal." I had a good idea what mine looked like. Bane and I spent hours dissecting each other's auras. But it would be a good measure of his abilities to compare what Bane told me.

"You need a dress for dinner with my dad. Where are you staying?" Malachi slowed as we entered downtown Clarkston.

14

"Just along the Snake River."

Malachi stopped for a red light and looked at me. Our gazes locked for what seemed like an eternity. His hazel eyes surrounded me in the warmth of the forest. Old growth trees stood as sentinels while ferns blanket the floor. Squirrels scattered, birds chirped. A horn honked, breaking the moment.

Malachi put the car in gear and drove along Diagonal Street to the bridge adjoining Lewiston and Clarkston. At the confluence of the Snake, Salmon and the Clearwater Rivers, I breathed in deeply, swallowing energy, pushing it to my center and through my extremities.

"Whatcha doin?" Malachi looked askance at me. The narrow draw bridge didn't leave room to be inattentive while driving.

"Just refilling my chi. The confluence is a very strong magical point for me." We drove off the bridge and entered Lewiston.

Malachi pulled into a parking lot in front of a dress shop on main street. The mannequins in the window wore beautiful, skimpy dresses.

We exited the vehicle. Behind his car, Malachi assessed me. "Wow. You are the most beautiful creature I have ever seen."

I blushed and looked to the ground. "Thanks." I mumbled.

We walked into the boutique. I hate shopping for clothes. Usually, my sister shops for me.

I followed Malachi as we walked around the racks. He found two dresses, grabbing an aqua blue and an emerald green. "You're about a size six? Try these."

I entered a dressing room and tried the blue silk first. It brought out more of the blue in my eyes and offered a stark contrast to my coppery hair with the platinum highlights. It showed off my dark skin, hugging my curves. The spaghetti straps crisscrossed in back, tying at my neck, dangling rhinestone encrusted balls on the ends.

I walked out to show Malachi. He looked me up and down, caressing my skin with his eyes. He swirled his left pointer finger and wrist, indicating to turn around. The silk mini skirt twirled. "We'll take that one," a smile in his voice.

Next, I tried the emerald satin. The green of my eyes leapt out. With my dark skin, it gave me an earthy look. The front and back necklines V-ed, diamond cutouts on the sides. The skirt hugged my thighs.

15

Malachi pulled out a credit card. "Leave that one on." "I suppose I need to wear shoes?"

"Yep. What size do you wear?"

"I have some. I'll grab my clothes." I returned to the dressing room, opened a portal to my closet, threw my clothes in and grabbed bamboo gladiator style sandals adorned with emeralds on gold braided strings.

Malachi flirted with the sales girl while paying for my dresses. The sales girl's name tag said "Carly". She blushed profusely as she handed Malachi his card.

"Ready?" He asked me, his eyes appraising my face, breasts, waist, lingering on my crotch, sliding down my legs, to my toes, then slowly his eyes returned to mine.

"Yes." I smiled as he placed his hand on my back, his thumb caressed my spine, opening the door with his right. We walked to his car. He beeped it open and I climbed in.

He slid into the driver's seat, "Where did your shoes come from?" "I opened a portal to my closet and grabbed them."

"Where's your closet?"

"In a cave in the rain forest."

Malachi raised an eyebrow, pulling into another parking lot. "Okay." We stopped at Mario's Restorante. Malachi held the door as we entered.

The maitre 'd recognized him. "Mr. Delrikkio, your father and brother already arrived. Follow me."

Malachi walked slightly behind me with his left hand gently caressing the bare skin peaking through the cutouts of my dress. I surveyed the restaurant patrons. Several different kinds of Weres. I felt some people with magical abilities, but none posed a threat. I looked at the table we headed towards. To my surprise, Dick Tracy and his sidekick were seated. I glanced over my right shoulder at Malachi, quizzically.

What? Malachi asked me.

I sort of encountered them yesterday.

Malachi's father and brother stood as we arrived at the table. "Dad, Dylan, this is Shyenne. Shy, my father, Ryan and brother, Dylan." Malachi made the introductions.

Dylan punched Malachi hard in the right bicep. "I swear to fuck- ing god, Malachi, how in the hell do you always get the gorgeous witch?" Dylan exclaimed, exasperated.

"Ah, well you know. I'm naturally lucky." Laughing, Malachi rubbed his muscle, while taking a seat. "We met at the Pride house. Where did you run into Shyenne?"

"We assisted the police issuing an arrest warrant on a witch. She just showed up."Dick Tracy, Ryan, placed his napkin on his lap, raising his gaze to me. "What were you doing there?"

"I felt magic residue being forced into the earth and the earth repelled it. When I searched for the source, I ended up at the house."I shrugged my shoulders, opening the menu. The three men gaped at me.

"You want a job?" Ryan asked me. The waiter came to our table. After placing our orders, Ryan, again, offered me a position. "Seriously. We need a witch of your caliber."

"What do you do, exactly?"Picking up a piece of bread from the basket on the table, I tore off a piece and put it in my mouth.

"Typically, we work as consultants on situations where paranormal ac- tivities occur. We assist law enforcement or are hired privately to investigate and handle paranormal disturbances." Ryan drank some of his ice water. "Currently, we're assisting the Sheriff's office with a significant increase in witches obtaining controlled magic components without licenses."

I hadn't considered employment. Hell, I hadn't thought about where to live. I just wanted out from my grandfather's Pride. A job solved many needs. I never had a job before. "Sure."

The waiter brought our drinks. "Tell me about yourself." Inwardly, I sighed. I hate this part. "My father was a Were bobcat. My mother was a witch."

"Are you from the Lewiston area?" Dylan asked, picking up a piece of bread. The waiter returned carrying our salads.

"Kooskia actually. We grew up on the Nez Perce reservation. My father's father is the leader of the Clearwater Pride. My mother's family resides outside of Lowell. Mom died a few years after my birth. My dad died recently. My grandfather hates me and excommunicated me from the Pride."

"What type of magic do you practice?" Dylan asked.

"Earth magic primary, water magic secondary and am classified as a catalyst."

"A catalyst? I've never heard that before." Dylan commented.

"I make things happen. I don't worry too much about the 'how'. I just accomplish what I want to accomplish," I explained.

"Only one coven classifies witches by type. The Nez Perce

Coven." Ryan furrowed his brow.

"Alberto Mendoza is my uncle. He has been our teacher of magic for most of our lives." I took a bite out of my salad. Ryan stared at me wide eyed, then dug into his entree.

After we finished eating, we walked out to the parking lot. Ryan and Dylan walked over to the Excursion they drove before. I hesitated in front of Malachi's car. "I really hate riding in cars. I can teleport us to your house."

Malachi looked surprised, then hollered, "Yo, Bro! Take my car!" Hardly able to contain his excitement, Malachi threw the keys to Dylan.

"What do we do?"

I looked around and spotted a pine tree. "Do you have a pine tree near your home?"

"Yes, we have several blue spruces lining the driveway."

We walked over to the blue spruce. I slipped out of my shoes and dug my toes through the pine needles into the dirt. Placing an arm around Malachi, "Put both arms around me. We need to touch body to body, as much as possible."

"Oh, the horrible things I endure in the study of magic." Malachi rolled his eyes, wrapping his arms around me. My head fell at chin level. My breasts rubbed against his chest. My thighs pressed into his. I felt Malachi's cock press into my groin. We fit together perfectly. I drew a breath in. A tingle coursed between us, like an electrical current. I looked into Malachi's eyes as he gazed into mine. I lost all thought. In his, a river flowed through a canyon with pine trees lining the banks. The untamed water tumbled over rocks, plummeting into pools, racing towards the convergence.

"Now what?" Malachi's question interrupted my ride down the river of his eyes. Shivering, I shook the image out of my mind.

"Close your eyes and focus on the blue spruce tree in your yard." I looked into his mind and saw the tree. I took the picture of the tree into my mind. I placed my left hand on the spruce tree. The pine needles poked and scratched my arm and fingers. Closing my eyes, I focused on the spruce. Malachi's body melded into mine as I melded us into the earth. We became one. We flowed. Slowly, I unmelded us from the earth. With a sigh, I separated molecule by molecule, feeling pine needles scratching my arm, hand and feet. "Open your eyes, Malachi."

Malachi and I appeared in the driveway of a house over-looking the Snake River. "That is too cool!" Malachi said as he walked up the steps. I started after him, then stopped, sensing the working of a spell. It wasn't active but I felt the intent. The intention forbade entrance to magic users. I pinpointed the spell attached to a porous lava rock. The spell had been cast and placed but not hooked up to an energy source or initiated. Seemed odd to go through the trouble to conjure the spell but not use it.

"Is this ward supposed to be active?" I asked as he opened the door. "Yep.

Is it not letting you in?"

"Oh, I can come inside. It isn't active." I informed him. "Out of respect for your father I won't enter without his per-mission."

Malachi bobbed his head back and forth, plopping down on the steps next to me. The periwinkle blue house was in-credibly large. It sat back a little from the neighbors, with trees providing a sense of privacy. From this side, I couldn't see the Snake River, but I smelled it. Blue spruce trees lined the drive-way of white crushed rock. The closely planted trees obscured the view from the driveway towards the neighbors' homes.

Ryan and Dylan pulled into a few minutes later. "Nice to see the ward works," Ryan stated, walking up to the porch.

"Actually, it doesn't. I could enter but out of respect for your intention, I chose to wait until your arrival." I responded.

"The spell is easily detected and a personal friend of mine whom I trust implicitly conjured it." Ryan said with disdain.

"Do you know the mechanics of a spell?" I questioned.

"Hum a few bars and I'll try to catch on." Ryan smirked.

I raised an eyebrow at his tone, turned around, walked up the stairs, opened the door, walked through the door, created three balls of water and rotated them in circles orbiting his head. Then, I splatted the balls at his feet. "I suggest re-evaluat-ing your relationship with this person."

He was obviously shocked.

"The caster conjured and placed it in the lava rock correct-ly. I can sense it and it can be detected. But it wasn't initiated or activated. I could activate it for you, but I would cast a better spell. The way it's cast, I could manipulate it to get in. If I could, so could others."

"Malachi, can we trust her?" Ryan's skepticism dripped

from his tone.

"Dad, we can trust her with our lives. She has the most beautiful aura I've ever seen. As soon as I saw her, I just knew..." Malachi's voice trailed off as he locked eyes with me.

Ryan took a deep breath, exhaled slowly and nodded "I apologize, Shyenne. I didn't treat you with the respect you deserve. Thank you for your help and I would greatly appreciate if you cast a better spell."

I don't think anyone ever apologized to me in my life. Dumbfounded and speechless, I nodded.

"All right. Let me gather a few things." I stepped off the porch and walked along the left side of the house. As I walked around the corner, the yard opened up to a beautiful overview of the Snake River. The perfectly manicured lawn looked like green waves leading to the river.

I picked a hand full of grass and shook the dirt into my right hand. A table and four chairs set on a patio near a swimming pool. A bull pine tree stood sentinel over the backyard, providing shade and protection. I picked up a pine cone and broke off a petal. Pine cone petals were my "go to" for spell vessels.

I breathed in deeply of the river, smelling the pine trees guarding the Salmon River as it journeyed through to her convergence with the Snake. I smelled the canyons holding back the forests. I smelled the musk of wild animals that relied on the river. I smelled the fish swimming in the waters. I felt minerals, gems, gold and silver hidden by the river.

I let the essence of the river fill me. I let the earth in my hand and at my bare feet seep into my soul. I closed my eyes and found the right words. I imbued the words with the essence of the river and the soul of the earth. Malachi, Ryan and Dylan stood at the patio watching me. "You want your sons to be able to enter, correct?"

"Yes."

"Is there anyone of your blood who can't enter? Ryan thought a moment, then shook his head.

"It will be stronger with Malachi's blood." I took the pointy end of the pine cone petal and pricked Malachi's finger, smearing his blood over the petal. Then, walking clockwise, I walked the perimeter of the house. I pulled a crystal the size of a dime out of my pocket. Along with pine cone petals, I carried crystals at all times. A wrought iron stylized sun hung by the French door. I placed the petal behind one of the rays and the crystal where it would be warmed by the actual sun. Initiating the spell, a protec- tion field encompassed the house. The crystal held the spell while the sun provided continual power.

"Wow. I just learned more about spell casting than I ever did at school. Shit! That was awesome!" Dylan laughed after the spell initiated.

"That was incredible." Ryan agreed. "Now that we are safe, shall we enter? Shyenne, you are welcome in our home."

We walked into the foyer where a couple of jackets hung on hooks above a bench. The foyer opened up into a kitchen. Black appliances accented the kitchen with cherry wood cabinets. A tan, black with flecks of red granite counter top covered a bar with cherry wood bar stools surrounding it. A light tan color, the kitchen felt very homey. To the left lay a formal dining room. The men continued through the kitchen - dining room area into the great room with a sweeping staircase leading to the second floor. The light tan great room sported black leather couches and a couple recliners with a bar set up to the left. The great room provided a panoramic view of the Snake and Salmon River as well as Clarkston and the Heights.

"Wow!" I walked over to the floor to ceiling windows displaying the river to the sky. The house was on a point overlooking the river. Upriver, I could see for what seemed like miles, almost to Hells Canyon Park. Downriver, I saw where the convergence of the rivers occurred. "On a full moon, I bet the view is spectacular! With the full moon reflecting off the river, in ripples!" I shivered. Not sure if it was the thought of the river or the full moon.

I don't know how long I stared out the windows before I returned to the present. The guys watched a baseball game on tv. I noticed a book- case. I went over to check out the titles. Quite the menagerie, everything from Chaucer, Shakespeare, Stephen King, Scott Cunningham, Laurell Hamilton. I found an old text entitled, *The Irish Druidic Handbook*. "Ryan, is it okay if I read this book?"

"Huh. Someone who reads voluntarily. Please, be my guest! I'd love your take on it when you finish." Ryan looked up from the game.

"Like my uncle says, 'You are never done learning about

magic.' You never know what you might be able to do using magic from here and there." I took the book and sat next to Malachi on the couch.

Ryan looked at me, surprised. "Can you use magic from different practices?" He swirled a drink around his ice in his glass.

I nodded my head. "Mostly our magic is a fair amount of Shamanistic practice, but I mix in a little Wiccan, a little Druid, whatever feels right for the circumstances," I shrugged my shoulders as I opened the book. Wow. It was published in 1615, prior to the Mayflower sailing to America. Huh. Touching each page reverently, I read about the author, publication and dedication before starting in on the actual text. It didn't take long before I found myself lost in the Druidic World of yester centuries ago.

4

MALACHI AND I walked upstairs to his room. He opened the last door on the right of a long hallway. The room faced the river, through open French doors, dominated by a king size poster bed. Off to the right, a door led to the bathroom. Large mirrors covered one wall. A two headed shower stall was visible. I couldn't see the commode but it must have been tucked in somewhere.

"I've waited to get you out of that dress ever since you put it on," Malachi walked behind me, brushing my hair to the side. He tugged the zipper down to my hips, pushing the dress forward, baring my back, exposing my breasts. He grasped my hair in his right hand, pulling my neck back, kissing the exposed carotid artery. His left hand snaked around me and cupped my breast. I moaned at the quick, intense onslaught. His left hand kneaded my breast, pinching my nipple into erectness.

I did the only thing I could, grinding my hips into his. He moaned as he grew. Pulling my neck further, he crushed his lips to mine. Our tongues dueled, exploring, fighting for dominance. His right hand hopelessly entangled in my hair, his left pushed the dress over my hips and it slid to the floor. With nothing on but a thong, I ground my hips into his again. I reached behind me and unzipped his black leather pants. He wore nothing underneath. I turned, breaking our kiss.

I looked up into his eyes and sank to my knees, his hand still entangled in my hair. He smiled as I took his rapidly growing cock in one hand and slid it into my mouth. I sucked it hard, taking as much down my throat as possible. I worked it in and out, massaging his balls. Moaning, he pulled me up by my hair. Stepping out of his pants, he pushed me down on the bed, pulling his shirt off, following me down. I parted my legs and

23

he rammed his cock deep into me. I moaned as he slid through my slickness and teased me deep inside. I arched my back giving him more access as he quickly pumped in and out of me. I wrapped my legs around him, urging him to pump harder. I roared as he punched my g spot with his cock, again and again. I arched my back and held him tight against me as my orgasm dove through me and plunged over the waterfall. I dug my nails into his back as I continued to hold him for each wave I rode. He yanked on my hair, loosening my grasp, pumping into me, hard, again.

I gazed into his eyes as we fought for dominance, for control, for release. Well, release for me, again. He pounded into me as I accepted it, my juices providing all the lubrication we needed. I contracted my vaginal muscles, squeezing his cock. He moaned in pleasure. With each thrust, I pulled on him, he teased me by not entering me fully. I whimpered my disappointment and he laughed. I continued to use my muscles to milk him as he thrust. I felt his body tense, then he pounded as deep into me as possible. I held him tight inside, as he tickled my g spot. We both came to the edge of the waterfall and rode over together, wave after wave rolling through me, and I pushed it through him, and he pushed it back to me, again and again. We shared the orgasm between us, pushing the waves through each molecule into the other. As our minds intertwined, my essence seeped into Malachi's, and his seeped into mine. Our minds, thoughtless, as the physical needs of our bodies overtook everything else.

I don't know how long it took before the waves ceased, our breathing eased. It took even longer to separate from one into two. When my sentient thought returned, the weight of Malachi held me down. His body touched mine, skin to skin, pore to pore. Every available surface touched either him or the bed. His right hand still helplessly entangled in my hair. His cheek rested against mine. His breathing, almost normal in my ear, my breath, almost normal in his. Slowly unmelding from one to two, both physically and mentally. I never felt sex like this. I experienced sex as a cat and as a human, but nothing like this. Was it because of the magic between us? The Were cat?

"Holy fuck. I mean that was a holy fuck! Wow! Babydoll, I never orgasmed like that before. Must be the witchy witch voodoo sex appeal!" Malachi laughed as he rolled to his back, pulling me onto his chest. "It might take a shit load of Pantene conditioner to disentangle my hand from your hair."

I laughed as I kissed his pec. "Yeah. Wow!" I couldn't offer more than that yet. Still in recovery mode. His left hand caressed the curve from my breast to my hip as he slowly worked his right hand out of my hair. At some point, we moved under the covers, but still tangled together. We slept a little and fucked a lot.

I awoke to a cool breeze drifting over my body as the scent of the Salmon and the Snake entered my dream. Malachi spooned me. As the scent of the rivers permeated my senses, I moved my hips. I felt Malachi's instant response. He rolled me over on to my stomach, used his knee to force my legs apart, wrapped his right arm around my midriff, pulling me to my knees as his cock beat into my aching cunt. I moaned with pleasure as we entered the sexual battle arena once again.

After showering and dressing, we entered the kitchen. Ryan and Dylan sat around the island, sipping coffee.

"About time you two got up. I imagine you are teleporting to the office?" Ryan asked as he looked at us over his coffee mug.

"Hell yeah!" Malachi answered as he opened a cupboard door and took out two coffee mugs. "Do you want coffee, Shy?"

"I prefer tea, if available," I requested, pulling a bar stool out and sat next to Dylan.

He nodded. "Our latest, greatest, ex-stepmother was a tea drinker so we have some around." He pulled out a couple different boxes. "Earl Grey, Orange Spice, Red Chai?"

"Orange Spice, please."

Malachi placed the tea bag into a mug with hot water, handing it to me, with a drop dead smile. I melted into the bar stool. He started his coffee.

"So, what are we doing today?" I asked, sipping my tea.

"I'm not sure. We usually wait until we get a case." Ryan stood up and rinsed his mug at the sink. "Shyenne, if you want to bring the book you started reading, feel free. It would be great to have someone actually do what I suggest. At work." He strongly emphasized 'work'. Malachi and Dylan exchanged a laughing look behind their father's back.

"Well, us working stiffs lacking the ability or a hot girlfriend who teleports, better hit the road, or we'll be late." Dylan got up, rinsed his mug, setting it next to his father's. "You know how ornery the boss man gets when we're late." Dylan directed this at Ryan. Ryan rolled his eyes.

"We'll meet you at the office." Ryan responded flatly, smacking Dylan on the back of the head. Dylan laughed as he grabbed a set of keys off of a hook, heading towards the front door.

As the door closed, Malachi walked over to me, kneed my legs open and pulled my stool so that he stood between my legs. He tipped my chin up and kissed me thoroughly. "Did I say 'good morning' yet?" He whispered into my lips.

"Yes, a couple times." I laughed into his lips. He chuckled, ducking his head.

Malachi grabbed his coffee mug, added creamer and took a swig. "I'm gonna need this today. I don't think we slept much last night."

Smiling, I said, "I'll grab my book, do my morning salutation, and then I'm ready whenever you are." I carried my tea as I made my way back to the great room.

"Morning salutation?" Malachi asked, sipping his coffee.

"Yeah, it's thanking Mother Earth and Father Sky for bringing us another day. It's part of my mother's family, magical heritage. It's supposed to remind us there are forces larger than us in control." I shrugged and headed out the French doors to the backyard, overlooking the rivers. Facing the rising sun, I knelt down, into the yoga pose, child's pose, with my forehead touching the earth as I spread my knees, lowering my torso to the earth. I kissed the earth and then started my salutation.

Thank you, Mother, for the water we drink, the scents of the wild, the ground we walk on, the air we breathe, the beauty we see.

I pushed up into down dog, walked my hands to my feet, then inhaled deeply as I rolled up. I extended my arms to my sides, circling my arms above my head then exhaled as I dropped my arms into prayer pose.

Thank you, Father Sky, for the sun that rises, the moon that sets, the stars that guide us, the rain that falls from your clouds. Thank you for feeding Mother Earth with your sun and rain.

I honor my mother and father by treating both with great respect. I treat my fellow humans with love and kindness. I will continue to learn, exude patience and understanding each day as I walk through life.

Let me keep this day so when I am called I can come to you, Father, with clean hands and straight eyes. When my life fades as the fading sunset, my spirit can come to you without shame. Let my body feed you, Mother Earth, as I continue as a small part in the cycle of life.

I created water and let it rain down on Mother Earth.

I took a deep breath, then returned inside. Malachi waited for me at the French doors. "Wow. That was incredible and beautiful on so many levels."

Smiling, "Thanks. As long as I remember, we performed the morning salutation. It goes along with our elemental based magic."

Malachi flashed me his sexy little grin. "As much as I like," pausing briefly, "studying your salutation, we better head to work. Dad is kinda neurotic about being in the office on time"

Nodding, "What kind of trees do you have at the office?"

"Big 'ol blue spruce in the courtyard," Malachi responded as he rinsed out his coffee mug and set it next to the others. I followed suit, rinsing and placing my mug next to his.

Together, we walked out of the house. I went to the blue spruce we used last night. We stepped together, our thighs brushing, our arms wrapped around each other, lips touching, groins rubbing. As we kissed, I searched his mind for the blue spruce we sought. His mind tarried on - more carnal endeavors.

"I need you to picture in your mind where we are going for me to teleport us there," I said, breaking the kiss.

Malachi shook himself, smiling. "I'm easily distracted. All my teachers said so."

We appeared in a cobblestone triangular courtyard surrounded on two sides by a brick building, facing the Snake River. As I looked around, Malachi commented, "As much as I love fast cars I admit your way of traveling is a hell of a lot better." An umbrella covered deck table stood in the center of the courtyard. Pathways lined with rosebushes, led to different doors entering the building. Malachi started down a walkway leading to a French door. Malachi punched in some numbers on a keypad at the entrance and the doors unlocked.

"This is my office," Malachi commented as he held the door open for me. A stormy blue room faced three walls of floor to ceiling windows dis- playing the Snake River as it lazily flowed by. A dark brown leather couch angled towards the view, and a matching recliner sat opposite, in middle of the room. A large roll top desk stood against the solid wall. A deep blue guitar sat on a stand in the corner of the office. Next to the recliner a coffee table held a lamp and notepad.

As I took in the ambiance of Malachi's office, I asked, "What do you do here?"

"As little as possible." Malachi laughed. "I usually just play my guitar. I'll give you the grand tour before Dad and Dylan show up. Slackers. Driving to work." He shook his head, as he led me out into a hallway.

Malachi's office lay at the end of the hallway. The next door on the left sported a name plate reading, "Dylan Delrikkio". "Obviously, Dylan's office." A deep sage color, Dylan's office furniture included a brown microfiber reclining love seat with cup holders between the seats. The love seat faced the river. A cherry wood roll top desk stood against a wall with a brown microfiber chair pushed under it. At the junction of the two wings we came to glass double doors. He pulled one of the doors open for me. The room faced the river, the middle part of the V. Books lined the solid walls. An elaborate cappuccino machine with coffee mugs hanging from under the cabinets took up the left corner. Comfy easy chairs and a couch scattered across the room.

"If we aren't working, Dad wants us reading." Malachi walked over to the cappuccino machine and brewed tea for me and started his cappuccino. I walked over to the shelf and perused titles. Different types of magic.

Commercial magic books mixed in with text books, as well as research papers and histories of different magics. That reminded me of the book I "moved"when I assisted with the arrest of Reynolds. A book with an aura. I perused the research books, looking for one that might know something about auras. *Auras: A Historical Analysis Throughout Magic.* Looked like a good starting point.

"You're already gonna be employee of the month in your first five minutes of work," Malachi laughed, handing me my tea. "Let's finish the tour, then you can read." He led me out of the library. A foyer and the main entrance lay to the right. A young blond woman with bouncy curls sat behind the greeting window. Malachi walked up to the window and leaned in. "Good morning, Rosie. How are you this morning?"

"I'm fantastic! Were you already here? Early? That's not like you!" Very perky, with a teasing smile, Rosie greeted Malachi, then noticed me. Her perkiness deserted her and I saw nastiness instantly pop in her attitude.

"This is Shyenne. We just hired her. Shyenne, this is Rosie, receptionist extraordinaire!" Malachi waved his arm towards her. "Shy's a witch and can teleport! I loved the morning commute! I'm giving her the grand tour! Anything you need, just ask Rosie and she'll get it for ya!"

"Nice meeting you, Rosie," I said over my shoulder, as Malachi put his arm around my waist and led me down the right wing of the building.

"Yeah, you too." She didn't sound very genuine.

We turned down the hallway to a glass door opening into a conference room. A large cherry wood table dominated the room surrounded by plush soft black leather captain chairs. Someone must really like cherry wood. This room, too, faced the river, with a magnificent view. In the corner, sat another large coffee machine. "Another coffee machine?" I questioned, as we continued.

"Yeah. When Dad scheduled a meeting in the conference room, Dylan and I headed out 'looking for coffee'. Dad decided a second ma- chine was necessary to the productivity of the office." Malachi explained as we continued down to Ryan's office. "To the right is the supply room. Assorted papers, pens, cleaning supplies, etc, can be found in this room. Also, back up coffee supplies. We'll get a list of what teas you like and have them on hand. Here's Dad's office." Malachi pointed to a closed door, with "Ryan Delrikkio" on the nameplate. Ryan's desk was a large ornate cherry wood with a black plush leather chair, matching the ones in the conference room. His desk faced out towards the river. Two other chairs sat in front of his and a cherry wood filing cabinet with several drawers stood in a corner. Like Malachi's office, he had views of the river on all three sides.

"So, that's the office. Want to sit in the library or in my office?" He asked as we headed back towards the left wing.

"Your office has the best view. How did you score that?" Curious, I asked as we entered the stormy blue room.

"It is a part of a long held brotherly pact that shall forever remain secret and unmentioned between us." He answered solemnly and then flashed me a wicked smile.

Smiling back, "I totally understand. There's a few of those in my family, too. So, what are you going to do now?"

Malachi picked up his guitar. "Play my guitar, 'til I have to do something else," again the wicked smile. Ahh. It melted me.

I raised an eye- brow and returned the smile. I sat down cross legged at one end of the couch and started reading the book on auras. I believe you determine the authenticity of a book by reading the publishing data. The book was initially published in London, 1852. The table of contents looked promising. After taking a sip of my tea, I settled in to read up on auras.

About an hour later, Ryan came to Malachi's office. "We just got a call. Dwayne Reynolds is dead. He made bail last night. This morning when the WPO came by, half of his head was missing." Ryan motioned for us to come. "Shyenne, you're up!"

"WPO?" I questioned as Malachi and I stood up to follow Ryan. "Witch Probation Officer."

We get our own probation officers. Huh. I didn't know that. Made sense though. A normal human stood no chance against a witch with significant abilities. Ryan and Dylan walked out the front door and headed for the Excursion. I smiled and waved at Rosie as we passed by.

"We're out, Rosie. Not sure when we'll return." Malachi stated off-handedly as we exited the foyer.

I sighed, hesitating in front of the vehicle. "Are we headed to Dwayne's house?"

"Uh, yes we are." Ryan answered in a belittling tone.

"Great!" sighing deeply. "I'll meet you there. I really don't like vehicles." "I'm with you." Nodding towards his father, "We'll see you there, Pops." A large cottonwood tree grew beside the street. Malachi caught my left hand. I placed my right on the rough bark of the old tree. Malachi pressed his body against mine, bending my arm behind my back with our fingers clasped. Malachi touched his smiling lips to mine. As our lips met, I stepped out of my shoes, sinking my bare feet into the green grass and soil. I brought energy from my feet, through my legs, coursing through me to Malachi and back to me, converging in my right hand and through the cottonwood. As Malachi's tongue entered my mouth, his lips caressed mine and his teeth nipped my lips. His left hand tangled in my hair. The smell of decomposition and blood replaced roses. Reluctantly, we eased apart. .

"Not sure what I like more. Kissing you or teleporting. It's a toss-up." Malachi smiled down at me. We landed at the cottonwood tree next door to Reynolds' house.

A squad car and an unmarked sedan parked in front. One

officer stood on the stairs and the other waited on the sidewalk. A man sat on the stairs with his head down, arms stretched out on his legs, breathing raggedly. Another squad car pulled up as we walked across the lawn. The driver was the detective from yesterday. He met us at the stairs.

"Officers, I'm Malachi Delrikkio, from 3-D Investigations. This is Shyenne, our witch for hire. Bring us up to speed." Malachi made the introductions easily, with a smile. God, I wished I possessed his self- confidence.

"I'm Jake Williams, WPO. I came out this morning to make contact with Dwayne Reynolds." Jake looked up and climbed to his feet, shaking some of the shock out of his system. "I noticed the inactive ward of protection. When I reached the door, I saw him lying face down in a pool of blood and knew he was dead."

Jake's aura was lavender with sparkles. His sparkles looked like bubbles of air, air witch. He ran a hand through his salt and pepper hair.

"I disabled the ward yesterday when serving the arrest warrant. Reynolds didn't possess the skills to cast the ward." I informed the officers.

"His file says he attended Lewis and Clark School of Magic, flunking out his first year, at age fifteen," Jake read from a file in his hand. "It doesn't say what his field of magic was or his skill set."

"Fire. He tried to fry us yesterday with a fireball. He must possess the innate ability to create fire. His spell casting was at a very low level, judging by his house. I didn't see any components for spells or potions." I noted as I waited at the bottom of the stairs.

"Actually, I'm kind of surprised he could cast a fireball. But I'm not a fire witch. Maybe it's easy for them?" I shrugged my shoulders.

"If he didn't know how to cast spells and didn't keep any compo- nents, then why would he be trying to buy Were pituitary glands?" The detective asked.

"Is he part of a coven? An earth witch cast the ward of protection. My guess? He's an expendable lackey. A witch with a higher skill set wants the pituitary gland." I answered.

Jake tried the door knob but it was locked. He flicked his wrist and whispered *Adaperio* We heard the lock click open. Jake entered, with his gun drawn. "Nez Perce County Sheriff!

31

We are entering the house!" Detective Swanson followed him with the two uniforms behind.

"We'll wait 'til they clear the house." Malachi stated, as he moved to the top of the stairs, back against the house, he motioned me to the other side of the door.

Shaking my head, "There isn't anyone inside. I don't feel any other auras." I replied, standing at the bottom of the stairs.

The Excursion pulled up to the curb and Ryan and Dylan headed over to us. "Law enforcement is clearing the house." Malachi informed them as they walked up.

"All clear!" Jake yelled from the great room. As we entered, I smelled the remnants of gun powder, blood, excrement and brain matter. Swanson and Ryan studied the body while one uniform started taking pictures of the crime scene.

The other uniform went back outside and stood on the porch. I noticed books strewn about the room. "Where was his casting center?" Jake asked as he stood near the hallway leading to the bedrooms.

"It's hidden off the master bedroom. I'll show you." I offered as I walked passed him and into the bedroom. The door to the casting room stood ajar.

"This is it."

Jake opened the door and entered. The room was a wreck. All the books lay scattered. Broken candles crumbled on the floor. Someone broke the altar into pieces. I scanned the room, looking for his spell book. "His spell book is gone." To destroy a witch's altar was a crime within witch society, akin to desecrating a church. Mr. Reynolds pissed off the wrong person.

"Why are all the books scattered everywhere, but nothing else? The rest of the house isn't torn apart, other than books. In here, books are thrown around. Destroying the altar is the biggest disrespect enacted against a witch." Jake observed as he looked around the casting room.

I might know what the killer wanted. I 'pathed to Malachi.

What do you think it is? Malachi looked at me and 'pathed back.

I picked up a book with a nasty aura, yesterday. I haven't had a chance to look at it. I sighed inwardly. *Based on it's aura, I didn't want just anyone to find it.*

I've never seen a book with its own aura. That sounds pretty freaky.

Malachi hesitated, then asked, *How do I telepath my dad?*

Follow me in your head. This area here. I went to the base of his neck and then up just a little. *Imagine this door opening.* I helped him open the door. *Now try to talk with your Dad.*

Malachi moved out of the room and back to the living room, where his Dad surveyed the body.

Jake, Dylan and I sorted through the room, verifying the only thing missing appeared to be the spell book.

Where's the book now? Malachi asked me.

I have it in my pack.

He was quiet for a moment. *We'll look at it back at the office. Can you talk with my Dad?*

Yes I can. I felt for Ryan. *Hi.*

With the connection made, Ryan could 'path to me. *Can you find anything identifying who killed Reynolds?*

I "felt" around for any sign of magic. *I don't feel any recent remnants of another witch. The only thing I sense that isn't Reynolds' magic is the ward on the door. And the remnants of the fireball from yesterday. Someone else cast it but Reynolds initiated it. I can tell now as I stand in the rubble.*

What's the deal with the book? Ryan asked as he moved a pile of books on the floor with his foot.

It had a black oily aura, which is typically very bad for auras. A book with an aura must be even worse. I knelt down and studied the ash where my icicles collided with the fireball.

I didn't know books exude auras," Ryan responded.

Studying the ash, I realized a lower level witch than me created the fireball. *It's very rare. It's usually either really good or really bad. In this case, I'm pretty sure it is really bad.*

Once we return to the office, we'll look at the book and discuss you removing evidence. Even though we communicated telepathically, I felt the censure in his thoughts.

"Shyenne, can you identify anything about the witch who cast the ward of protection? That looks like all we have, at this point." Ryan asked aloud, standing up from Reynolds' body.

"A higher level witch cast the fireball but Reynolds initiated it. It would be difficult to cast the spell but leave it in," I hesitated, looking for the right word. "Suspended animation?" I headed to the front door." I'll take a look at the ward of protection and see what I can tell." I walked out on the small porch. An earth witch initiated the spell. "I dispelled it fairly

33

easily, so the witch was either a low level initiate, or didn't really care about protecting Reynolds. I think a different person cast the protection spell. I'll research what it takes to place a spell in suspended animation."

"Wouldn't it be like a charm or a spell held in a vessel, waiting for activation?" Malachi asked, lounging in the doorway.

"I'm not sure how you hold such a volatile spell without destroying the vessel. I'm not very familiar with fire type magic. Water being directly opposed to fire, I try to stay away from it."

"Well if he's a witch with fire as his magic, wouldn't he be able to innately cast a fireball?" Swanson questioned.

"Not at his skill level. He lacked control on a minute level, let alone the advanced ability required to create and control a fireball," Jake replied. "Another witch with fire abilities cast it."

Swanson glanced up at me from over the body. "So, at least two higher level witches were involved with Reynolds. One, a higher level fire witch and the other, a lower level earth witch. That gives us a starting point. Thanks, guys." Pulling out his iPad, Swanson took down the info.

"Okay, call if you need anything further. We'll meet you two back in the office," Ryan stated, looking at Malachi and me. I knew he wasn't happy about the book.

5

MALACHI AND I 'ported to the office, entering through the library. Malachi made a beeline to the cappuccino machine. "You want tea?"

"Yes, please?" I asked. "Here's some hot water. We keep tea on the top shelf."

I looked on the shelf and found orange spice tea. Malachi made himself a double caramel cappuccino. As I dunked the tea bag in my hot water, I gazed out at the river. I watched the undulating waves caress the shoreline. The waves and rhythm mesmerized me. I felt the energy of the water roll through me, taking all the stress back out to the center of the river. I shivered as the familiar power of the Clearwater soaked into my es- sence. I grew up on the Clearwater as it ran through the Nez Perce Indian Reservation along Highway 12 to Lewiston. Both my Grandfather's home and my Uncle's home were on the Clearwater, just different forks, pouring into the main body.

"Got a chill?" Malachi whispered in my ear, snaking his left arm around my waist, fitting his body to mine, sending another shiver through me. Malachi laughed.

"It's kinda like getting drunk off the energy of the river," I said, leaning against him, clasping my hand over his. "Watch the waves of the river as they sneak on to the shore and then slowly roll out. Match your breath to the waves. Feel the rhythm within your body." As energy seeped into me, I moved it into Malachi, through our bodies. I felt Malachi hiccup as the first of the power dripped into his thighs from my thighs. Slowly, I pushed it through our clasped hands. Malachi relaxed all his muscles, allowing the energy to meld within. Next, I let the energy sink into his chest, and then his groin. He moaned and ground his hips into my ass. His lips sought out mine and he kissed me.

His tongue plunged into my mouth and I met his. Together, we dueled, each trying to dominate the other. I pushed energy from my mouth to his, and he returned it to me. The waves from the river flowed through me, building, cresting and overflowing. I rode the waves of my orgasm and Malachi joined me. Together, we pushed the orgasm back and forth between us, until it eventually sunk into our essence. We lost time, holding each other, eventually returning to our bodies, to our minds.

"Wow." Malachi breathed in my ear.

I laughed. "Yeah, wow. Your dad and Dylan just pulled up."

"I'm gonna take a quick trip to the bathroom." Malachi kissed me on the cheek, winking. Malachi disappeared through a side door.

A few moments later, Ryan and Dylan entered the library. Dylan made a beeline to the cappuccino machine. Ryan headed to me. "So, where is this book? And how did you 'lift' it?"

"I consider it 'moving' items." I stalled waiting for Malachi to return. *Is it okay for me to explain how I "acquire" and "move" things magically?*

Yep. Just wait for me. Malachi responded.

Okay. "I love your location here. I could watch the river all day long." I smiled at Ryan and sipped my tea. Dylan brought his father a cappuccino. The machine dripped out his beverage as Malachi walked in through the side door.

"Where is the book?" Ryan demanded, ignoring my comment.

I looked at him and raised an eyebrow at his tone. I opened a small portal, reached in, grabbed my backpack, closed it, then unzipped it. I removed the book, reading the title before handing it to Ryan. *The Physiology and Anatomy of Were Animals for Spell Casting.*

"Holy shit!" Malachi slapped the book out of my hand and it landed on the floor between us. "Don't touch it! The aura! What the fuck?"

Ryan jumped away from the book, at Malachi's response.

"It's okay, Malachi. I touched it." I tried to calm him. So much for our "relaxation exercise."

"Darlin' you could touch Satan himself and not be harmed. You possess a strong aura. You can't be tempted or converted to evil. Dad, DO NOT TOUCH THE BOOK!" Malachi moved between his dad and the book.

Dylan walked over cautiously and looked down at the book on the floor. He took a sip of his cappuccino. "*The Physiology and Anatomy of Were Animals for Spell Casting.* That doesn't sound like a best seller on the We R Were book club list. Malachi, can you read it?"

"I am not touching that fucking thing! Nooo fucking way!" Malachi stretched his arms out, like he was blocking access to it.

"Malachi, explain to me what is wrong." Ryan spoke in a soothing yet fatherly tone, holding his hands up in a non-threatening gesture.

"Take a deep breath, Malachi." I said softly, gently taking his hand. He did. "Take another deep breath." He did. "Take another deep breath. He did. Ryan started to interrupt. I held up my hand stopping him. "Exhale slowly. Feel the energy of the river through your thighs, your hands, your chest, your groin, your mouth." I said softly. "Breathe in, then exhale slowly." He did. "Now, tell your dad what the aura of the book looks like." I suggested softly.

"It is black, oily black. Octopus black ink oily black nastiness. The ugliest thing I ever saw. I'm pretty sure evil looks just. like. that." Malachi said pointing at the book, then roughly stroked his hand through his hair.

"Okay, Malachi. I won't touch the book. Who can? Shyenne? You? Dylan?" Ryan asked, gently.

"I am not touching that book!" Malachi exclaimed and went to move away from it, but then decided to stand between it and his father. He took a shaky breath, exhaling slowly. He took another, steadier breath and ex- haled again. "Dylan could read it safely. Shyenne, do you agree?" He gazed at me.

"Yes, I think Dylan can. I think you could, too." I said encouragingly.

"Not happenin'." Malachi replied, shaking his head, vigorously. "Not touchin' the book. No way, no how." He remained between it and his dad. I wondered who he protected who from. My cattiness shining through. Cattiness came naturally to me.

"I think, I'll read over Shyenne's shoulder, if that's okay with her. After seeing your response, I'm not touching the book, Malachi. Sibling rivalry, and all." Dylan said seriously, though smiling to take a little of the sting out.

"Doesn't bother me. Shall we start?" I reached down to pick

up the book, then thought better of it. "Malachi, can I pick up the book?" I asked him softly.

He turned so he could see me and his father, then backed away from it. He nodded quickly, then said, "Wait!" holding up his hands. "Cast a circle. Someone as ugly as the book is probably looking for it."

I tilted my head, then replied, "Shit. That's a good idea." I focused on my center then expanded it to include the book and Dylan. I picked it up. "Dylan, move over by me, stay within the circle." He scooted next to me. "Let's head to the double recliner." With my tea, his cappuccino and the evil book, we settled into the double recliner and began to read.

Part way through, we took an emotional break. Not sure about Dylan, but I wanted to puke. I tried not to think about how many Weres suffered and died in the name of spell casting science via Were body parts. I left the book in the circle, exiting through a door leading to the river. A dock extended into the river adjacent to the office property. I walked to the end of the dock and dove in, shedding my clothes as I broke the water. I executed a shallow dive, sinking to the bottom of the river. I slid along, feeling the mud and sea weed brush against my body, scrubbing away the evil taint from the book. Once I felt cleansed, I slowly worked my way back to the surface, breaking the waves, gasping for air. I inhaled deeply, slowing my breathing, working my way back to shore. No hurry. Getting back to the evil book was not a priority, in my book. I treaded water, feeling the under currents buffeting my body, pushing and pulling me in one direction, then the other. I let the water just take me.

As I bobbed along with the current, I felt another aura. Malachi snuck up behind me. He grabbed me, pulling me around face to face. He wore shorts. I took them off and slid down on the shaft of his cock, spearing me to the center. Our lips met in a crushing blow. We held each other by the hips and we furiously fucked, allowing the current to caress and tease us as we floated in the river. I met him, thrust for thrust, tongue for tongue, my legs wrapped around his hips, I broke contact with my breasts against his chest and laid back on the river, letting go of my hold on him. He still held my hips and thrust himself in me, over and over, matching the currents of the river. I sucked in energy from the water and fed it to him. We orgasmed together, riding the waves of our orgasms, and the river. As we finished, and returned to reality, we circled back, to the dock at the office.

I dressed us as we stepped out of the water. We entered the library.

Ryan and Dylan walked in as we did.

"Why don't we call it a day? Sounds like Dylan and Shyenne need a break from the book. I'll pick up Chinese and we can compare notes over dinner at the house." Ryan suggested from the doorway.

"Works for me." Dylan agreed, looking a little green around the gills. "Okay. Ryan, if you don't mind, I want to put a ward of protection on the office." I suggested, walking over to the end table, picking up my empty tea cup, and heading to the sink.

"I'd love a ward of protection on the office. But I'm not sure how to place it allowing entrance to the public." Ryan rubbed a hand through his hair, scratching his head. "Let me think about it and we can come up with a plan. Can you keep the book safe?"

"Yes, there isn't a protection or locate spell on it. I think it would be difficult to try and find it without a spell. I can keep it in my library, 'til we need it." I rinsed out my cup and went back to the book. I dropped my circle, picked it up, opened a portal to my library, placing it on a shelf, then closed the portal.

Ryan, Dylan and Malachi just stared at me. I looked back at them and raised an eyebrow.

"Uh, where's your library located?" Malachi asked me.

"Same place as my closet, in a cave in the rain forest." I shrugged my shoulders and walked to Malachi. "Are we headed to your house, now?"

He hesitated momentarily and then said, "Yep." He took my hand and we started towards the door. "Grab new hire paperwork from Rosie. You can help her fill it out while we pick up dinner." Ryan said as he and Dylan walked past Rosie's desk, towards the exit.

"I hate paperwork!" Malachi groaned, stopping at Rosie.

She laughed and spun around in her chair, stood up and opened the top drawer of a tall filing cabinet. She thumbed through a couple files and then pulled out the one she searched for. "Fill out these three pages, I-9 and w-4 forms. I'll need copies of her Social Security card, driver's license and birth certificate." Smiling, Rosie handed the file to Malachi.

Malachi grabbed a pen from her desk, meeting her smile. "Okay. Thank you, Rosie."

"Have a good evening." I said as we exited the building. We walked over to the blue spruce and 'ported home. Malachi handed me the file and pen. "Here, start on this and I'll grab us ice tea."

"Okay." I smiled as he handed me the forms. I sat down at the patio table and opened the file. The first page was labeled, "Application". I filled in my name, Shyenne Joey de la Angelino. Date of birth, Social Security Number, Address, Emergency Contact, Education, Race, Ethnicity. I sighed and read through the rest of the pages, then looked at the I-9 and W-4. Fuck.

Malachi came out with two glasses of ice tea. "Here ya go." He glanced over my shoulder and laughed when he saw I only wrote my name. "You're as good as I am when it comes to paperwork. For Address put 1456 River Bluff Road, Lewiston."

"Thanks. That helps." I sighed, gratefully, and pulled out my cellphone. I clicked on Favorites and found Bane. I sighed again and clicked send. *We Will Rock You* by Queen started playing and then Bane answered.

"Hey! How ya doing?" I heard the smile in his deep voice.

"Doin' great! I found a job and need help filling out the application. Can you help me, please?" I asked hesitantly.

"Yep. Let me walk outside. Where are you?" I heard a door close and then the Clearwater River in the background. I knew Bane stood on the bank, watching the river flow by.

"Lewiston. I got a job with an investigation agency for paranormal activities."

"Wow." I heard the surprise in Bane's voice. "That is awesome. Perfect for you."

"Yeah, if I can get through this paperwork." Sighing, I asked "When is my birthday?"

"June 6, 1996. You're 18 years old." Bane answered. "Okay. Social Security Number?"

Bane groaned. "Skip that one."

"Emergency contact. That would be you, right?" I asked, sucking on the end of the pen.

"Yes. Put my phone number."

"How do I do that?"

"Copy the numbers programmed into your phone for me," he explained. "Okaaaay. Education?"

He groaned again. "Fuuck."

"Yeah, that's what I said. It also asks about my magical training. And I need a copy of my birth certificate and picture ID. Race. Ethnicity."

I heard him breathe out deeply. "Race is Were, ethnicity is Native American." Bane sighed. "Well, you both will need this stuff. Let me talk with Jadan and see what he thinks. Uncle Alberto can answer the magical training stuff."

"So, I should call him?" I asked.

He hesitated. "Yeah. Take pictures of all the forms and send them to me. Jadan and I will procure what you need."

"Okay," I breathed a sigh of relief. I had no idea where to start and was grateful for my brothers' assistance

"No one expected you girls to reach maturity so none of this was ever taken care of." Bane explained from the other end of the call.

"Yeah. Shame on us." I retorted angrily.

"Send me the pictures and I'll get back to you." Bane ignored me.

"Alright. Thanks." I ended the call and snapped pictures of each page.

"Are you going to be able to get what you need?" Malachi questioned as I sent the pictures off to Bane.

"I think so. My brothers will take care of it," I answered.

"Why don't you have that stuff ?" Malachi asked me as he took a drink of his ice tea.

I didn't want to answer the question. Malachi had already done so much for me. But he knew the short version of my story. And it won't be long before he figured out the rest. It's surprising it hasn't come out yet. I sighed deeply. "My sister and I were born as bobcats. We couldn't change to human until adolescence. We always possessed innate magical abilities and my brothers use to read aloud to us. They taught us a lot of the information they learned. Except numbers and math. I can read and repeat numbers, but I don't understand the concepts behind them, counting, adding, subtracting, etc."

"My paternal grandfather was our Pride Leader. He firmly believed my brothers should have been fed me so they would obtain my abilities. Luckily, my older brother, Bane, refused. Bane taught himself how to 'port. He 'ported us to a Latin American

41

rain forest as kittens when things sucked at home. He taught us to 'port, so we traveled back and forth as needed." I took a long drink of my ice tea.

"Once I learned to hold human form, I read everything I could get my hands on. I taught myself to read Spanish and Latin. A little Arabic and French. Our maternal grandfather served as the leader of the Nez Perce Coven. Bane told Grandpa Mendoza as soon as we displayed magical abilities. Creating water, moving dirt, making plants grow. Grandpa Mendoza insisted our magical abilities be developed. But he didn't feel capable of caring for us, so we stayed with Grandpa de la Angelino. Our father did the best he could to stand up for us but once he died, my brothers told me I better leave, before my grandfather killed me. So, I came to Lewiston." I took another long drink of my tea, afraid to look at Malachi. "Longer version of the short story.

"I'm always shocked at the prejudice in Prides. You'd think Prides would accept any form of Were!" He shook his head in disgust. "I'll handle my Dad. With your magical abilities, he isn't going to be concerned with a high school diploma."

"I can call my uncle and ask about my magical status." I offered.

Malachi shot me a hopeful look. "If it isn't too much of a hassle, I know Dad would love that."

I picked up my phone and found Uncle Al in my favorites. After a few bars of Chopin, Al answered.

"Hi Uncle Al. It's Shyenne. How are you?"

"I'm fine, dear. How are you? Where are you? Shaylenne said you left?" Al questioned, inhaling on his pipe, probably sitting in his den, reading some book of magic.

"Yes, I did. I'm in Lewiston. I got a job with a paranormal investigation company. I'm trying to fill out the application, but don't know what to put for my magic status." I explained.

"Which company?" Wariness crept into his voice.

"3-D Investigations. Ryan Delrikkio and his sons own it," I explained.

My uncle breathed a sigh of relief. "Delrikkio is an honorable man. Quite the magical scholar."

"I've told them I am an elemental witch primarily of earth with water as secondary and I'm classified as a catalyst." I said.

He laughed. "You are the epitome of a catalyst. I don't know

42

how you do some of the stuff you do. We need to revise the level system. You two blow it out of the water, no pun intended. Let's put you as a level three point five. I think you could pass as fours but at your age, it brings too much attention to you."

"Am I in a coven?" I hated to ask. I knew it was a painful subject.

He sighed and fell quiet for several moments. "For your own protection, I need to list all of you in the Nez Perce Coven. With the reputation of the Coven, you'll be accepted. I'll do licenses for you, Shaylenne, Tristan and Lance. I'll test Bane and Jadan for their licenses and levels.

"Thank you, Uncle Al." Relief flooded through me.

"What's the fax number for 3-D Investigations? I can fax your license and certification so you have it."

"Hold on a sec, Al. Malachi, what's the fax number?" He rattled off the number and I passed it on.

"Take care of yourself, Kitten." He ended the call.

"Well, I got the magic form filled out and he'll fax my license and certification to the office." I offered the form to Malachi.

Malachi took the form and looked it over. "Level three point five? Member of the Nez Perce Coven? My Dad will orgasm when he sees this! That'll buy a few days for the rest of the paperwork." Malachi said with a smile.

"What am I orgasming over?" Ryan and Dylan walked out to the patio carrying bags from a Chinese takeout.

"Shyenne's Magic Form. Her uncle, Alberto Mendoza, the Nez Perce Coven leader, is faxing her certification and license to the office. Here's her qualifications." Malachi handed the form to his Dad, not concealing his smugness in the slightest.

Ryan set the food down on the table and took the form from Malachi. Malachi and Dylan started taking boxes out of the sacks. Ryan read the form. "Impressive. What's a three point five?"

"My uncle didn't want to put it at a four due to my age. He said it would draw unnecessary attention." I replied as I grabbed a plate and started putting rice on it. Levels refer to how talented a witch is. The scale is one to five with five being a coven leader. One is a new initiate with some innate abilities and limited spell casting.

43

"How old are you?"

"I'm eighteen."

"Where did you receive your magic training?" He asked, looking up from the Magical Abilities Application.

"My grandfather and then my uncle taught us."

"So, what's the deal with the book? Why were you two so freaked out?" Malachi forked a mouthful of Moo Goo Gai Pan.

"The book detailed the care of Weres to harvest body parts for different types of spells. For instance, the book recommended invoking fear in a pregnant Were in her second trimester to harvest her ovaries as that has the right level of adrenaline, estrogen, and progesterone for a polymorphing spell." I explained, adding fried wontons and sesame chicken to my plate.

"So there's no waste, use the developing fetuses for healing traumatic brain damage as the developing cells will replace damaged cells. But they must be "harvested" before the adrenaline from the mother reaches the babies. Adrenaline interferes in the developing cells and is less effective in replacing the damaged ones." Dylan shook his head as he dished out fried noodles.

"Wow. It has the actual spells? Traumatic brain damage is curable?" Ryan sounded excited at the prospect.

"Yeah, Dad. At the expense of a pregnant Were and her children!"Dylan shouted. "People, Dad, real people are tortured and killed for these spells. Keep in mind that includes your son, Malachi. Malachi is the perfect specimen for developing muscle mass, increasing sexual stamina and increasing cock size. It only takes his balls just as he's about to orgasm. You want someone to torture your son to make their cock bigger?" Dylan exclaimed as he grabbed wontons. "It's horrific what someone did to Weres creating these spells. How many Weres suffered in the making of this book? It's like a modern day Auchwitz. Hopefully, on a smaller scale." He shook his head popping a wonton in his mouth.

"I certainly wouldn't advocate for the torture and dismembering of Weres." Ryan said as he started eating sesame chicken. "I was just shocked that spells exist to fix something as debilitating as a traumatic brain injury." Swallowing a mouthful, "So Reynolds tried to buy a Were pituitary gland. What kind of spell are we looking at?"

"The pituitary gland has many different uses within spell casting. We can narrow down the number of spells if we know what type of pituitary gland he wanted. Different spells call for female versus male, sleeping versus excited, flight versus fight. Do we know what specifically he tried to buy?" I questioned, mixing fried rice with my sesame chicken.

"I'll call Detective Swanson and see." Ryan pulled his cellphone out of his shirt pocket and dialed a number. I heard it ringing and then Detective Swanson answered. "Hi. Ryan Delrikkio. Dylan and Shyenne are researching spells. They need to know what kind of pituitary gland Reynolds tried to buy."

"I didn't know pituitary glands came in types." I heard Detective Swanson's side of the conversation thanks to my bobcat abilities. The realization hit me. I realized Malachi overheard my conversations. Fuck.

"Me either. Apparently, the spell depends on the sex of the Were and the emotional state and/or physical state of the Were body." Ryan explained. "Huh. I learned something new today. Not that I wanted to learn about spell uses for the Were pituitary gland. Let me see if I can reach the informant and get back with you."

"Great. Let me know." Ryan ended the call.

Quietly, we all ate, focusing on our plates, rather than the conversation at hand. After a few minutes, Ryan's phone started chirping like crickets. "It's Swanson. What did you find out?" He asked, as he answered the call. "Reynolds wanted an adolescent female Were at rest pituitary gland. Is that specific enough?" Swanson responded. I nodded my head at Ryan.

"Can you two finish the research by lunch tomorrow?" Ryan asked Dylan and me. We looked at each other, dreading the assignment. I nod- ded my head again. "Meet us at our office at noon tomorrow. We'll share what we found."

"Perfect. Have a good night." Swanson ended the call.

Dylan swallowed a mouthful of food. "We came across spells calling for male adolescent pituitary gland. It was a healing spell, I think."

"We'll need to finish the book, though. The "at rest" part is quite specific." I sighed, popping another wonton in my mouth. I dreaded reading anymore of the book. It made me sick that someone treated Weres in such an inhumane way, experimenting with spells. These were my people being killed for their body parts. And my people using the body parts in the name of magic. I choked back tears, and finished dinner. Everyone focused on eating, lost in their own thoughts.

I needed to change into my bobcat and just run. *I need to change to my cat. Do you want to come with?* I 'pathed to Malachi.

Hell, ya. Malachi responded. He finished his ice tea and started picking up empty containers. I followed his lead and gathered up empty glasses and plates. "We're going go for a run. We'll be back late tonight."

"Alright. Be careful. Where are you going?" Ryan asked as he handed me his plate.

Malachi looked at me. "Want to run up the Snake River, maybe swim back down?" I suggested, picking up Dylan's plate.

"Anywhere you go, I will follow." Malachi smiled, placing his right hand over his heart, his left holding empty Chinese takeout containers.

Okay, I melted like chocolate, I'll admit it. Not out loud, but I'll admit it. Mmmh. He has such a great smile. I followed Malachi through the great room and into the kitchen. He opened a cupboard door and placed the garbage in a trash compactor. I rinsed off the dishes in the sink and placed them in the dishwasher.

Dusk fell outside, a mild mid summer night. We returned to the patio, walking over to the row of blue spruce trees lining the drive. Malachi led me between the trees. A small grassy clearing appeared encircled by blue spruce trees. The perfect spot to undress and transform. I took off my t-shirt and shrugged out of my cut-off shorts. I stood in front of Malachi in a black bra and black lace thong, smiling. Malachi took off his t-shirt, his six pack abs rippled with the movement. We looked each other in the eyes, as he kicked off his loafers and peeled off his trousers, baring his thighs and calves.

"I'll show you mine, if you show me yours," he joked as he stood in front of me in blue trunks, with that melting smile. His cock visibly grew. I unhooked my bra and my breasts popped out, my nipples hardening like his cock. I hooked my thumbs into my thong and bent over straight legged and stepped out of them. I stood in front of Malachi, naked, with my legs apart and my arms crossed behind my back. Malachi duplicated my movement in taking off his underwear. He stood in front of me, naked, with his cock standing at attention, his legs spread, his arms at his hips.

I fell to my knees, placing my hands on the ground. I closed my eyes and stretched from my neck, to my shoulders, through

46

my arms, to my hands, along my spine, down my thighs, into my calves and toes. My whole body shivered. My skin rippled as the brown, black and white fur covered me. I roared, announcing my presence. I looked to Malachi. He stood in human form watching me. His desire for me was obvious. I walked over to him and licked the tip of his cock. He laughed and dropped to his knees. He petted my head and ears, looking into my eyes.

"You are so fucking beautiful. "

Change for me. I demanded.

Malachi stretched forward as his hands hit the ground, white fur springing forth as they changed to paws. The white fur raced up his arms, over his shoulders, his head, along his spine, down his hips, thighs and feet. His tail whipped around. His hazel eyes met mine. We circled each other, our eyes locked. He was a snow leopard! I walked towards him, meeting him, eye to eye. Cautiously, I leaned forward and licked his face, and he licked me back. I leaned back and then sprung over top of him, through the spruce trees, racing down the bluff.

Malachi roared behind me. Scents invaded my soul. Blue spruce, sage brush, the river. I heard his paws pound the ground behind me. The bluff was steep, with sage brush clinging to the side. I hit the bottom and ran towards the river, following the smell of fish, silver, gold, minerals, Oh! I loved the water! I crashed through the brush lining the bank of the Snake, finding a game trail used by deer and other animals. Their scents intermingled. I also smelled the scents of Weres. I raced down the path, with Malachi right behind me. The sky darkened and the stars popped out as we ran. I don't know how long we loped along, before I slowed. I didn't outrun the images in my head from the book, but I felt like I ran for them, the victims of the evil witch that thought torturing others for magic was okay.

Finally, I stopped, panting while my heart beat pounded in my chest. Malachi halted beside me, breathing heavily, too. We walked to the river and drank deeply. I waded out to cool my overheated body and continued drinking. Malachi moved past me and began to float in the current, back towards his home. I swam out with him. Together, we let the currents of the river propel us back, as the water soaked into our fur, cooling our over-heated bodies. I ducked my head under, washing away the taint of the day. I allowed the energy of the water to soak into my fur, my skin, my essence and my soul, washing away the im-

47

ages of tortured Weres.

The lights of Asotin came into view, Lewiston across the river. We were almost back to Malachi's house. We started swimming towards shore. My paws hit mud and I walked out of the river, with Malachi next to me. We both shook off the excess water from our coats. Malachi loped in front of me, down the trail we followed earlier. He veered off through the thick brush. I ducked under branches and burrs, following him. After a few minutes, we reached the bottom of the bluff about a mile from the house. We followed a narrow trail leading to a rock outcropping and came to a cave. Malachi walked in and I followed. It was snug, but we both fit inside and could turn around. A thick old buffalo hide lay on the floor. The scent of natives wafted from it.

Sometimes, I like to sleep here, in cat form. Malachi 'pathed to me.

This is fantastic. Quite the lucky find. I'll show you my cave sometime, I offered.

Malachi rubbed his face against mine, scent marking me. He licked my face. I smelled his pheromones as he became aroused. My body responded to his and I knew he wanted me. Like this. Malachi moved behind me. I spread my legs and lifted my tail. He stood over top of me, his front legs behind mine. He moved up until his prickly penis entered my vagina. I roared as he entered me. He bit down on my left shoulder as he started pumping into me. My vagina tightened around him. He covered my front paws with his claws sinking into my paws. The pain swirled around me, between his pheromones, the pain, my vagina tight around his prickly cock, and the building climax, I was lost. He pumped so hard, my vagina burning, we finally crested and came together as I roared and he sank his teeth into my shoulder and clawed my paws. I fell to the buffalo rug, with him on top of me. I don't know how long we laid together. I remember hearing purring in my sleep, not sure if it was Malachi or me. We lay curled up on the buffalo rug.

We woke up just before dawn and headed home.

6

WE ENTERED THROUGH the main office. I handed a cappuccino to Rosie. "Good morning."

"Oh, well thank you. A fax came in for you from the Nez Perce Coven. You're a member?" She asked as she took the cappuccino and handed me the fax.

"Yes. Alberto Mendoza is my uncle." I answered, scanning the fax. "Ooohhh."

At her odd tone, I glanced up at her.

"Here, I'll take that to my dad. You head for the library." Malachi said as he took the fax.

"Okay." I entered the library and went over to the easy chair. I opened a portal and took the book out. Sighing heavily, I opened it where we left off. Notepad and pen. I closed the book and went out to Rosie's office.

"That just pisses me off! Oh, gotta go!" Rosie hung up her cell. "Do you need something?" She asked me, smiling overly bright.

"Notepad, pen? I'm not sure where to find stuff like that." I asked, leaning on the counter dividing her office from the entrance. She swiveled around in her chair and stood up. Opening a closet door behind her, she grabbed a pad and a couple pens.

"Here you go. Is there anything else I can do for you?" Rosie handed me the pad and pens. Once again, her tone seemed slightly... off.

"No, thank you. Back to my reading." I grimaced, pivoted and headed to the library.

Back in the easy chair, I made columns on the page. One column I labeled 'spell'. The next: 'result,' 'age' and 'activity level'. I placed the spell I had already read fitting my criteria into the chart. It was definitely some sort of healing spell. No other type of spell called for an adolescent Were pituitary gland.

I sighed, picked the book up and started reading where I left off yesterday. As I read, I charted the different spells fitting the criteria. None of them specifically called for an adolescent Were female pituitary gland, at rest. The spells calling for adolescent female Were pituitary gland healed assorted medical conditions, including brain cancer, leukemia, dwarfism, infertility, and kidney dysfunction. Different levels of activity seemed to play a key role in the spells. Not seeing a spell calling for a pituitary gland at rest, I wonder if someone was trying to tweak a spell to cover a different type of illness not mentioned in this book. If so, the spell caster needed to practice and perfect it. A shiver coursed through my body. This required more … spell components.

Sighing, I started back through the spell book, paying close attention to the different diseases treated and the activity level at time of "harvest". Instead of looking at age and sex, I researched activity level, locating spells calling for a pituitary gland at rest.

Malachi, Dylan and Ryan walked into the room. "What the fuck are you wearing?" Ryan exclaimed as he headed over to me.

"Good morning, Ryan. I'm fine this morning, thanks for asking. And how are you?" I set my pen down and picked up my tea. "I am wearing Levi cut-offs, naturally distressed along with a sky blue low v-neck t-shirt. Do you want to know what's underneath?" I teased, very sarcastically. I put up with that shit from my grandfather and didn't need to deal with it from Ryan.

"Dad. Chill. Shyenne is performing the one task none of us can, nor want to do. We aren't paying her to look like a super model, even though she has most of them beat." Malachi walked over to the cappuccino machine and started his second of the day. "Found anything yet?"

Glancing away from Ryan, hesitatingly, I met Malachi's eyes. Holding up my chart, I explained my research. "I'm reading the book a second time, categorizing and classifying the spells."

Ryan walked over, picking up my legal pad. He looked at it and wrinkled his brow. "What language is this? I can't understand any of it!" He stated, frustrated, tossing it back in my lap.

I repeated the Latin alphabet in my mind as a way to control my anger. Quietly, I replied, "It's a form of Latin. For spell casting, Latin has a more precise language describing and interpreting the wording, components, intent, and execution of a spell. My grandfather and uncle taught me to perform magic in our form of Latin, as it carries more power and potential because it

50

is the language of magic. If you like, I'll explain the birth of Latin, its progression as the magical language and how the power came to be behind the words. Our grandfather required we understand it prior to teaching us casting." My temper simmered.

"Shy. Summarize for us." Malachi stepped between us.

I turned my gaze away from Ryan and focused on Malachi. "There aren't any specific spells calling for a pituitary gland, at rest, whether male, female, toddler, child, adolescent, adult, middle aged or elderly. So, I am cross referencing between level of activity versus diseases affected."

"Dad. Back to your office. Shyenne, awesome job. Get back to it. I'll shop for a new wardrobe for Shy. Dylan, do whatever it is you do." I rolled my eyes, but smiled at Malachi as he returned to the cappuccino machine, retrieving his drink and start Dylan's.

"Can someone research Reynolds' background?" I asked. The Delrikkio men stopped, turning almost as one to look at me.

"What do you expect to find?" Ryan asked me.

"He possesses little magical talent, negligible latent abilities. Minor to major criminal history, starting as a teenager. Desire to be accepted into the magical community. Maybe a sibling or cousin more successful with magic and accepted into a coven. We may be able to narrow down at least which coven the other witches are linked to." I stated, putting my tea down and picking my pen up.

The men stared at me. Dylan grabbed his drink from the machine and started my refill. "I'll work on it." Ryan said, wonder in his voice. The brothers tried to suppress smiles as Ryan walked out.

"Good job, Babydoll! Love it when my dad is shocked." Malachi kissed me, with a little tongue. "Off to shop for my girlfriend. Catch ya on the flip side!" He headed out.

Dylan brought me a tea. "Do you need my help?" He asked as he set a cup down on the table next to me.

"No. I have a couple ideas but I want to go through the spell book once more."

"Great," Dylan said, sighing with relief. "I'm still recovering from yesterday." He shook his head. "Holler if you need anything."

Malachi returned a little before noon with my "office appropriate" attire. He handed me a navy blue silk skirt and vest to change into. I pulled a pair of blue satin ballet slippers out of my closet. Professionally dressed, I gathered my research for our meeting.

"Swanson's here. Let's head to the conference room." Ryan stuck his head in the door. I put the book back in my library, picked up my pad and tea. I topped off my mug and headed to the conference room. At the large table, I sat facing the river, nodding to Swanson.

Once Malachi and Dylan sat, Ryan took charge of the meeting. "Shyenne, why don't you start?"

"Okay. Detective Swanson, can you check on female Weres reported missing, probably from Western Montana to Northern Idaho to Eastern Washington?" I sipped my tea.

Swanson and Ryan looked shocked. "Um. Yes I can." He pushed some buttons on his iPad. "I'll let you know when the results come through."

"Okay. So, I couldn't find a spell specifically calling for an adolescent female Were pituitary gland at rest. Using a process of elimination, I ruled out medical conditions the caster is not trying to cure. I think the spell targets an auto immune disease."

"How does that relate to Reynolds?" Detective Swanson asked, skeptically.

"Well, I surmise someone offered Reynolds a place within a coven if he provided an adolescent female Were pituitary gland at rest. Reynolds was willing to do about anything to be part of a coven. I bet a significant number of adolescent female Weres have been reported missing in the area I mentioned. I haven't found a spell to cure the ailment the spell caster desires. The witch must experiment with different pituitary glands to create a spell to cure the ailment. Reynolds jeopardized the spell caster when he was arrested, so he was killed. I suggest we look at the members of the coven he has a familial relationship with to determine who has a sick relative that is an adolescent female, with a possible autoimmune disease."

Swanson's iPad tinged. He looked down at the screen, his eyes widening as he read. "Holy shit. There are two girls missing in Montana, three in Washington, one in Sand Point and one in Coeur de Alene over the past six months. There's also a male Were missing from Spokane within the time frame. Since it occurred in separate states and counties, it wasn't obvious."

I sighed. "Where in Montana and Washington?"

"Within a few hours of Lewiston." Studying his iPad, "Son of a bitch. The disappearances occurred within a five hour radius of Lewiston."Swanson swiped at his screen."But none in Lewiston or Clarkston,"surprised.

"There's a higher population of Weres in Lewiston than in most cities in the Northwest." Ryan seemed puzzled.

"Unless the perpetrator is from Lewiston. Doesn't want to hunt in his own backyard."Malachi grabbed a donut off the table and dunked it in his cappuccino. Everyone looked at Malachi. "What? Just pointing out the obvious." We mulled over the information and the missing Weres.

"Did you find anything on Reynolds?" I asked Ryan, grabbing a maple bar.

"Actually, I did." Ryan clicked his iPad and pulled up his notes. "You're right on the money. Sealed juvenile record. As an adult, he was convicted of DWI, destruction of personal property, possession of marijuana, vandalism. Numerous places of employment at menial jobs. He isn't listed with a Coven. A search of his family tree revealed his family tends to be mediocre witches with fire as their area of study. Only one family member initiated into a coven, his cousin, Robert "Bobby"Reynolds. Bobby is a level 2 in the Orchards Coven."

As Ryan recited his findings, Detective Swanson entered information into his iPad. "His juvie record was for fire starting. The destruction of personal property and vandalism plead down from arson."

Dylan picked up after Swanson, "Education history reveals expulsion from Lewis and Clark Magic School at age fifteen because he lacked basic skills. His abilities were unpredictable. More than fifty percent of the time, he failed to conjure a simple flame. His innate magical abilities appear mediocre at best," Dylan summarized his time at Magic School."In public school, he exhibited behavioral issues and poor grades. He dropped out at age sixteen."

"So, what's next?" Malachi asked, munching on a donut.

"We'll look into the Orchards Coven, which will lead to who procured pituitary glands, killed Reynolds, and kidnapped the adolescent Weres," answered Swanson, sipping his coffee. "Hopefully."

"You're deluding yourselves if you think the missing Weres live. Given the location of the pituitary gland, they wouldn't survive the "harvesting" of the gland." Dylan pointed out, finishing off his donut.

A moment of quiet settled over the table.

"When arrested, was Reynolds wearing a ring or some other piece of jewelry?" I asked.

"What does that have to do with anything?" Ryan asked, looking at me, totally bewildered.

"Unless he had some sort of talisman to boost his magical power, he couldn't have created the fireball he threw at us. So, he either wore a talisman," I fingered my tea mug. "Or someone was in the house with him at the time of the arrest."

"His magical abilities could have improved in five years." Swanson stated as he typed info into his iPad.

"Not true. With his innate abilities so negligible, he wouldn't improve without talismans or power transfers from family." Ryan drank from his cappuccino. "Studying magic won't improve your magical abilities if you lack the capacity to perform. Power transfers from family members might boost his abilities, but at the levels his family members achieved, he needed to receive transfers from at least four just to cast a fireball. Four family members didn't die in the last five years," Ryan stated, explaining about power transfers. "To transfer power from a living family member is very difficult, requiring a level five, coven leader. It is frowned upon due to the extreme danger it places on the owner of the power and the receiver of the power."

Swanson looked at his iPad and scrolled down the page. "Got my les-son out of the way for today." He looked up at us and smiled. "I like to learn something new every day. To your question, Shyenne, no, he didn't wear any jewelry, not even a watch, at the time of his arrest."

I nodded. "His watch lay on the dresser. I 'ported to his home when a high level witch attempted to deposit negative residue into the earth. At the time, I didn't realize it wasn't him. He didn't cast the fireball. The other witch was there when we went in."

"The open bedroom window," Dylan sighed, swallowing the last of his cappuccino. I nodded again.

"You picked up no residual magics. If negative residue was being deposited into the earth, would you notice it once on site?" Ryan asked.

"I should have." I mulled over the situation, watching the

river flow by. "A clean up spell. It neutralizes all magic to avoid contamination. Reynolds lacked the skill to cast a clean up spell."

"We could gather fingerprints at the window and see if we come up with anything." Swanson suggested.

"A clean up spell or charm probably failed to cover the window. Definitely worth looking into," I finished off my tea.

7

WHILE SWANSON AND Ryan researched the members of the Orchards Coven, I started working on the ward of protection for the office. How to allow the general public but protect those within? If I incorporate a spell of detect ill intent into the ward, then it should bar anyone meaning harm. I wrote out the spell for the ward and interlaced the ill intent within. Wanting to check with Ryan, I headed to his office.

"Ryan? I put together a spell for the ward of protection for the office and thought I would run it by you." I sat down in a chair opposite his desk, leaving me kitty corner to the view of down river.

He looked up at me a little surprised. "Really? What did you come up with?" He pulled a pipe out of his top drawer, filling it with tobacco and then lighting it with a lighter.

"I used a ward of protection spell and interwove a detect ill intent spell into it. It should provide access while inhibiting passage to those with ill intent toward us." I explained.

Puffing on his pipe, "Sounds good. Initiate the spell after hours. I'm curious to see how it works. It may need tweaking."

I rocked my head, side to side, doubting imperfections lay within my spell, but figured we'd see. "Okay. I'll round up the components I need to initiate it." I said, heading to the door.

"Thanks, Shy." He called out as I closed the door.

I returned to Malachi's office. He played *Stairway to Heaven* on his guitar. I smiled, opening a portal to my closet, and pulled out a copper pot. Once Ryan, Dylan and Rosie left for the day, I walked out the French doors and down to the river, gathering about one-third of the pot with water. I scooped half a handful of silt from the bank. A pine tree stood sentinel between the river and the office. I picked pine needles and a cone from the ground, then off the tree. Walking clockwise around the building, I gathered dirt, gravel and leaves from the perimeter of the building. *Proteja aquellos dentro de aquellos sin ese deseo hacernos daño.* I repeated these words strolling the perimeter twice to ensure full coverage. Facing the river, I continued to recite the spell while stirring the contents of the pot using my hands. Combing my hair with my fingers, I mixed the contents, incorporating my magics into the spell. With the power of the river, the earth, my spell and my essence, I once again, walked the perimeter of the office, reciting the words dumping the contents along the way.

I returned to Malachi's office. He still strummed his guitar. He picked the notes to *Witchy Woman.* I smiled. "I'm done with the spell." I sank into the recliner, listening to him play, allowing his music to wash over me, like the waves of the river. Slowly, pulling me deeper, wave by wave, sinking to the center of the river. The river currents taking me to the bottom, down river.

Malachi touched me on the shoulder. "Are you ready to go home?" He asked me. Totally the witchy man. Totally.

I entered the land of the living and smiled up at him. He took my hand and we headed to the blue spruce to 'port home. We appeared in the drive- way, walked up the stairs and entered. Ryan and Dylan sat in the kitchen, digging into pizza.

The next morning, Malachi and I returned to the office, after morning salutation. Rosie waited in front of the doors. "For some reason, I can't en- ter. I can't move beyond this point. I'm not sure why." She stated, stamping her feet, frustrated.

"Huh. Malachi, dial your dad's number into my phone. I'll figure it out." I handed it to him. Malachi dialed a number and returned it.

I walked away from the entrance. Ryan answered. "Ryan, we're at the office. Rosie isn't able to enter due to my spell."

"Well, let her in." Ryan stated, disdainfully.

"If she can't get in, it's because of the spell." I informed him. "Well, let her in." Ryan repeated.

"Ryan, if she can't enter, there's a reason for it." I ran my hand through my hair.

"Yeah, your spell is screwed up. Let. Her. In." Ryan repeated, strongly.

I hesitated. "Let. Her. In."

Sighing deeply, I opened a gate large enough to allow her

in. Malachi took my arm and we went to his office. "Did you screw up the spell? Or is she a danger to us?" He asked after closing the door.

Shaking my head, "I didn't screw up the spell." I told him, but expected him not to believe me. He sighed and said, "She's worked for us for several months. Let's see what happens.

Dejectedly, I nodded

I pulled out my phone and looked up my favorites. When I got to "Lance" I pushed dial.

"How is my favoritest cousin?" Lance answered, causing me to smile.

"Pretty damn good. How are you?" I answered.

"Not bad. Found Uncle Al's stash of whiskey. Ridin' high and goin' out for a long one!" I groaned at Lance's football reference.

I laughed. "Okay. Login to your magical expertise and riddle me this: A coven member needs a female Were pituitary gland at rest for a spell and asks for help from a level one. Why?"

"Because the coven member needs a low, low level spell of some sort?" He answered.

I stopped to think. "A low degree fire?"

"Yep. A low level initiate would happily sustain a low degree fire to get noticed." Lance reasoned.

Huh. "What do you think a high level witch would utilize a low level witch for?" I asked.

"A two tier spell."

"Huh?" I asked bewildered.

"Don't you ever listen when Uncle Al lectures? A spell that is a precursor to a larger spell. Instead of utilizing his, or her, power for easy shit, a witch uses a low level witch, utilizing their power for the really important spell casting." Lance responded. I could see him swirl- ing Uncle Al's good whiskey in a crystal tumbler as he educated me. I recalled Al's course on casting conservation. After Lance's short lecture.

"Thanks for the re-education." I smiled as we said our goodbyes.

So, a high level spell requires an adolescent Were female pituitary gland aimed at curing some illness. The development of the spell occurs through trial and error, after consulting a book utilizing Were body parts. A low level witch obtained the pituitary gland and cast the initial foundation of a two tier spell. I felt the earth reject the negative residue of the spell. We interrupted during the casting. Reynolds threw a fireball at us while the witch grabbed up the spell components, and exited via the window, after dropping a clean-up charm. If we disrupted the spell at the wrong time, the witch may need another pituitary gland. I sighed. I need to inform Malachi and Ryan that the witch might be searching for another adolescent Were.

All three men sat in the library. Ryan read a book on the couch, Dylan made himself a cappuccino and Malachi gazed out the windows, watching the river, strumming his guitar, in time with the waves. "I talked with my cousin, Lance. We think the high level witch used Reynolds to cast the foundation of a two tier spell. We disrupted the casting while serving the warrant. The witch gave Reynolds a fireball to provide himself time to escape, with the spell components." Sighing deeply, "Depending on the stage in the casting, the pituitary gland may no longer be viable."

"Two tier?"Ryan asked, setting his book down, paying close attention.

"When casting a difficult spell, another witch performs the foudation work, casting the smaller spells and preparing the components. Then, the higher witch fully concentrates the extent of their power on the more difficult aspects," I explained as I made myself a cup of tea. Ryan raised his eyebrows, waiting.

"So, the witch may need another Were." Malachi took a couple deep breaths. "We need to warn the Pride. Now." He walked over to me, took my arm and started out of the library.

"Wait a minute, Malachi. We are in middle of an investigation!" Ryan jumped up from the couch.

"Shyenne provided invaluable information regarding the magical aspects of the case, identified a series of disappearances no one else linked, and narrowed down who we are searching for. We can't do anything else until the police get a list of witches within the Orchards Coven. Now, while you and the police do your part, we are going to warn our Pride of the danger. Call Swanson."

Malachi's tone towards his father surprised me. Taking my arm, he propelled me into the hall and past Rosie's desk. I gave her a little wave as we walked out the front door. At the spruce tree, I walked into Malachi's arms, touching the tree with my left hand. As our lips met, I pulled energy up from the earth, and circulated it between us. We moved through the tree and earth, then appeared in the driveway of the Pride home. We opened our eyes as our lips parted. I gazed into Malachi's ha- zel eyes. He flashed me a little smile and we turned to walk up the stairs to the porch. He knocked at the door, waving into the camera. The door opened and Muscles blocked entry.

"What the hell, Malachi! Where did you come from?"

"Shy can teleport." He answered smugly. "We need to talk with Mac, about an investigation we're doing."

"Shy is hhhotttt." Muscles licked his lips, smiling at me. I returned the smile and ducked my head, shyly, letting my hair fall half way over my face.

"Let 'em in," announced the intercom. Muscles opened the door wider to allow entry. I walked behind Malachi as he headed down the hallway, to the great room. Kyle McCormack, Mac, sat behind a large desk, with papers in his hand. A young lady lounged on a couch reading a magazine. Mac looked me up and down.

"You clean up nice, Shyenne. Did you forget to mention you're a witch?" I heard the irritation in his voice and saw lust in his eyes.

"Sorry. My last Pride frowned at my being a witch."

"Why don't we start over and you tell me the whole truth." Mac demanded.

"Actually, we're here about an investigation we're consult-ing on with the Sheriff's department. It appears young female Weres are being kid- napped and probably killed. We need to warn families with young fe- males," Malachi interrupted.

Mac looked completely surprised and stood up from his desk. He hit an intercom button. "Alisa, come in here with your laptop." He moved towards the bar, grabbed a tumbler and poured himself a glass of scotch. "What's going on?" He asked Malachi.

"I can't provide you any specifics because its an ongoing in-vestigation. But young female Weres need to be closely super-vised and not left alone in public places."

Alisa, the woman who thought Malachi crazy for taking me, entered the room carrying a laptop. She did a double take when she saw me. "Do a search of the Pride for young females. Notify the families the girls need to be strictly supervised." Mac ordered as he swallowed the scotch.

Alisa sat down on the couch, placing the laptop on the coffee table. She punched some keys. "What ages are we looking for?" she asked Malachi. Malachi looked at me.

I thought about the ages. "School age." Malachi could decide what details to include.

Mac looked surprised. "Uh, that's a pretty wide range. Are you serious?" "Yes. We're serious. This needs to stay within the Pride. It's only Were girls at risk."

"Okay, Alisa, send an email out to all members with school age female Weres." She nodded and started tapping keys.

Malachi took my arm. "Thanks, Mac. We need to go. My father is waiting on us. I needed to ensure the safety of our Pride."

"We need to discuss Shyenne and her lying to me." Mac stated, sharply. "She didn't lie to you. She just didn't tell you she was a witch. I knew it. Why didn't you?" Malachi acted surprised as he looked back at Mac.

Mac clenched his jaw. "What pride were you kicked out of?"

"Clearwater Pride."

"Leonardo de la Angelino?"

"My grandfather."

He took a deep breath and blew it out slowly. "Holy shit. And you're still alive?" he asked, incredulously.

I smirked at his response. "Through my father, my brothers protected me. But once he died, my brothers told me to leave before Grandfather tried to kill me." Mac looked at me, measuring me. "So, to protect you, you had to be excommunicated from the Pride." He shook his head. "Your fucking family, I swear."

I shrugged my shoulders and sighed.

"What's your stance on Shyenne, now?" Malachi asked, his voice devoid of emotion.

"She's all yours. I want nothing to do with the de la Angelino's." He swallowed the rest of his scotch. "Especially an excommunicated *bahema* witch granddaughter."

Instantly, I flicked my wrist to open a portal and grab a weapon. I gritted my teeth, took a deep breath, then exhaled slowly. I fucking hate being called a *bahema*. My grandfather always called me that, a derogatory word for a Were born in beast form instead of human. I swallowed my disgust, then looked to

Malachi.

He nodded and said, "We do need to leave. My father wasn't pleased we left when we did." Malachi took my arm and guided me out the door.

We went to the spruce tree and 'ported to the office. Upon our re- turn, we entered the foyer. Rosie looked up from her desk, talking on the phone. "Oh, Malachi and Shyenne just walked in." She hesitated, listening to the caller's response. "Okay, I'll inform them. Thanks." Rosie hung up the phone. "Detective Swanson is headed over to meet with all of you to discuss the Reynolds case. What's the deal with that?" She asked curiously, twirling her hair around a pen.

"The stuff of nightmares." Malachi shook his head. He turned and looked at me. "This calls for donuts. Tell Dad Swanson's on the way. We're off to find donuts." He grabbed my arm and swung me out the door and back to the tree.

"Do you think I can teleport?" Malachi asked.

I considered this. I tried to remember how Bane taught us to 'port. "I'll show you how I learned and I guess we can see."

"Ya know, if all my teachers were as hot as you, I'd have earned straight A's and developed more magical skills." He sighed dramatically. "Such is the nature of our educational system." He opened his arms and I readily stepped in, smiling up at him. As our lips caressed each other, I breathed into his mind. *Do you feel me?*

Yes, I do. Follow me.

I took him through the maze of his own thoughts. I saw the part of him that was Were. *This here combines You with the Were. Yours is different than mine. Must be the snow leopard.*

We continued through the maze. I found the spot where magic resides. Malachi held immense magical potential but appeared blocked. Like someone locked it. I stepped back, mentally, and looked at him.

Your magic is blocked. Not blocked, locked. Well, unlock me.

I looked at the lock. The lock intertwined around his magic. I would have to -

"Hey are you guys getting donuts or making out?"

Abruptly, we jerked apart. "Uh, ha, uh!" Malachi knelt down, grabbing his head. "Fuck! That hurt!"

I put a shaky hand to my forehead. My head felt like an ice cream headache. I groaned.

"Whatcha two doin?" Dylan asked, leaning out the window of his office.

"Shy was teaching me to psychically kiss. It really hurts to be interrupted."

"Well, save it for after work. Go get donuts." Dylan shook his head and closed the window.

"Let's work on you tonight. I'll need to study the lock. I really don't want to fry your brain."

"Yeah, that would suck. Let's get donuts."

8

A LITTLE WHILE later we returned with a dozen donuts. We entered through the foyer. "Rosie, want a donut?" I offered her the box.

She seemed a little surprised, smiled and stood up. "Thanks! Ryan and Dylan are in the conference room already."

We walked into the meeting, placing the donuts in middle of the table. Malachi started his cappuccino and poured hot water into a mug for my tea.

Within a few moments, Rosie opened the door, announcing, "Detective Swanson arrived." She held the door open and Detective Swanson came in, with two others accompanying him. The second man was a witch. Wiccan, medium level. I checked his aura. Pretty lavender. He wore several charms: a protection charm, a protection bubble and a fireball. He sized me up. He looked young, clean-shaven, in a hand me-down suit and tie. The woman appeared older. Her dark hair was pulled back in a tight chignon.

"Hi Ryan. This is Detective Finn Fielding and Detective Karen Newman," Swanson introduced as he took a seat at the table.

"Hi. My sons, Dylan and Malachi, and Shyenne, our magical consultant. Please, take a seat. Do you need coffee, tea or cappuccino?" Ryan offered as he waved the newcomers into chairs around the table.

Dylan took orders and handed drinks out as everyone found a seat and a donut. Rosie stood the door. "Thanks, Rosie. That's all we need."

"Do you want me to take notes?" Rosie asked, hesitating.

"No, we're fine. Thank you." Ryan stated and waited pointedly until she walked out. "Please close the door."

64

"Did you cast the protection spell on the office?" Finn asked me. I nodded. "Very impressive. How did you do it, if you don't mind me asking." He took a sip of his coffee.

"I intertwined an intent spell with a protection ward." I said. "Did you have any issues entering the building?" Ryan asked.

"No, not at all. I felt the tingle of the intent spell. But it was perfectly cast, a work of art, for a spell," Finn complimented me.

"Thanks. I tried to find a way to allow the common public entry but keep out anyone who wished harm." I sipped my tea, hoping Ryan took note of another witch's opinion.

"After obtaining a list of members of the Orchards Coven, we cross referenced it with family members suffering medical ailments. Because of the confidentiality of health records it may be incomplete." Swanson passed out copies.

"Do you know what level the witches are?" I read over the list. "Can you tell us what we should look for?" Swanson countered.

"What are your thoughts, Finn?" I asked Finn, wondering about his background.

"I'm playing catch-up. Our captain asked me to consult since I am a witch," Opening a file, "I'm a member of the Heights Coven, level three, Wiccan. I work with fire. After reading the file, it sounds like someone wants to cast a healing spell."

Malachi jumped up from the table. He grabbed a couple packets of sugar and walked over to the intercom on the wall. He clicked a toggle switch and then returned to his seat.

"I'm a member of the Nez Perce Coven, level three point five, elemental witch, primarily of earth with water as secondary, and I'm classified as a catalyst."

"I saw the spell you did. You're definitely higher than a three point five." Sipping his tea, Finn stated, "I couldn't begin to cast a spell like that, let alone figure out how to do it."

"I believe a witch requires an adolescent Were female pituitary gland to cast a high level spell aimed at curing some major illness, probably an auto immune disease. A low level witch, Reynolds, was used to cast the foundation of a two tier spell." I sipped my tea, "While in the process of casting, I felt the earth reject the negative residue of the spell. We disrupted their work. The witch gave Reynolds a fireball to throw at us while grabbing up the spell components and exiting through the window. If we interrupted the spell prior to finishing, then the components are ruined. The witch needs to start all over." I sighed deeply, "And may need another pituitary gland."

The room fell silent as they assimilated my theory. "How did you know about the missing Weres across the Northwest?", Karen asked, taking notes on her iPad.

I dunked a bear claw in my tea. "A female Were adolescent pituitary gland at rest is incredibly specific. It would be difficult to find a spell requiring that component. I researched a lot of spells and haven't found one." I explained further. "Most covens and magic users tend to frown upon magic calling for the death of higher species, especially humans, Weres, and witches. More than likely, a high level witch developed or tweaked a spell to cure a medical illness. You can't go to a grocery store and buy Were parts. There isn't a legal way to obtain components like that."

"How do you know the spell treats a medical illness?" Karen questioned as she took a bite of her maple bar.

Agreeing with me, Finn explained, "Spells calling for glands, hor- mones or lymph nodes treat assorted illnesses or polymorph. It changes cell structure on a basic level. I never heard of using a Were pituitary gland, but I know of spells utilizing rabbit, trout, and lizard pituitary glands. Those spells deal with healing minor medical issues. A Were female pituitary gland must treat something major." Finn explained, sipping his tea. "It's scary to think of the process the witch used to discover specific traits required for the spell." Finn shuddered.

Nodding, I continued, "Well, more than likely it's a higher level witch, probably four to five. To develop and cast the spell requires significant knowledge and skill. The witch who cast the ward of protection performs earth magic. Earth magic may not be the primary ability as the ward wasn't very strong."

"So, to summarize: Level four to five fire witch in the Orchards Coven with earth magic secondary," Swanson noted.

"Or tertiary."

"Or tertiary, with a young female relative suffering from an auto-immune illness. Does that cover it?" Swanson asked, looking around the room.

"Or it may be a second witch that is the Earth witch, level two to three." I nodded my head.

"Finn, do you agree?" Karen asked, reading the list of names.

Finn evaluated the summary of the profile for a moment. "Yes, it sounds accurate to me."

"Okay. We'll narrow down the list of coven members matching the criteria. We may need your assistance, Shyenne, when we arrest the witch. As soon as we know who we're looking for, we'll contact you." Swanson packed up his notes and iPad. Finn and Karen followed suit.

"Shyenne, if you ever need assistance with anything, I'd love to work magic with you. I'm totally impressed with the spell you designed for the office. It is beautiful," Finn commented.

"Thank you. I appreciate that." I hoped Ryan noted Finn's observation.

Malachi followed after them. Ryan finished his cappuccino and rose up from the table. He started making himself another cup.

"You drink more cappuccino than anyone I've ever known!" I laughed as Ryan and Dylan chuckled.

"That's why I bought a cappuccino machine. We never accomplished anything because someone always ran out to grab cappuccinos." He loaded coffee into the machine and started it perking. "You did awesome today, Shyenne."

I ducked my head, letting my hair cover my face and looked up at him. "Thanks, Ryan." I wasn't use to compliments.

My cell phone started playing Queen's *We Will Rock You.* Smiling, I answered, "Hi Bane! What's up?"

"We obtained documentation to acquire you and Shay's ID and Social Social Security cards." Bane explained. "Are you busy?"

"Hold on a sec, Bane." I glanced up to Ryan. "Do you need me? My siblings are coming to help with my ID."

"Nope. We're on hold until Swanson calls." He shook his head.

"Okay. We're on our way." With bobcat hearing, Bane heard Ryan's response. I ended the call, finished my tea, rinsing my cup.

"When will they arrive?" Dylan asked.

"In a minute or two probably" I explained, "They'll 'port."

A few moments later, Malachi walked in with my siblings, Bane, Jadan and Shaylenne. "I assume the two guys are your brothers and am fairly certain the girl is your sister. Did you forget to mention you're an identical twin?"

"I'm an identical twin. Ryan, Dylan, my brothers, Jadan, heir apparent to Clearwater Were Pride, Bane, Sargent at Arms for Clearwater Were Pride, and my sister, Shaylenne." I made the introductions, properly, fitting their place within the Pride.

"Pleasure to meet you all," Ryan stated, eyeing the three of them.

"Shyenne, did you cast the protection spell on the building?"-Jadan asked.

I knew Bane reviewed auras while Shay smiled at Dylan, who smiled at her. "Yes, I did," responding to Jadan's question.

Jadan nodded his head. "Very cool. What is it?"

Shrugging, "I combined a protection spell with an intent spell."

Raising his eyebrows, pondering my spell mashing, "Impressive."

"Did you have any trouble entering?" Ryan asked.

"No. I felt Shy in the spell." Jadan shook his head. He opened a file and held out a piece of paper to Ryan. "Here is Shy's birth certificate, if you want a copy of it. We're obtaining her Social Security card and ID card now."

"Great!" Ryan took the birth certificate, "I'll make a copy."

Bane and Malachi sized each other up. I compared auras as they stood facing each other. Both had a lavender base with sapphire spikes. Emerald offshoots with twinges of teal colored Malachi's, while Bane sported cherry red waves. White iridescent threads flowed throughout both. "Wow. You two standing together," breathless, at a loss for words, "Your auras."

"You should see you two." Both Malachi and Bane spoke together, then looked at each other, smiling.

Breaking up the aura gazing chain, "Well, let's get you two turned into actual citizens of the US of A." Jadan stated.

After a fun-filled day (not) with my brothers and Shay, I returned to Malachi's house. They went back to Kooskia. The Delrikkio men watched a baseball game on tv. I perused a book out of Ryan's library, *Celtic Druids of Ireland*, when Ryan's cell rang.

"This is Ryan. Shit. What's the address? Okay, we're on our way," Ryan ended the call, then announced, "A female Were disappeared from East Lewiston. The police want Shyenne onsite. Shy, can you teleport somewhere you haven't been?"

"If someone with me knows where to go or if I have a picture of the location, I can find it," I explained as I put my shoes on.

"If someone sends a cell picture of the location you can teleport?"Ryan questioned.

I thought about it a moment, nodding. "We can try." I shrugged. I'm always up for something new. Always the first to jump out of a tree, dive off a cliff, tinker with magic. Growing up, between dares from Lance and Jadan, Bane seemed to rescue me often.

"Where is it, Dad?" Malachi slipped his shoes on.

"Near the little grocery store on River Road."

"I know where it's at. Let's go, Shy." Malachi grabbed my hand pulling me out the patio door. "Do we need a tree the same species as one by the store?" Malachi asked,as he sprinted across the lawn.

"It's easier." I jogged, keeping up with him.

"There's cottonwood trees nearby." We ran around the house to the large cottonwood tree shading the front drive. I touched it as we stepped into each other's arms. We 'ported to a little store in East Lewiston. I came aware of sirens and traffic, abruptly breaking away from him. We landed next to the front door. Two patrol cars parked in the lot, askance to two other parked cars. I saw Swanson and headed towards him.

"What happened? Malachi asked, dread coloring his voice.

"An eight year old Were coyote girl was abducted right off her bicycle. She bought candy at the store and rode down the street."He ran his hand through his hair, and looked at me. "Shy, you totally called it. Can you tell anything from the scene?"

Hesitating, "I'll try." I walked over to the bicycle and breathed deeply. I smelled Were coyote. Breathing deeper, I caught the scent of cologne. The cologne smelled of cedar. I stepped back and "looked for magic". I saw remnants of a detection spell. Probably Were detection. The spell held overtones of fire. Not the same caster as the fireball at Reynolds house. Lower level. "Our suspect recruited a new sidekick. Low level witch with fire skills. I think at least three people took part in the abduction, a caster, a grabber and a driver. The grabber wore cedar smelling cologne."

"I smell the cologne, too. Givenchy, I believe. We'll recognize it if we smell it again." Malachi stated. Swanson and I looked at Malachi, surprised. "Hey, I know my colognes." He said with a wry smile.

"Any description of the car?" I asked, glancing around the

scene. River Road was two lanes with little traffic at this time of night. Closed shops lined the street. Further up, lights from a larger grocery store illuminated the night.

"The camera pointing at the parking lot caught the right side of the back of the car. A four door passenger sedan. We enhanced the image to get the license plate." Swanson ran a hand through his hair. "How much time do we have?"

"I don't know." I thought for a moment. "They need to wait for the adrenaline to disperse from her body. How long does that take?"

Everyone looked around at each other. "Hold on a sec. I'll google it," Malachi pulled his iPhone out of his back pocket, hit a button, then asked, "Siri, how long does adrenaline stay in the body?"

"Hold on a moment while I look that up, Rock God." The sultry female voice responded to the question. Several officers laughed, break- ing the solemnness of the moment. "It can take anywhere from half an hour to a couple of days for adrenaline to dissipate from the human body, Rock God."

We mulled the information over. "Williams, start pull- ing traffic cams, surveillance cams, anything recording imag- es. Maybe we'll catch the license plate, or at least the make and model." Swanson refocused on what could be done at this point. "Shy and Malachi? Thanks for your help. I'll call when we need you. Appreciate you arriving quickly." He saluted Malachi.

With a weak smile, I nodded.

"Just call." Malachi put his arm around my back and we turned to- wards the cottonwood tree. As an afterthought, Malachi added, "Good luck," over his shoulder.

We returned to Malachi's house.

Well, we had time to investigate Malachi's mind. We went up to his room. He laid down on the bed and I next to him. "Get comfortable and relax." We intertwined our fingers. "Breathe deeply and feel all the stress seep out of the pores of your body." I matched the rhythm of his breath- ing, flowed gently into his mind, our hearts beating the same pattern. I found him in the maze. We moved passed the Were area, then to the magic. I studied the lock.

Someone interwove a spell through his magic center. It looked as if sweet pink thread laced around the area. Mala- chi's magic fueled the spell. Breaks appeared along the thread.

Strange, the spell still worked even with gaps. It was incredibly intricate. I noted elements of a protection spell, a binding spell, but the rest I failed to recognize. I couldn't identify the caster.

What do you think? Malachi questioned as he stood next to me, gazing at the site.

I'm not sure, yet. I moved closer to one of the places where the spell broke. Malachi's magic outgrew it, almost like it was a rubber band and broke when stretched too far. But fueled by Malachi's magic, it still worked. Someone cast it when he was young. As he grew older, the spell failed to grow with him but slowly deteriorated.

I'm nervous about cutting or dispelling it. I'm not even sure I can. I'll call my uncle or cousin and ask their opinion. I wasn't sure about effects if I altered the spell in any way. *Do you know who cast it? Should we talk to your dad?*

No, I don't want to ask him. Malachi moved closer to the area. *I dream where I'm a baby and make lights dance. I moved my toys and blankets around. At ten years old, I saw auras. At thirteen, I gained the ability to detect magic and identify magic users, witches, warlocks, etc. The abilities resulted when the spell broke? So, when it's dispelled, will magic overwhelm me?*

That's kinda what I'm wondering. Nodding, virtually from Malachi's mind, *I'll ask my uncle how to proceed.*

Malachi nodded. *Ok. I'd prefer to not fry my brain. I vote we take a shower, fuck, then go to sleep.*

I laughed aloud. *Sounds perfect to me!*

9

THE NEXT MORNING, Malachi and I teleported to the office. Again, Rosie stood at the barrier, unable to cross. Wearing a white flouncy skirt with red polka dots and red sleeveless top, she typed on her phone.

Malachi looked at me, raising an eyebrow. "Open a portal for her."

I nodded, "Good morning, Rosie. How are you this morning?" Smiling, I flicked my wrist and opened the portal.

"I'm   great!   How   was your evening?" She smiled   b   r   i   g   h   t   l   y   .

"Eventful." Malachi punched a code into the pad, then the door swung open.

"Oh, really? How come?" She asked eagerly.

Malachi looked at her quizzically as he held the door open. "Got called out on the case. Someone abducted a Were girl."

"Gees. Are there any leads?" She gushed, walking into the foyer. "Do you know who was involved?"

"Law enforcement pulled traffic and surveillance cams to obtain details on the car. We left before they analyzed the footage." Malachi held the door open for me. "Shy, call your uncle. I'll make your tea and my cappuccino. As soon as Dad and Dylan arrive, we'll call Swanson for an update."

"Okay." I headed to the library, pulling out my phone.

"What is her uncle helping with?" Rosie questioned, interest piqued, voice, wary.

"Oh, it's another matter we're dealing with." Malachi answered following me to the library.

"Huh," Rosie mumbled as she moved behind her desk.

I looked Uncle Alberto up in my phone and clicked on his name. A few bars of Chopin played before he answered. "Shy. How are you?"

"Great! I wanted to ask about a magical binding." I said

72

as I gazed out at the Snake and Salmon, flowing towards the convergence with the Clearwater.

"On how old of a person?"

"About my age. It looks like a fairly old spell. In places it appears worn, torn through. Like the magic outgrew the spell." I shook my head. I heard like an echo or feedback. Not sure where it originated, I opened the door and stepped outside the building. "I hesitate to dispel it. Is it safe?"

"Who cast the spell?" Uncle Alberto asked, as he sipped something.

"Unknown. He remembers performing some innate magic like making light, moving objects. At different ages, he gained more abilities."

"What did the spell look like?" Albert questioned.

"It looked similar to a protection spell interwoven with a binding spell but I didn't recognize the structure or some of the parts."

Alberto paused for a few moments, pondering my information. "It's broken through in a few spots?"

Malachi walked outside and handed me a mug. "Yes. It looks like the spell stretched due to growth of the area. In some parts, it broke. In others, it reminds me of a rubber band stretched to it's breaking point." I described as I sipped my tea.

"Is it powered by his magic?" Alberto questioned.

"Yes it is. It still works even though it broke in places."

"That's because the spell is powered individually throughout rather than at a certain point. It was probably conjured with the intent to eventually release the magic slowly over time, slower than natural." Alberto paused for a few moments. "Start with spots where the spell is already broken. Release a small amount and observe the effects. Dispel just a little at a time. Since he has been bound for so long, you don't want to overwhelm him with magic. He needs to learn to control it as he assimilates it."

I watched the river flow by. "Okay. I'll start in a single spot. Thanks, Alberto." We said our goodbyes and hung up.

Malachi looked at me wordlessly, with a raised eyebrow. With his kitty hearing, he knew my uncle's thoughts. "Should we start?

"Hell, yeah! How long will it take?" Excited, Malachi opened the door, leading to the library.

"Just a few minutes. I'm already familiar with the area. Lay

73

on the couch." Malachi kind of danced over and laid down, resting his head on the armrest, crossing his legs at the ankles. I swear I heard the echo again. His eyes met mine, and then closed. I knelt beside him, taking his right hand in my left, closing my eyes. We headed to his magic center.

Whatcha gonna do next? Malachi questioned as we gazed at the spelled area.

I'm going to dispel a small section and see what happens, I shrugged as I moved closer. Like the brain, the area of magic isn't clearcut as to what areas control what abilities. This scenario presented the perfect study of mapping magical functioning of the brain. I needed to record which areas I cut and what magical traits appeared. I found a broken section of the spell, still embedded. Carefully, I pinched an end of the sweet pink thread between my pointer finger and thumb on my right hand. *Discuitate, discuitate, discuitate.* I repeated as I rolled the thread between my pointer finger and thumb. The thread dissipated from my pinched fingers to the other end. I moved back. *Let's return and see the effects.*

Back in the library, Malachi and I hesitantly opened our eyes. "Whaddaya think?" I asked.

"I feel the same." Malachi sat up slowly. "Don't notice anything different."

"You seem the same to me. Give me a sec to look at your aura." I backed away, then checked. The colors all seemed to be the same. Then, I noticed the blue outlining the lavender seemed to be a little more teal and a little thicker. I didn't know if the gradual change was my imagination or not. The emeralds remained the same, as did the sapphire spikes "Your teal might be a shade more teal than before, but I don't know what that means."

"Me either." Malachi stood up as Ryan and Dylan walked into the library.

"Swanson and his crew are on their way to update us. They want to take both of you to a couple of homes in hopes of identifying one of the kidnappers. By smell."

"Sounds good. We're ready." Malachi reached a hand down to me. I nodded as I stood up from the floor. The two of us followed Ryan and Dylan to the conference room. Malachi freshened up our drinks as we set- tled into seats and readied for the Sheriff's Department to arrive.

After a few minutes, "Detective Swanson and his team are

here,"Rosie announced over the intercom.

"Send them to the conference room." Ryan responded.

"Okay." An audible click signaled the disengaged intercom. Moments later, Rosie opened the door, admitting the trio. She held a tablet and pen in one hand. She glanced up, doing a double take as she gazed at Malachi. "Can I get you another cappuccino, Malachi?" She smiled, flirting and twirling her hair.

"Uh, no. But thanks. Do any of you want anything?" Malachi asked the new arrivals as he sipped his cappuccino.

"We're good. Let's catch you up on our investigation." Swanson pulled out a chair as Finn and Karen took seats around the table. Rosie moved towards the table reaching for a seat.

"Thank you, Rosie." Ryan remarked, pointedly.

"Don't you want me to take notes?" She inquired as she waved the notebook and pen, pausing behind the chair.

He shook his head. "No, we're good. Thanks."

"Oh, okay." She waved her hand as she walked out, closing the door behind her.

"Well, they stole car from the paper mill a few miles away just prior to the abduction. We recovered it along Lindsay Road within thirty minutes, in a hayfield. No fingerprints or identifying info left behind. An elderly couple own the property. They're not magical or Were." Swanson paused as he sipped his coffee.

"The suspects cleaned the car with a charm. The magic felt like earth. A surveillance camera picked up the car with four people, before it turned up Lindsay." Finn picked up where he left off. "It took most of the night, but we identified the front passenger and two potential residences."

Strange. I swear I heard an echo. Again.

"Was the "clean" a spell or a charm? I thought the witch was a fire," I questioned Finn.

He pondered the question for a moment. "I think it was a charm." "Shyenne, come with me to the first house. Malachi, Finn and Karen head to the second." Swanson stated. "We obtained search warrants for both places. Glean all the information possible while inside. Ryan, Dylan, jump in with whoever." Swanson detailed the plan. I noticed Karen shot interested looks towards Malachi, gazing at him below her eyelashes.

"I'll go with Malachi. Dylan, go with Shyenne," Ryan stood up, pushing his chair back.

I followed Swanson, with Dylan behind me. Rosie ended a call on her cell, smiling brightly. "Where ya'll headed?"

"Not sure. We'll be back in a few hours. Keep the cappuccino hot!" Malachi shot her a gorgeous smile.

"Anything for you." Rosie said softly.

I raised an eyebrow, as I followed them through the foyer. In the parking lot, I groaned inwardly. I had to ride in a vehicle. Sighing, I dropped behind Dylan. We approached a white SUV of some sort. Dylan opened the passenger door for me, but I declined. "I'd rather sit in the back," I replied as I opened the rear door, sliding in. "It gives me a little more time to 'port out if I need to." I shuddered.

Dylan laughed. "Typical cat. Hates car rides."

Swanson started the car and pulled out of the parking lot, into traffic. "The suspect we identified is a sixteen year old earth witch named Shamus Brownley, a low level hopeful for the Orchards Coven. The two address- es we found are for his mother and father. He bounces back and forth between the two homes." Swanson checked his side mirror and changed lanes, turning up towards the college. "We don't know which house he's at, so we want to hit them simultaneously. Then there's no warning we're coming. Even if we don't catch him at home, we hope to gain intel on the coven and who is behind the abduction."

"Any idea who else was in the car?" Dylan asked.

"We're checking his known associates. While we search, look for information possibly indicating other culprits."

"What background do you have on Shamus?" Dylan asked as we switched lanes.

"Not a whole lot. He attended LC Magic school for two years but performed the bare minimum to be enrolled." Swanson turned left. "His school records are being obtained as we speak."

"So, another low level witch with elementary magic skills," Dylan remarked. "I imagine Shamus is willing to do anything to garner the approval of a coven witch."

"Why in the world would a coven bother with these wannabes?" Swanson asked, confused.

"A coven wouldn't. These activities aren't coven sanctioned. The witch uses the wannabes to distance himself from the mundane, illegal activities." I closed my eyes as Swanson navigated in and out of traffic.

"Where is the other residence?" Dylan questioned.

"In the Orchards. It will take the other team longer to arrive." Swanson turned on a back street.

"What are the parents like?" I asked.

"Mom teaches 4th grade at Webster elementary school. Dad works out at Potlatch. Magic is on Mom's side of the family but skipped her," Swanson explained, driving down several neighborhood streets. "Shamus and a twelve year old sister possess magic abilities. The sister's abilities are negligible."

"Magic tends to manifest more at puberty." I remarked. At least we drove slower, but I felt queasy from the motion.

Swanson stopped, made a left hand turn, and drove down a couple blocks. "The white house, with the flowering crab apple tree? That's Mom's house."

"I feel earth magic. No major magical works. No protection spells or wards on the house," Looking at the aura of the lot, "Male and female earth magic. They practice their magic on the crab apple tree and the flowers along the house."

"You can differentiate between male and female magic users?" Swanson turned to look at me in the back seat.

"Yes. A female tends to cast with softer edges. Their spells melt and blend. Males will be sharp edged, abrupt, rough."

"Learned my new thing for today." Swanson remarked.

"I swear, Shy, I learn more from you than three years at magic school. You should teach." Dylan commented.

"I agree. Hanging with you, it's easy for me to get in my lesson for the day. When we finish this case, I'll talk with Ryan and you, Dylan, about having Shyenne do some sort of a workshop," thoughtfully, Swanson smiled in the rear view mirror. "We really need to integrate magic and Weres into law enforcement as they factor significantly in many investigations."

Just then, Swanson's cellphone chimed. He pulled it out of his shirt pocket and answered it. Finn's voice was on the other end. They arrived at the father's house. Swanson flipped the car around and pulled into the driveway. "Alright. We're here too. Call me if you find anything." He returned the phone to his pocket, grabbed a leather portfolio, and opened his door. Dylan and I followed. Dylan touched my right arm and motioned me behind him. At the door, Swanson knocked and called out, "Law enforcement! We have a search warrant!"

With no response, Swanson turned to me. "Can you open

the door?"

I nodded and with a flick of my wrist, the bolt slid back. Swanson opened the door and again, announced our presence.

"I don't sense anyone," I said, standing behind Dylan. Dylan entered and I followed into a small living room with a wraparound couch facing a large television. Plants grew throughout, vines and leaves encircled the room. The plants thrived from the nurturing of a female earth witch. A fireplace stood off to the side of the living room. On the mantel two crystal lights glittered.

"Uh, I remember crystal lights. The first real magical item a witch creates," Dylan remarked.

"What's a crystal light?" Swanson asked as he scanned the living room, looking for clues.

"A witch learns to charge a crystal to feed a spell. The crystal charges the light and the light charges the crystal. It should be a perpetual light charm." I explained as I studied the crystals. One barely glowed, while the other shown like the Northern lights, with a wide array of colors. The sister's charm. She possessed significant magic potential. I never saw the aurora borealis effect in a charm. Intently, I studied the spell she weaved within layers of light entwined into the crystal, refracting at different angles. Incredible.

"Shy, we're searching?" Drawing out the statement, Dylan reminded me as he headed into the kitchen.

"Yeah, right. Sorry. Awesome woven spells are my weakness." Truly amazing a witch as young as the girl could weave a spell already. Wow. I reluctantly turned away and scanned the living room. I saw nothing of interest, so I headed upstairs to find the bedrooms. At the top of the landing, bedrooms lay to the left and to the right. The left emanated the muskiness of male and the right, smelled of female. I entered the left one. The room was a disaster. Dirty clothes covered the floor, bed unmade. I noticed several magic projects either unfinished or not properly executed. Numerous plants grew in his room, but none flourished. With a view out the window, sat a desk. On top, an open laptop flashed images. I found a trail through the dirty laundry and studied the screen saver. A revolving collage of pictures of teenagers, probably his friends, played across the screen.

"Hey, up here!" I started recording on my phone the slide show.

Swanson and Dylan ran upstairs and entered the bedroom.

Swanson pulled out his cell and dialed a number. "We found pictures of Shamus' friends on his laptop. I'll take a video and send to everyone. Start identifying who they are."

"I already recorded it and sent it to Malachi." I pushed the button, sending the file.

Dylan fingered the touchpad, waking the computer. He paged through open windows. "Does the search warrant cover his laptop?" Dylan asked as he pulled up Shamus' Facebook page.

Swanson nodded. "Yes, it does."

I wanted a closer look at his magic projects. The crystal light and his barely living plants showed examples of his magic prowess. I ran my finger along the bookcase. Dust. Obviously, he couldn't cast a clean spell. Half burnt candles of a variety of colors lined the shelves, along with assorted spell books. One of the books was Shamus'. I opened it and thumbed through the pages. Very reminiscent of Reynolds' spell book. It appeared he attended the same Dr. Seuss class on spell composing.

I walked out of the room, across the hall and into the sister's room. Here's where all the magical talent landed in this family. Wow. I entered a jungle. Plants grew in abundance. I saw species only grown in Hawaii and the tropics. The plants formed a canopy over her bed and along the ceiling. Woven in the canopy, more light crystals. In the corner of her room lay her altar, where she practiced spell work. with several spell books next to it. She individually made each book, as a true witch does. *Isabella's Spell Book*. Numbered one through three. I opened the first one. Wow. Her first spells showed more complexity than Shamus or Reynolds spells. The second and third books were incredible. Along with earth magic, she demonstrated an affinity for light. I felt something watching me, and heard breathing. Sniffing, I didn't recognize the scent. I slowly turned my head towards the open window. A furry creature came through and stared at me. A chinchilla? Huh. It climbed up a lemon tree and hid among the leaves. Isabella found a familiar. This young girl would grow into quite a witch.

I nodded at the chinchilla and exited the room. I stuck my head back into Shamus' room. Dylan and Swanson poured over the computer. They continued to scope out Shamus' Facebook page. I headed to mom's room. Her tidy bedroom held a few magical items made by Shamus and Isabella in school. I didn't sense anything else in the room of interest to us. Back in Shamus' room, Swanson had his cell on speaker.

"Okay, so we identified Dave Oswald, Charles White, Mario Sanchez, Derek Turner, Bobby Baker, Jing Wong, Dante Kane and Leon Del Rey. We identified them from their pictures through Facebook. Kids these days make it so easy for us! Bring 'em all in for questioning, alonwith Shamus and his parents."

"Stepmom said Shamus went out with Dante Kane last night and stayed at his house." Finn said. "She took one look at Malachi and spilled her guts." Laughter came across the other end of the line. "Anything Malachi asked her, she answered readily."

"Okay. We'll head to Kane's next. Wilcox, get me an address for Dante Kane. And start accessing cell numbers and GPS locations." Swanson said as he turned to leave the room.

"Can we take the laptop? It'll probably be the easiest and quickest way to find numbers. More than likely, Shamus backed up his cell to his laptop which stores his contacts. Yup. Here are his contacts." Dylan said as he tapped keys on the laptop. "I'm emailing them to you, Swanson."

"Yes. Take the laptop. Shyenne, did you find anything interesting?" He asked as he turned towards me.

"His sister shows incredible talent as a witch. Her first spell showed more insight and talent than anything he cast. He couldn't begin to hold a candle to her."

"So, his story is similar to Reynolds, a witch with very little skill or ability and a family member possessing real skills." Swanson nodded, digesting the information.

"Okay, I found an address for Dante Kane. Swanson, he's a few blocks from your location. I'm sending it to your phone now. I'll round up the rest of the kids and put them in separate interrogation rooms. Is there anything else?" Karen asked.

"That's it for now. I'll let you know what we find." Swanson motioned to Dylan and I as he headed out the door and down the stairs. "Shyenne, can you lock the door?"

"Yep."

As we returned to the vehicle, I started thinking about what Finn said regarding stepmom and her response to Malachi. Rosie and Karen appeared more attracted to Malachi than in other interactions. When I cut the thread barring his magic,

I wonder if it affected his charisma? *Malachi, does it seem like women are more friendly to you than typical?*

Yeah. I picked up on that. Do you think it has something to do with the string you cut?

I think so. I laughed.

"What are you laughing about?"Dylan asked as we slammed the doors.

Swanson gunned the motor and headed towards the Kane residence. "Malachi and I were just talking."

Dylan shook his head, teasingly, "Young love. Sigh."

We made a left hand turn, drove a couple blocks then turned right. Swanson stopped in front of a pale blue three story house. Immediately, I felt a ward of protection, a ward barring ill intent, a ward against unknown magic users. "This house is warded, heavily. I must stay outside the wards unless granted permission."

"We have a warrant. It's okay for you to dispel the wards and enter." Swanson stated as he exited the vehicle.

"It may be all right from your point of view, but from a witch's, it's very rude. I'll wait here until given permission or until we are attacked. It's all right to enter in the case of self defense. Besides, I'm not exactly sure I could dispel the wards." I stopped on the side walk. Swanson shook his head and walked up the stairs, with Dylan behind him.

Swanson knocked on the door and identified himself. "Nez Perce County Sheriff's Office."

"Multiple people inside and one is answering the door. Female."I said, loud enough for Swanson and Dylan to hear.

The door opened to a middle aged woman with dark brown hair pulled back from her face. She wore a light green t-shirt and a black pair of yoga pants. "Can I help you?"

"Yes. Mrs. Kane?" Swanson asked, flashing his badge.

She studied the badge, comparing the ID with Swanson. She did a quick spell detecting lies and ill intent. She relaxed a little when she saw he was being truthful and meant her no harm. She looked past the men and focused on me. I nodded, respectfully. She did the spells again on me. "You may enter our homestead. Your aura is beautiful. I've never seen one quite like it. You're an earth and water witch?"

I walked up to the porch. "Yes, ma'am, I am. My name is Shyenne de la Angelino of the Nez Perce Coven. You're Wiccan." I checked her aura. Orange-pink. Good hearted person. I noticed the smell of Givenchy cologne emanating from within.

She nodded and smiled. "Nez Perce Coven? I didn't realize the Coven still practiced. I'm a member of the Orchards Coven. How may I help you?"

"Mrs. Kane, we need to speak with your son. Is he here?" Swanson questioned, placing his badge and ID in his pocket.

Her smile faded. "Which son? I have three." "Dante."

"He isn't here. He spent the night with his friend, Shamus. What do you need with him?" She questioned, hesitantly.

Walking back down the steps, Dylan pulled out his phone and dialed a number. "Dante's not here. He was supposed to spend the night with Shamus. We need the GPS location of their phones."

"Well, Dante and Shamus are wanted for questioning in the disappearance of a young girl in East Lewiston last night. We checked Shamus' house and they aren't there. We identified Shamus in the car involved in the abduction."

Mrs. Kane stumbled. "Whhaat? No." She shook her head. "Nooo!" She ran a shaky hand through her hair. "Maybe, they're at Shamus' dad's house, in the Orchards." Hope colored her tone.

Swanson softly shook his head. "We executed search warrants on both homes. We didn't find them at either place. I'm sorry, Mrs. Kane. May we come in?"

"Yes, yes. Of course. Please come in." She held the door open for us. Swanson entered first, with me and then Dylan, coming up behind, into a living room.

"Mom, what's going on?" A teenage boy, about my age, came into the living room, from the kitchen. He looked at me, interest in his eyes as he studied my magic. He was Wiccan, like his mother, with the same orange pink aura.

"Do you know where Dante and Shamus are?" Swanson questioned. The boy looked at Swanson and then at his mom. Indecision splashed across his face. Mom erased it. "Nathaniel, do you know something?" Her voice ended on a shrill note.

"What happened?" He questioned hesitantly.

"What do you know?" Swanson countered, flashing his badge. The boy hesitated.

"Nathaniel James, start talking right now." I recognized the don't- argue- with-Mom tone of voice.

"They went to a party with some friends." He answered.

82

His mother caught her breath.

"Why weren't you at the party?" Dylan questioned.

"I don't like the friends they hang with." Nathaniel replied.

"I hear that. I don't like some of my brother's friends. Who were they with?" Dylan nodded as he empathized with the boy.

"Going to a party at Derek Turner's. Staying at Bobby Baker's. They live up in the Orchards on Burrell Avenue, a few blocks from each other." Nathaniel swallowed nervously. "What happened?"

Dylan pulled his cell out and pushed a button. "Hit Derek Turner and Bobby Baker's residences. Party at Turner's, sleeping it off at Baker's."

I heard Malachi's, "Gotcha."

"A young girl was abducted from East Lewiston last night. We iden- tified Shamus in the car involved in the kidnapping." Swanson stated.

An "oh fuck" look crossed Nathaniel's face. He dropped his eyes, glancing askance at his mother. "Zeke! Get down here!"

A younger version of Nathaniel bounded down the stairs and came up short in front of us, surprised. "What?"

"Take Mom into the den and help her call Dad." Nathaniel stated, motioning with his head.

As usual with younger siblings, Zeke asked the age old question, "Why?"

Nathaniel looked at him sternly and stated, "Now."

The boy rolled his eyes but took his mom by the arm. "C'mon, Mom." He looked back over his shoulder at his broth-er, quizzically. His aura matched his Mom and brother. Mom and the two boys possessed better than typical magical abilities. I placed her level at about a four, Nathaniel a three and Zeke a two.

Nathaniel put his hands in his front pockets of his jeans and rocked back on the balls of his bare feet. Obviously, he wanted to say something. He took a deep breath and said very quietly, "Was it a young female Were?"

I raised an eyebrow and nodded. Nathaniel shook his head. "About a week ago, a friend," correcting himself, "an acquain-tance of mine, contacted me. He wanted help with working a healing spell involving a female Were organ. Naturally, I re-fused. I knew he had no hope of writing a spell on his own."

"Who was the friend?" Swanson questioned, pulling out his

phone, taking notes.

"Acquaintance. Dwayne Reynolds. We were friends in first and second grade, then lost touch. His family moved to Clarkston." Nate explained as he slid his hands out of his pockets. "We attended Magic School together, but he lacked the skills to hack it. He stayed one semester."

"Why did he contact you?" Swanson asked.

"I figured I was the only witch he knew who possessed the skills to write a spell. He told me he had a shot of initiating into the Orchards Coven if he helped with the spell and components." Shrugging, Nate continued. "I told him you truly wouldn't know if the spell worked unless you test it. I got the feeling that "obtaining" the organs might be part of the bargain. He said he'd put in a good word for me with the Coven." Shaking his head, Nathaniel stated, "I told him, no thanks."

Swanson met his gaze, "You didn't want a chance with a Coven?"

He shrugged his shoulders. "My parents belong to the Orchards Coven. I stand a very good chance of assuming one of their spots. I'll get one and Zeke will get the other."

"What about Dante?" I asked.

Nathaniel shook his head. "Dante doesn't possess the magical skills. If not for Zeke and I, our family would lose one or both of their spots. Dante's skills are on par with Dwayne's."

"Do you know who in the Orchards Coven he worked for?" Swanson questioned.

"No idea." Nate stated strongly, "Definitely not my parents."

I agreed. Their auras indicated honest, good people. "Why do they want the spell?"

"I don't know and don't want any part of what he got mixed up in." Nate re-affirmed, "I didn't think he would get anywhere. Like I said, his skills suck."

"Do you know he's dead?" Swanson asked gently.

Nathaniel looked like somebody sucker punched him. "How?" "Someone shot him after he was arrested for trying to buy an adolescent female Were pituitary gland." Swanson informored him. The color drained out of Nate's face. "Oh, god, Dante."

Dylan's phone started playing *Jukebox Hero*. "Yeah? Okay. Dante's older brother has some information. I'll let you know if we find anymore leads." He ended the call. "Dante and Shamus weren't at either residence. No one saw or heard from them since yesterday afternoon. They failed to show up for the party. No one knew anything about their whereabouts. Kids said another friend, Charles White, was with them."

I smelled Givenchy cologne on Nathanial and Zeke. "What cologne are you wearing?" I asked.

Caught off-guard, Nathaniel hesitated, "Givenchy. I buy it but my brothers always steal it." Dylan and I exchanged glances. We knew one of the Kane boys was involved with the abduction.

"Nate? Dad wants to know what the hell is going on. I got Mom doing laundry. She wasn't making much sense." Zeke held a cordless phone out to his brother. Nathaniel looked to Swanson. Swanson took the phone. "Mr. Kane? This is Detective Swanson with the Nez Perce County Sheriff's Department. We are looking for Shamus and Dante in connection with the abduction of a young girl in East Lewiston last night. Shamus was identified in the stolen vehicle associated with the abduction."

Swanson informed the father.

"Ah, gees. Dante!" Nathaniel said under his breath.

"Nathaniel informed us the boys planned on going to a party and staying with a friend last night. We've already talked with the friends. They didn't show up at either residence last night."

"Has Nathaniel tried to call him?" Mr. Kane asked. Standing close enough to Swanson to overhear the conversation, Zeke looked like his eyes would pop out of his head.

"No, sir. We're still questioning him," Swanson explained.

"Dante will probably pick up if Nathaniel calls him." Mr. Kane stated. He took a deep breath and then offered, "I can call my coven to help locate the boys."

"No." I said quietly, but forceful.

"No, sir. Not a good idea. Could we talk with you and your wife before you contact your coven?" Detective Swanson hesitated, "We are at your house now. Your help with this situation may be crucial for us to move towards resolution without any further crimes being committed or anyone else coming to harm. How soon could you meet us here?"

Pausing a moment, "In about twenty minutes. May I talk with Nathaniel? My wife..." Mr. Kane hesitated. "My wife is fragile. My boys need to keep her," he paused, "occupied."

"Of course. Here's Nathaniel." Detective Swanson handed the phone to the older boy.

"Yeah, Dad." Nathaniel spoke softly into the phone.

"How much does your Mom know?" Mr. Kane asked quietly.

"She knows the boys are wanted for questioning in connection with the abduction. That's it. As soon as I heard voices, I came downstairs. Zeke took her out of the room while I spoke with the officer and the two witches."

"Okay. Do a forget spell and a sleep spell on her. I'm already on my way. Keep Zeke with you. Don't let him do anything stupid before I arrive." A car door beeped.

"Don't do anything, Zeke." The implied warning, thick in Nathaniel's voice. "I'll take care of Mom."

"I already cast the forget. She starting getting worked up." Zeke looked up at his brother. "What do you want me to do?"

"Whatever they want you to do." Nathaniel headed to the back of the house.

Zeke nodded his head, looked up at Dylan and then me. "Wow. Your magic... It's so cool! What are you?"

I smiled. "I am an elemental witch. Earth as primary, water secondary and I'm classified as a catalyst. I see you're Wiccan. Your aura matches your brother's. Are you in magic school yet?" I was a little surprised he could tell my magic was unique. Most magic users sensed I was a witch, but nothing more.

"Yeah, this is my first year. I never thought I would like school, but I love magic school. What year did you graduate?"

"I didn't. I was home schooled. Why do you cast forget spells on your mom?" I asked gently.

Zeke sighed and shrugged his shoulders. "A few years ago she worked a spell with the Coven. Something... backfired. Now, she upsets easily. When she gets upset and works magic..." He sighed again. "She's very powerful but doesn't..."

Nathaniel walked in the room, carrying his sleeping mother, passed us and up the stairs.

Zeke sighed again. "Her ability to regulate intensity is extremely im- paired. One time, she was cooking dinner. A fire started in the frying pan. She flooded the entire house with water. We can't leave her alone. If one of us isn't available then the coven sends someone over to watch her."

I nodded. "My mom died during a coven spell. One of my uncles suf- fered what sounds like your mom. As a young witch, you must learn from this and be very careful performing magic, especially with others, even coven members."

Nathaniel walked down the stairs as I shared my loss. "Yes. We definitely have to heed the knowledge gained by the loss of others in the coven. I'm sorry about your mom. At least we still have ours."

I gave them a weak smile. I looked towards Swanson. "What do we do next?"

He took a deep breath, weighing the options. "Dante is probably our best chance of finding the girl. Do you think he will answer if you call?"

"Better chance if I text him. I'm sure by now the boys know you're looking for them." He sighed. "Dante has his issues, but he's a good kid. He'd easily be talked into doing something to get noticed by a coven." Shaking his head, "I can't imagine he'd go this far."

Swanson dialed a number. "Any luck with getting GPS co-ordinates from the boys' cell phones?"

I heard a female voice, probably Karen, respond. "No. GPS is turned off."

"Alright. We have another way of locating them. Mr. Kane is headed here so we'll glean as much info as we can from him regarding the coven. Nathaniel, the older brother, may be able to contact Dante." Swanson ended the call. He looked at Nathaniel and nodded. "Whatever you think is the best way to contact him."

"We use code words for dealing with Mom." Nathaniel pulled his cell phone out of his back pocket, hit a key, then text. "I can send him a message that looks innocuous to most people, but will let him know he needs to come home right away."

Hopeful, Swanson gave him the go-ahead. "Okay."

Nathaniel explained as he typed the message. "Our code in-volves eggs. Mom always likes to have lots of eggs on hand. I'll text to see if he can pick up eggs on his way home. That means come home quick." Nathaniel finished typing, then sent the message. While we waited for a reply, I asked about Dante's friends.

"Most of his friends are magical. But Shamus and Chaz don't possess the abilities to be initiated. They always try to prove themselves." Nathaniel's phone rang. "It's him." He hit speaker phone. "Hey."

"So, Mom is doing bad this morning?" Anxiety was palpable in Dante's voice.

"Yes, can you pick up some eggs on your way home?" Nathaniel responded.

I heard whispering in the background of the call. An adult female voice, then, "Why can't you?" Dante asked.

"I got called into work, Zeke is at Mario's house working on a school project. Dad said to call you to come home." Nathaniel answered smoothly.

Again, whispering in the background. A hand placed over the phone muffled the exchange. I couldn't make out words or really hear a voice.

"Dante?"

"Alright. I'll head home and grab eggs on the way." Sighing, his anxiety increased.

"Great! Hurry, I need to leave." Nathaniel exhaled in relief. "On my way right now." Dante signed off.

"I'll move the car down the block further. We don't want to spook him. Nathaniel, call your dad and tell him to pull into the garage and close the door. I'll walk through the alley and enter through the back." Swanson said, walking out the front door.

Nathaniel nodded as he hit a number. "Dad, he's on his way home. Detective Swanson wants you to pull into the garage and close the door so we don't spook him."

"I'm almost home," relief colored Mr. Kane's voice. Hesitantly, he asked, "How did he sound?"

"Freaked."

Mr. Kane sighed heavily, "Did he say anything?"

"No. It was obvious someone stood next to him," Nate explained further. "We heard whispering in the background."

Mr. Kane exhaled with a sound like a fist banging on the steering wheel, "What the hell did he get himself into? I'm pulling into the garage now." At that, I heard metal on metal and a car engine. Moments later, a door opened in the kitchen. Mr. Kane looked like an older version of Nathaniel. "I'm Stephen Kane. Call me Steve." Steve's aura shown the same as his wife and sons. He was Wiccan as well. A very powerful witch. He sized me up. "I am Wiccan, Second in the Orchards Coven."

"I'm Dylan Delrikkio and this is Shyenne de la Angelino

from 3-D Investigations."

"And I'm Detective Swanson, NezPerce County Sheriff's Department," Swanson stated as he came in the back door.

Steve glanced at him, but returned his attention to me.

"I am an elemental witch, earth, primary, water secondary and am a catalyst. I belong to the Nez Perce Coven." I introduced myself. Steve was definitely surprised.

"de la Angelino? Maria's daughter?" Steve questioned, shock coloring his features.

That surprised me. "Yes. My twin sister and I grew up within our father's Were Pride, after her death."

"Who trained you?" Compassion bled through his tone. "My Uncle Alberto." I responded.

Recognition dawned his features. "I knew your Mother. She was a wonderful person and a terrific witch."

"I've heard that about her."

He nodded. Turning his attention back to Swanson, "I will ensure my son's full cooperation with your investigation. What exactly occurred? Why on earth would my son kidnap a girl?"

"We appreciate your cooperation. We're hoping to resolve the situation without anymore charges or injuries," Swanson hesitated for a moment. "The child is a Were."

Steve looked bewildered. "Why would my son kidnap a Were child?" Swanson looked to me and nodded. "It appears someone within the Orchards Coven is trying to obtain female Were adolescent organs, specifically a pituitary gland."

Bewilderment turned to horror, then anger. "How do you know it's someone within my coven? I've known the members for decades. No one performs that kind of magic!"

"The caster is trying to create a healing spell. Possibly for an auto-immune disease. Someone offers a coven spot to young witches whose magical skills are rudimentary in exchange for obtaining the organ." I explained. "Is there a witch within the Coven who has a family member suffering from an autoimmune disease with rapidly failing health?"

"The Clarks." Steve and Nathaniel said in unison.

"Their daughter, Kayla, has Diabetes Insipidus. This past month her health took a drastic turn for the worse. As a coven, we researched and performed numerous healing spells." Steve rubbed the back of his neck. "But nothing involving human or Were body parts. Or even blood magic."

"I can't imagine any of the Clarks harming another person." Nathaniel shook his head.

Steve looked directly into Nathaniel's brown eyes. "Wait 'til you have a child," he paused. "Dante's here."

I moved back from the door out of line of sight. The door opened and a scruffier, larger version of Zeke burst through, then stopped abruptly. "Dad! What's going on?" He looked around, noticing Swanson and Dylan.

He turned to run out the door. I blocked the exit, locking it with a flick of my wrist. He whispered, "Unlock!", but nothing occurred. For a second, he considered bowling me over.

"I could think you unconscious, kiddo." I laughed and put my hand on his chest, pushing him back.

"Dante, I'm Detective Swanson with the NezPerce County Sheriff's Department." Swanson took out his badge and showed it to Dante. "This is Dylan Delrikkio and Shyenne de la Angelino. We want to talk to you about last night."

All the color drained out of Dante's face. "Dad! Help me!"

"Here are your options. One: sit down and answer all of their questions truthfully. Or two: I hit you with a truth spell and you answer every question. Now sit down and start talking." The anger was palpable in his father's tone.

Insolently, he stomped over to the table, jerked the chair out at the head and threw himself into the chair. With an ornery look on his face, he crossed his arms and slouched down in the chair. "Shoot."

"Dante! You will address them respectfully." Steve ordered.

"Dante, you're in a shit load of trouble. You are caught. If you cooperate FULLY, maybe you won't be in prison for the rest of your life." Nathaniel stated in gentler but no nonsense terms. "Between stealing a car and abducting a child you're looking at serious time."

"I'm a kid. I won't get any time. Besides, the coven won't let anything happen to me." Dante said, a cocky smile on his face.

"With the severity of the crimes, there's a very good chance you'll be tried as an adult. If the little girl is harmed in any way...," Swanson informed him as he took a seat at the other end of the table.

"I'm the second highest ranking member of the Coven and I didn't hear about this...this...this ludicrous scheme. This is not a Coven sanctioned activity and the Coven will not condone

90

kidnapping a child to use the organs in spell casting. It doesn't matter whose benefit it is for! This is serious, Dante. You are in big trouble. And I don't know if I can even help you." Exasperated, Steve sat in a chair on Dante's right. Nathaniel took the seat on Dante's left side. I sat next to Nathaniel to keep an eye on Steve, calculating him as the biggest threat. Dylan sat across from me. Zeke plopped down on a stool at the breakfast bar. He looked scared to death.

Dante mulled over what Swanson, Nate and his father said. "They told me we were helping obtain spell components for a coven sanctioned spell. They wanted kids to do it because a kid wouldn't get in as much trouble as an adult."

"Where is the girl?" Swanson asked, cutting to the chase.

Hesitating, Dante looked to his older brother. He nodded. "She is in the old abandoned barn in Cooper's field."

Swanson looked questioningly at Dante then Nathaniel. "It's off of Elm Street, overlooking the river."

"Who is there with her?"

"Shamus and Chaz. Mindy comes in and out, checking on the girl," Dante explained, dropping his attitude. "Apparently, the adrenaline has to dissipate before they can collect the spell components."

"Who is Chaz and Mindy?" Swanson asked, taking notes.

"Chaz is a friend of Dante's. Charles White. Mindy serves as the nanny for the Clark girl. She's a mid level earth witch," Steve explained.

"Does she possess the ability to create a healing spell including a Were organ?" I questioned.

"An organ? You mean like heart, liver, pancreas? Those kinds of organs?" Dante exclaimed, freaked out, sitting up straight in his chair.

"No, to her ability. Yes, to organs." Nathaniel replied looking at me and then Dante as he fielded the questions.

"Oh fuck! Oh my god! Oh fuck! I didn't know anything about no or- gans! I figured it was like Were sweat or somethin' like that!" As Dante quickly processed the ramifications of his actions, "I had no idea they would hurt her! Dad! Please believe me. I wouldn't hurt a little kid. I played rummy and fish with her! I tried to calm her down. And let her know she was safe. I didn't know they would hurt her! Dad, please." Dante begged, tears falling.

Swanson pulled his phone out and dialed a number. "They're holding the girl at an old farm building off Elm street, in a field overlooking the river. What level of magic user is Chaz?" Swanson directed towards the Kanes. Nathaniel and Steve looked at Dante

"He's worse than me." Dante responded. "Shyenne?" Swanson asked, looking at me.

I weighed Dante's ability and then added another one. If Mindy knew how to use lesser witches to magnify her spell casting, Finn may be out maneuvered. "I'll go. It could get dicey if Mindy is there."I stood up and pushed my chair in.

"What about this?"Dylan asked, indicating slightly towards the Kanes. "These are good people, with pure intentions. Even Dante's. Holler if

you need me." I 'pathed to Malachi. *Where are you?*

Here I am. I felt his smile and found him on the astral plane.

As I de-materialized, I heard Zeke say, "Wow! That was totally cool! Not only is she smokin'hot, but that was the coolest thing ever! Dad, when do I get to learn to teleport?

"One day after I learn."

10

I RE-MATERIALIZED NEXT to Malachi. They stood outside a residence, entering a car.

"We just finished. They haven't been here either." Malachi stated as he put an arm around me.

"Who's place is this?" I asked as I leaned into him. "A friend named Chaz."

"Dante said Chaz is with Shamus. Both are basic level witches. But there's another witch, Mindy, that might be there as well. She's a moderate level earth witch. She is in and out, checking the status of the adrenaline in the child." I explained, sharing the information we gained from Dante.

"Swanson sent the address to me. It's not too far from here. Let's load up."

I groaned inwardly. Yeesh, I hate vehicles. We drove for a short time, then Karen pulled over near an open field. "The building they're talking about is over the rise. Finn and/or Shyenne should determine if the building is magically protected."

Finn and I looked at each other. I shrugged. "Let's both go up. We can compare notes," Finn suggested.

"Okay." We both started walking towards the rise. As we came closer, we lowered ourselves to the ground. We finished the trek belly crawling. At the crest, we peeked over. An old pole barn stood down in a recess. Outwardly, the barn appeared unused and abandoned. There were no vehicles visible. I didn't detect a protection spell or ward.

"I don't detect anything. What about you?" Finn whispered.

"Nope. Me either. I smell four people inside, one is a Were. Mindy must be there." I thought for a moment. "I can 'port us to the door. If you subdue the two wannabe's I can handle Mindy."

"If they're next to each other I can, but I can't take both out if they're separated." He rubbed his scruffy beard, contemplating the situation.

"As long as Mindy is out of play, I don't think the other two pose a concern. It sounds like they possess rudimentary skills." I took a deep breath. "Ready a spell for when I 'port us. You hit Mindy. I'll bat clean up on the other two." I decided.

After a hesitation, Finn said, "Okay. My spell is ready." I nodded, touched his arm, then 'ported just outside the barn door. I quickly opened the door as we materialized. Finn hesitated a moment or two, readjusting to our new location. He lobbed a sleep spell at a female standing over a little girl, knocking her unconscious instantly. I hit the two males, dropping them like a sack of potatoes. We scanned the area, looking for others. Seeing no one, smelling none, I let Malachi know all was well.

The young Were sat in a chair, facing us. I approached her quickly and said, *"Acutum sakim"*, freeing her from the rope binding her to the chair.

Crying aloud, she rushed into my arms. "You're okay sweetheart. We'll take you home to your mom and dad." I whispered into her brown curls. I swung her around, so I faced the open barn door. Finn gazed towards us, ensuring no unforeseen attacks. He walked over to the female, kicking her roughly to ensure she was out cold. Then, he went over to the two males, kicking them as well. None of them would wake any time soon. I held the little girl, scanning her for injuries, detecting none. She wrapped her arms tight around my neck.

Malachi et al burst through the door. "Cuff the female with spelled zip ties, first. She is the bigger threat." Karen nodded and pulled the special zip ties out of a side pocket of her vest. She bound the female's wrists, then moved to the males securing them as well. Malachi and Ryan headed towards me. The girl whimpered in fear, clutching me, stopping them in their tracks.

"It's okay, Kit. These are my friends. Ryan, can you call her par- ents? Let her talk to them?" I suggested, cuddling her close. He nodded and pulled his phone out, dialing a number. The kit relaxed a little, but trembled.

"We need a crime scene crew and a paddy wagon." Karen reported into her cell. Surveying the suspects, Karen raised her eyebrows. "Are the suspects sleeping or injured?"

"Just sleeping." Finn pronounced, as he bent over Mindy,

searching her. He pulled off charms around her neck and wrist. "We hit them quick before they readied a spell. All are sleeping peacefully with sweet dreams." He removed a ring from her left hand. "Sweeter than they deserve."

"Mr. Schneider, this is Ryan Delrikkio. We found your daughter. She's okay and has been very brave. Would you like to talk with her?" He smiled holding the phone out to her. She grabbed it, placing it to her ear.

"Daddy?" She spoke softly into the phone.

"Baby! Are you okay?" Fear and anxiety flavored his voice, colored with hope.

"Yes, Daddy. A Were cat found me. She knocked out the evil witches and made the ropes untie me!" She described the events succinctly. "I wanna come home, Daddy!"

"Of course! I'm sure the officers will let me come and get you. I love you and I am so glad you're safe!" Relief flooded through the phone, as his voice cracked. "Let me talk to the officer, Carrie. I'll meet them somewhere to pick you up."

"Okay, Daddy. I can't wait to see you and hug you!" She handed the phone back to Ryan, wrapping both arms tightly around my neck.

"Karen? Can the father pick her up at the precinct?" Ryan asked as he put the phone back to his ear.

"Yes. That works. Does she need medical attention first?" Karen asked.

She finished her search of one of the zip tied boys. "No, she's okay." I responded.

"Here, I'll take her to the precinct to meet her Dad," Karen said, walking towards us with her arms open.

"NO!" She shrieked, burying her head in my hair, squeezing my neck tightly as Karen reached for her. "I want to stay with the Were! She won't hurt me!"

Karen stopped and looked to Finn. He sighed and raised his eyebrows. "We really need Shyenne here to process the scene." Two uniformed officers pulled up outside the barn and entered.

"Hey, sweetheart. My name is Ki. I'm Shyenne's friend and am a Were snow tiger. Have you ever seen a snow tiger?" Malachi asked as he oozed charm her way. She looked at him, awestruck, and shook her head. His charisma abilities worked on little girls just as well as big girls. I smiled.

"Well, I'm about this tall, with ultra white fur and black

spots," holding his hand about three feet off the ground, he moved towards us. "What color are you?"

"I'm black and brown and white and tan. I have a bushy tail. Do you like your belly scratched?" She asked, hesitantly.

He shivered. "I love my belly scratched. And my ears. Right back here." He reached behind her ear and scratched. She giggled. "Shyenne has to stay here to work but I'll take you to your Dad. Would that be okay, Sweetheart?" He looked deep into her eyes. Almost mesmerized, she nodded, reaching for Malachi. He took her, winking at me. "Okay. I promise I won't let you go until you see your dad and I won't let anyone hurt you." The sincerity in his voice reassured her.

"'K." She smiled up at Malachi. Then, she remembered me. "Thank you, Shyenne for rescuing me from the bad witches."

"No problem. You're a very brave and strong girl." I smiled and smoothed her hair back behind her ear.

"Wanna ride in a cop car?" Malachi asked her as he and another patrol officer left the barn.

"Can I turn the siren on?" She asked, her voice filled with excitement. "You sure can! That way, we can race to meet your dad!" The patrol officer told her.

I smiled as they walked towards the patrol car, thrilled we found her before she had been harmed. Looking around the desolate building, I didn't see much evidence of magic being used here. It was decorated like a typical barn: dirty and stinking like animal feces. No barnyard animals had seen the inside in a lot of years, but the odor lingered. The boys and Mindy remained unconscious. The officer stood guard between them.

The chair where they secured Carrie was situated with bales of hay forming a semi circle wall behind it. Using a pen flashlight, Karen inspected the area around the chair. A garbage pile against the east wall boasted fast food, pop cans and beer bottles. By the size of the pile, kids hung out here routinely. Strewn about in several different spots, sleeping bags made up makeshift beds. They built a table using bales and a piece of plywood. Bales also served as chairs around the table. A deck of cards, pizza box and pop cans littered the table top. Ryan inspected items on the table. I walked over to the garbage pile, at the edge of the semi circle.

A narrow opening existed between the barn wall and the

hay. I squeezed through easily. My cat eyes kicked in, adjusting to the darkness behind the wall. I saw an altar placed diagonally in the corner facing the horseshoe shape of the hay bale wall. This small area was set up almost like a meeting room. Were the kids holding "services"? Their own coven? Only rudimentary spells had been cast. A few perpetual light charms hung from bales, but failed to re-charge.

It dawned on me suddenly that it was oddly quiet in the rest of the barn. Cautiously, I peeked around the bale wall. Ryan lay prone by the table. Shit. Mindy must have woken up. I figured the patrol officer was probably down, too. Maybe Karen. I didn't know where Finn was. Using easily accessible components, I twirled my left pointer finger through the dirt and started a little whirlwind. With the stealth of a cat, I carefully edged my way around the bale wall. A bare spot appeared where one of the boys had laid on the ground. I sniffed the air locating everyone's where- abouts. Karen was near me, which meant she was still by Carrie's chair. But I didn't know if she was awake or not. I smelled the two boys, one by the chair, the other still in the center of the room. The patrol officer lay there, too. Mindy's scent wasn't as strong, but still in the barn.

Stealthy, I stepped out from the wall, turning to face the rest of the barn. Mindy was sneaking up behind Finn. *Ayah turbo.* I tossed my tornado towards her. Expanding from the size of a pop can to a small car, the tornado sucked Mindy up and threw her out the top. Her body hit the ground, hard. The other boy stood wide eyed between Karen and Finn. Finn spun around, "Get on the ground! Now!" He whispered a word and a sleep spell smacked into the boy. Lights out.

Karen laid on the ground a few feet from me. She was alive but uncon- scious. Someone hit her with a sleep spell. I checked on Ryan. He'd been hit, too. Next, I approached the patrol offi- cer. He wasn't breathing. "Finn!" On closer examination, one of them created dirt— in his nose and mouth, suffocating him. I dispelled the dirt, but it was too late. "He's dead." Shaking, I went to Ryan. Sleeping. I sighed with relief and dispelled him, then Karen. Finn stood over the boy. Mindy didn't move. Ryan and Karen rose to their feet.

"What the hell happened?" Ryan rubbed his hand over the back of his neck.

"I think Mindy and the boy came to. One of them must

have something we missed that dispells or cuts zip ties." Finn pulled another zip tie out of his pocket and cuffed the boy. I walked over to Mindy. She remained unconscious. She wore a friendship bracelet on her wrist. At first glance, it appeared to be woven with multiple strands of rainbow hued string. I examined the bracelet closer, fingering the strings. It sliced through my finger. Razor sharp. *Acutum sakim.* The bracelet fell to the floor. I looked towards the boy failing to wake up. Yep, he wore one, too. *Acutum sakim.* That one was gone.

"Finn, is your kid wearing a rainbow hued friendship bracelet?" I picked up an empty cup from McDonald's. Using the straw, I placed both bracelets in the cup.

"Yeah. Fuck! That's sharp! What the hell is it?" The bracelet drew blood and he wiped it on his pant leg.

"Not sure. I'll research it. Can you zip tie her again? Maybe we should tie their legs, too." I suggested, sighing as I looked at the dead officer.   I should have thought about securing their legs. In the distance, sirens approached.

I moved towards the boy, thinking he may have come to, then woke up Mindy. Detecting magic on him revealed something glowing on his ankle. Huh. I raised an eyebrow as I pulled his pant leg back. Suddenly his leg kicked back, knocking me in the head, propelling me backwards. I rolled with it, back on my feet and reached for Eadala, a cross between a Klingon bat'leth and an Arabian sword. I pulled it back.

The kid shrieked and rolled up into a ball, like a hedgehog. "I'm sorry! I'm sorry! Please don't kill me!"

I moved into an offensive stance with my sword. "Remove the talisman from your ankle now, or I'll cut it off!"

"I don't think I can. My mom said never to take it off." The kid whined, peeking out from his defensive posture.

"I bet your mom told you never to kidnap little girls." I retorted.

"Not specifically." He said, slowly coming out of hedgehog pose. "But it was probably implied."

Not trusting the kid, I put a protection bubble around him. I doubted his magic could get through mine. "Take off the talisman, now." For good measure, I put a bubble around Mindy and the sleeping kid, too. "What's your name?

"Chaz. Charles White." He pulled his pant leg up, revealing a bright orange ankle sock. Several tightly woven strings appeared above his sock. It encompassed two different protection spells and a dispell, cast by an air witch, roughly around my level. Maybe higher since it dispelled my sleep spell. Unless the two protection spells and the dispell combined against mine. Hmm. I needed to research that. My research just list grew longer.

"Who's sleeping beauty?" Finn questioned, pointing to the other boy, still out cold.

"Shamus. And the girl is Mindy." Chaz worked at the knots and removed it from his ankle, placing it on the ground, about a foot away.

"How did you get free the first time?" I asked, watching him closely, putting Eadala back in my portal.

"My anklet dispelled the sleep spell. I touched my anklet to Mindy and it woke her up. We cut the zip ties with our friendship bracelets. Mindy cast the sleep spells on those two" nodding at Ryan and Karen, "and then she ... handled the officer." His cell phone started screeching in a high pitched voice. Chaz groaned. "It's my mom. I have to answer this or she'll flip out." He tapped his phone and hesitated a moment then said, "Hey, Mom. What's up?" He tried for nonchalance but totally missed. I'm not even a mom and I noticed.

"Why did you take off your anklet?"

"Um." He hesitated. "Because this lady told me to?" "Who?" She demanded in a high pitch shriek.

"I dunno. Some lady with a crazy ass looking sword. She said she'd cut my ankle off if I didn't." Chaz explained.

"Give me that phone," exasperated, Finn broke the protection bubble and took the phone from the kid. "I'm Detective Fielding with the Nez Perce County Sheriff's Office. You'll want to meet us down at the station. Your son is under arrest for kidnapping a child, stolen vehicle, accessory to homicide of a police officer, assault of a police officer, attempted assault of a police officer, and probably a whole lot more charges!"

"Oh, my god! What has he done?! Is this a prank? This isn't funny!" She shrieked again. I totally understood the kid's ringtone.

Finn pulled out his badge and held it up to the phone for the woman to see. "We'll be down at the Sheriff's office with Chaz in about twenty minutes. Are there any other magical items on him that need to be re- moved for our protection?"

"Nnno." She answered quietly. "Does he need an attorney?"

"Yes, he does. He is in a lot of trouble." Finn replied, softer. The sirens screeched loudly outside the barn as squad cars and ambulances arrived. "You'll learn more down at the station." Finn hung up the phone and put it in an evidence bag. "Up against the wall, Chaz." Finn frisked him for weapons or magic items. Typical of a teenager, he kept all kinds of junk in his pockets but nothing dangerous. Finn put the items in another evidence bag as Swanson, Dylan and numerous officers entered the barn.

Swanson immediately headed towards the fallen officer. "What the fuck? What happened to Johnson?" Swanson asked, bewildered.

"Mindy hit him with a create dirt spell in his nose or throat. Suffocated him." I answered quietly.

"Chaz wore a protection talisman that counteracted the sleep spell

He woke up Mindy and she hit him with the dirt spell," Finn explained. "Chaz's mother will meet us at the station soon. He's ready for transport."

An officer took Chaz by the arm, escorted him to the car, placing him in the back seat, climbed in, started the car and drove off. Meanwhile, Finn moved to Shamus. He removed the friendship bracelet from his wrist. Then detected magic on him. Nothing glowed. He searched his pockets, removing a small pocket knife, some change and a stick of gum. Finn dispelled the sleep spell. Groggily, Shamus gained consciousness. Aware he was bound, he started to freak. "Shamus, you're under arrest for kidnap- ping a child and stolen vehicle. This one is ready to transport. His parents haven't been contacted yet."

I stood over top of Mindy and detected magic. She glowed all over. "Finn, should I hit her with a sleep spell before removing her magic items?" I didn't want her waking while I searched her.

"Isn't she already asleep?" Swanson asked me.

"No. She's unconscious. I hit her with a tornado before she attacked Finn."

Finn walked over, nodding. "I think we should. She poses a definite threat. She killed one person today."

I spelled her, then Finn took off the rest of her magic items, placing them in an evidence bag, then searched her. I noticed the evidence bags appeared to be spelled, nullifying the magic items. After searching her, Finn zip tied her wrists. "We'll leave her unconscious until we arrive at the station. Her abilities aren't known at this time."

11

AT THE STATION, Swanson, Finn, Karen, Ryan, Dylan, Malachi and I met in a conference room. "Update. What do we know?" Ryan stated as he pulled out his iPad.

"According to Dante, the kids thought the coven sanctioned the abduction. Someone told the kids they were recruited because there wouldn't be much of a punishment due to their age. They didn't realize the child would be harmed. Mindy was the point person overseeing them. Steve Kane is the second highest ranking member in the Orchards Coven and was unaware of any of this. Our profile matches the Clark family within the coven. Their daughter suffers from Diabetes Insipidus and has deteriorated significantly recently. The Coven tried numerous healing spells but nothing utilizing human or Were body parts or blood magic. Mindy is the caregiver for the girl. Steve Kane and his sons will help out with whatever we need. Reynolds approached Steve's oldest son, Nathaniel, a couple weeks ago to assist with writing and obtaining spell components including a Were pituitary gland. Reynolds told him he would be initiated into the Coven for his assistance. Nathaniel said no." Swanson finished up, tapping on his iPad.

"1. You guys need a cappuccino machine, 2. It sounds like all of the other kids in this group were at a 'ragin'' Orchards party last night. No one saw Chaz, Shamus or Dante since yesterday afternoon, 3. I questioned Carrie on our way to the Sheriff 's Department. Carrie said a girl stopped her on her bike and asked her where the mill was. The last thing Carrie remembered, the girl asked her to smell a flower. The girl was blond and smelled sugary. 4. Dante seemed really nice and played games with her. Shamus tried to be mean but Dante wouldn't let him. Chaz tried to scare her and Dante made him stop. 5.

Mindy was really nice but Carrie could smell she was not a nice person. 6. Mindy wasn't the girl in the car. Smelled way different. 7. You guys really need a cappuccino machine." Malachi summarized succinctly.

"Cappuccino machine. Dually noted. How many of these parents are witches and Coven members? Kane- yes. White?" Swanson asked, looking up from his iPad.

"Mom made an intricate protection talisman which dispelled my sleep spell, so she is probably a level three or four. Shamus' mom is a no." I surmised.

"Shamus' dad is a no," Malachi stated.

"Okay. I'll take Kanes. Finn, Dylan and Shyenne take Whites, since she's the unknown. She is a Coven member, but we don't know her status amongst the Coven yet. Malachi, Karen and Ryan take Shamus." Swanson detailed.

"Can we trust the information from Steve Kane?" Ryan asked skeptically. "And you do need a cappuccino machine."

Swanson rolled his eyes, picked up the phone and hit a button. "Can someone make a coffee run before the DelRikkios' die of caffeine withdrawal? Might as well get us, too." He hung up the phone. "I think we can trust Kane. He set Dante straight real quick and made it very clear he didn't condone and wouldn't condone using human or Were body parts or blood magic. He's number two within the Coven. He stated this is not a coven sanctioned activity. He gave us the Clarks."

"I agree. The whole family, even Dante, their auras indicate they are honest people," I remarked. "I believe they can be trusted to do the right thing."

"Let's let Mindy cool off in a holding cell for a while once she's booked for deliberate homicide of a police officer. We can interview the boys first and figure out as much as we can prior to interviewing her."

"Is there going to be any kind of deal for the boys?" Malachi asked. Swanson sighed. "We'll have to figure out what they know, what exactly has transpired to this point and what laws they've broken. One step at a time."

A knock sounded at the door. A young woman came in, carrying an array of coffees.

Finn led Dylan and I down a maze of halls and opened a door to a small room. Inwardly, I groaned. I hate small windowless rooms. Chaz sat sullenly at a table next to a woman who looked like an older, female version of himself. Her aura glowed sweet pink, exuding selfishness. Right now, it was tinged with anxiety. A heavy set man with jowls sat next to her at the table. "My name is Oscar Grenell. I represent Charles White. Is Charles being charged with something?"

"At the present time, yes. He is charged with kidnapping a child, grand theft auto and accomplice to murder of a police officer. I'm Detective Fielding, Shyenne de la Angelino and Dylan DelRikkio from 3-D Investigations." Finn introduced us as we entered. "Due to the magical nature and Were involvement in this case, 3-D Investigations is consulting." Finn noted, pulling a chair out and sitting down at the head of the table. I sat down to his left and Dylan to his right.

Mr. Grenell, laughed, causing his jowls to shake. "I'm sure this is a misunderstanding. Charles is just a boy! What evidence do you have that my client did anything illegal?"

"Traffic cameras spotted your client, along with Dante Kane and Shamus Brownley in a stolen vehicle within minutes before and after the kidnapping of an eight year old girl in East Lewiston. A co-conspirator identified your client. Within hours, we located your client, Shamus and a young woman named Mindy in an abandoned barn with the young girl, tied to a chair. The suspects were subdued and zip tied while awaiting transport." Finn nodded towards Ms. White. "The protection talisman worn by your client enabled the spell to wear off sooner than anticipated. Charles aided Mindy to wake up. Mindy cast a spell causing the death of a uniformed sheriff deputy. In the victim's recounting of the kidnapping, she discussed her interactions with each of her captors, detailing her interaction with Charles."

Mr. Grenell didn't look as amused as he was moments ago. Ms. White's eyes filled with tears and she took a deep, shaky breath. "Charles, what the fuck did you do?" Her voice broke on the last word. Chaz gazed as his mom. I swear a look exchanged between the two. He turned to Mr. Grenell. Grenell paused for a moment, looking between his client and Ms. White. "What incentive does my client have to cooperate?"

"Well, gee, your client is looking at about five times the amount of jail time versus his age. By the time he smells freedom again, those black curls will be totally gray." Finn informed Mr. Grenell. "Oh, did I forget to mention the intention behind kidnapping the little girl was to kill her?"

"Whoa, whoa, whoa!" Chaz jumped up out of his chair. "We did not intend to hurt her! Are you crazy? We were supposed to get her and babysit for a little while until her lab work or blood levels or whatever were good. As soon as the coven got what they wanted —"

I saw Ms. White start a spell. Immediately, Finn dropped a protection bubble around Dylan and himself. I easily deflected it. It was a memory spell. "Not a smart move Ms. White," Finn stated. Circling his left pointer finger in the air, a whirlwind picked her up and moved her to the corner of the room. She remained pinned up against the wall. Finn dropped his protection bubble and approached Ms. White, pulling a spelled zip tie out of a side pocket of his cargo pants. "You are under arrest for attempting to perform a magical attack on an officer and two civilians." Again he did a movement with his finger. She turned to face the wall. As he zip tied her hands together, "Dylan, pick up the phone and dial star one one. Ask for an officer to report to interrogation five, please."

Dylan nodded and did as Finn asked. Wow. Finn had some skills. Grenell took a deep breath and slowly let it out. "Please, Detective, it was a rash reaction. She is very upset and worried for her boy. Any mother's response is to protect her child."

"That was a memory spell. How does that protect her child?" I asked.

The attorney looked at me quickly. "How would you know what she cast?"

Meeting his gaze, "I recognize some spells. Hers was a memory spell." I stated matter of factly. An officer entered the room.

Finn turned her to face the responding officer. "Take her down to booking." He handed her off to him. "She just tried to use a spell on us."

"Come on. This is a little high handed don't you think?" Mr. Grenell tried to assuage the situation.

"I need to be here for Charles' interview!" The officer placed a hand on her back as he escorted her to the door. She turned, fear in her eyes, look- ing towards her son. "You can't interview him without me present!"

"Your son is represented by an attorney who will ensure we respect his rights." Finn informed her. "You just attempted to attack a police officer and two civilians. You'll stay in a jail cell for a little while, at least."

"Anna, don't say anything. I'll take care of Charles and get you bailed out as soon as I can!" Grenell rubbed his hand through his gray sparse hair. Chaz looked terrified, swallowing a lump in his throat. He sat back in his chair while the officer led his mother out. He wiped a tear as it trickled down his face.

Finn sat back down at the table. "So, where were we?" Referring to his iPad, Finn asked, "What did the coven want from the girl?"

Chaz looked at Grenell, his breathing, quickening. Tipping his head to the side, Grenell laughed and said, "I'm sure the child misspoke. No coven would sanctify the kidnapping and murder of a child. Obviously, this is a childhood prank gone terribly awry."

"Start at the beginning. And keep in mind, we're interrogating Dante and Shamus, as well. Mindy is next. Your best chance at any kind of deal is total, complete honesty." Finn crossed his arms and sat back in his chair, waiting for Chaz's response. Chaz looked askance at Grenell and he nodded.

"They wanted us to find a Were girl. When her blood levels were right then they would take what they needed and we'd be done." Chaz stated and shrugged his shoulders.

"Who asked you to get a Were girl?" Finn questioned as he tapped his iPad.

He looked at Grenell again, who nodded, and said, "Mindy did." "Okay, so what was the plan?" coaxingly, Finn tried to pull more details out of the teenager.

"We needed to find a young Were girl and hold her until her blood levels or something were right. A friend of Mindy's came with us because she could cast a detect Were spell. Shamus stole a car from the mill. We found the girl and took her to the barn. Mindy checked on her several times." Again, he shrugged.

"How does the coven play into this?" Finn asked.

"Now, now. Like I said, the boy misspoke. The coven isn't involved in this at all." Grenell interjected.

"Are you representing Charles or the coven?" Dylan asked, pointedly. "I represent both. Right now, my focus is Charles." Squinting his eyes, he looked at Chaz. "Go ahead and answer son."

Chas took a deep breath and sighed. "She told us we would be initiated into the coven for our assistance."

"Who told you this?" Finn asked.

"Mindy." Grenell's facial muscles relaxed visibly at his response. "What's Mindy's standing within the coven?" Finn asked.

"She's an initiate and works for the Clarks. Richard Clark is the coven leader. Mindy cares for his daughter." The reverence was evident in his voice when he mentioned Richard Clark.

Pushing for more information, "How do you know Mindy?" Chaz fidgeted in his seat. "Whaddaya mean?" he stuttered.

"How did you meet her? How do you know her?" Finn elaborated. "You're a lot younger than she is. Why would she call you, a sixteen year old, to kidnap a child? It doesn't make sense."

Obviously uncomfortable with this line of questioning, Chaz didn't want to answer. He looked over at Grenell, hesitating. "So, will you tell the coven what I say in here?"

Surprised, Grenell responded, "No. I'm bound by attorney client privilege. I can't tell anyone what we discuss without your permission."

Breathing a sigh of relief, "Kayla is my girlfriend. I come and help with her homework. I met Mindy through Kayla."

"Why is your relationship something you want to hide from the coven?" Finn asked as he looked up at Chaz, confused.

"Because I usually enter and exit through her window. She doesn't think her dad is ready for her to have a boyfriend. And he'd probably turn me into a frog or something," Chaz crossed his arms. "Mindy knows about our relationship and is okay with it. She thinks Kayla should lead as normal of a life as possible. She asked me to help because Kayla's health is really bad. If a cure isn't found soon, she will die."

Yep, Grenell was definitely relieved.

"How did Shamus and Dante get involved?"

"I asked them for help." He exhaled loudly. "We're in the same boat. Our magical skills suck. Our chances of being initiated into a coven are highly unlikely. This was our only chance."

"Okay. What did you think she wanted with the Were girl?"

He shrugged. "I didn't think she would be killed. I just figured they needed something from her for the spell." Sighing,

"I guess I didn't think anything about it. I just wanted to help Kayla."Tears welled up in his eyes. "I don't want her to die."

"Whose idea was it to steal the car?" I asked, gently. Hedging a bit, "Shamus stole the car and picked us all up."

"Who was in the car?" I continued questioning.

"Me, Shamus, Dante and Daisy." "Who is Daisy?"

He shrugged. "A friend of Mindy's? I didn't know her. She could do a detect Were spell and a sleep spell. We needed her for our plan."

That surprised me. "You had a plan?"

"Yeah."

Everyone starred at him, waiting for him to elaborate, including Grenell. "And the plan was…"

"Steal a car, find a Were girl, get her in the car, hit her with a sleep spell, keep her at the barn until Mindy got the spell components right. Let the girl go." And he shrugged again. Keep it simple, stupid?

"What does Daisy look like?" I asked, reclining in my chair. "Blondish short hair, shorter than me, kinda heavy." He shrugged, again. "But I think she used a disguise spell. Towards the end, her hair darkened and her face seemed different. At times, when we said her name, she didn't respond."

"Why the barn?" Finn leaned back in his chair, crossing his ankles.

"It's our party barn. It's set up with the creature comforts. Everyone else attended the party last night. No one would stop by. We figured we'd have the place to ourselves while Mindy collected the spell components." "From the beginning, tell us what happened." Finn suggested tapping his iPad.

Sighing heavily, Chaz said, "Alright. I visit Kayla almost every night. She suffered a lot of issues lately and her health is failing. Mindy told me at the rate she was deteriorating, Kayla didn't have long to live. Mindy said there was a spell that would cure her but obtaining some of the components were tricky. She said they needed a young female Were but all these levels in her system had to be just right."

"According to Mindy, the coven decided teenagers should find the Were girl. As minors with clean records, we wouldn't get in trouble and the coven would protect us. If we did this, then we would be initiated." Chaz stopped for a breath.

"Why did you think you would be initiated?" Finn asked,

tapping his stylus pen against his lip.

"Mindy told me so. She said to get a couple friends, come up with a plan." He fumbled with his fingers as he spoke. "She asked if any of us could cast a detect Were spell or a sleep spell. None of us could. Mindy said she had a friend that could do both. Her friend's name was Daisy. We met her just minutes before we went looking for a Were female. "Shamus found a car at Potlatch. He picked us up an old dirt road off of Lindsay Road. We found the girl real fast. Daisy cast the detect Were spell and we pulled up alongside of her. Daisy asked her where the mill was. She gave her a flower to smell. When the girl smelled the flower she passed out. We grabbed her." He sighed, then continued. "We went back to where we left Dante's car, abandoned the stolen car and headed to the barn. Mindy met us there. She said the girl was perfect. But we had to wait until she wasn't scared and the adrenaline left her body.

"Daisy went with Mindy. Her part was done. Dante started playing cards with Carrie and got her laughing and stuff. But Mindy said it wasn't enough. We made a soft bed for her and took turns watching her all night while she slept. Mindy came by every couple hours and checked her levels. She said the levels were almost where we needed them to be.

"Just before you guys busted in, Mindy said the levels were perfect and she prepared to extract what she needed. The next thing I know, I'm laying on the dirt with my hands zip tied. I remember feeling the odd effect of my protection talisman waking me. I used my friendship bracelet to cut off the zip tie. While I cut it off, I touched my ankle talisman to Mindy's arm. I knew it would wake her. She dropped the cop, the lady and the guy. That's all I know."

"How did Mindy test her?" I asked.

"She ran this gizmo down her arm and the LCD display monitored the chemicals in her body." Chaz answered.

"How did you know your talisman would work to wake up Mindy?" Finn questioned.

"I'm a kid. We always push the limits, testing things out. One time, Shamus fell out of the loft- wait a second." Chaz hesitated. "If I admit to other crimes, will I be in more trouble?"

"What crime did you commit?" Oscar questioned, leaning towards Chaz. Chaz whispered in his ear. Oscar flashed a smile. "At this point, I'm sure that doesn't matter."

"I don't know if that's good or not."Chaz gulped, continuing his story. "So, we threw a roaring party in the barn. Shamus was drunk, fell out of the loft and got knocked out. None of us knew how to heal him so I touched my anklet to him and he woke up!"

"Did Mindy ever mention anyone else who was involved with the coven?" I asked Chaz.

He shook his head, "No."

"When did Mindy approach you?" Finn asked.

"Night before last, when I went to visit Kayla. After I visited with her for a couple hours, she told me Kayla was running out of time and she needed help. I said okay, I'd do it." He shrugged his shoulders. "I knew my buddies had my back."

"Does your mom know about you and Kayla?" Finn questioned as he continued entering info into his iPad.

"Yeah. She thinks it's great!" Chaz answered enthusiastically. "Why does she think it's great?" I quizzed him.

"Because her parents are like the top witches in Lewiston and Clarkston. If I get in with them, we're golden!" Chaz smiled.

"What do you mean by golden?" Finn asked.

"You know!" Chaz rolled his eyes as he explained. "I'll probably be initiated just for being with Kayla and Mom will move up within the coven because of our relationship!"

"Did your mom know about your plan to kidnap a Were?" Finn questioned nonchalantly.

Chaz nodded his head. "Yeah she said we needed to steal a car so we wouldn't get caught. She thought the mill would be a good place because no one would miss it for hours. What?"Chaz asked as Oscar tried to inter- rupt him and get him to stop talking, but it was too late. For Mom anyway. "My client is done. This interview is on hold for now." Oscar announced.

"That's fine. I got what I wanted." Finn picked up the phone and punched a few numbers. "Book White for accessory before the fact, kidnapping and conspiracy to kidnapping. We are booking her son, too. Get juvenile detention in here."Finn put the phone down. "Charles White, you are under arrest for kidnapping, accessory to homicide of a police officer and accessory to grand theft."

"Wait! What!? I cooperated with you! I'm a just a kid! The coven will protect me!" Charles looked wildly at Oscar. "Do something! I don't want to go to jail!"

Oscar sighed heavily. "Keep your cool! I'll figure out what we can do. You're probably going to be detained a few days while I work out a deal." He patted Chaz on the arm. "Detective, I want to speak with my client confidentially, please."

"Of course." Standing up, Finn opened the door. Dylan and I walked out. Finn closed the door, smiling. "Well, we got two adults. Let's see how the other interviews went." He led us back through the maze to the conference room. Everyone else waited for us. "How did the White interview go?" Swanson asked.

"Awesome. We got Mom for attempted magical attack on a police officer and two civilians, conspiracy to kidnap a child and accessory before the fact." Finn quickly summarized. "Chaz spilled his guts. What about your guys?" We began comparing notes. Shamus corroborated Chaz's accounting that Anna White knew of the plan and she proposed stealing a car from Potlatch. Dante corroborated the other boys' story. Steve didn't know who else might be involved and refused to speculate. Anna White was a level three and Mindy late level two to early level three.

"There must be a witch more skilled than Mindy and Anna," I stated. "I deflected Anna's spell easily. Mindy lacks the skills to cast the healing spell. The create dirt spell was an effective means to kill the officer but not one a witch would typically use as an attack spell."

Fynn nodded. "The attorney Anna called for her son works for the coven. It's safe to assume the coven knows who all is here. Grenell is focused on bailing the Whites out of jail, for now."

Swanson rubbed his hand across his face, then looked around the table. "Shyenne, Finn and I will interview Mindy. She's the key to who the real witch behind this debacle is."

Wondering, I asked, "Are the boys going to be safe? It seems like young witches end up as collateral damage."

Swanson bobbed his head side to side. "Reasonably safe. There's twenty-four hour supervision with video surveillance. Juvenile Detention is secure. For right now, they are being detained. They may need to get use to it." Swanson responded frankly.

12

FYNN AND I followed Swanson into another interrogation room. Mindy sat in a chair with her hands zip tied together. Her feet had been released. She immediately sized us up. She ignored Swanson like last week's newspaper. Finn, she studied for a few moments before dismissing him. Then she reached me. Her eyes widened and she gasped.

"Yeah, I have that effect on people. So, Miss Mindy. Let me sum- marize your situation. You convinced three hapless boys to kidnap a little girl in exchange for initiation into a coven. You don't have the ability to promise that. Three counts fraud, kidnapping a child. Conspiracy to murder a child. Murder of a uniformed police officer, assault of one civilian consultant and one police officer." I summed up for her.

"Why did you do this? Kayla, your charge, suffers from Diabetes Insipidus. To heal her. You're aiding with the spell. It requires, among other components, a Were female adolescent pituitary gland, at rest. You reached this conclusion after experimentation using other Weres. Result: three counts of kidnapping and three counts of murder." I purposely left out the other missing Weres.

"Your coven? Well, attorney, Oscar Grenell's focus is the coven. Not Chaz, Shamus or Dante. Not Anna White. Or, you." I emphasized by pointing at her. "Fall guy for this whole debacle?" I questioned and then again pointed at her. "You. You were involved with Dwayne Reynolds. You cast the crappy ward of protection on his house. He tried to find a Were female adolescent pituitary gland, at rest. He got caught. His head got blown off.

"Shamus Brownley, Dante Kane and Chaz White identified you as recruiting them to obtain a Were female." Adding another nail to her coffin, "You were identified by the latest victim."

"Bottom line: you are the fall gal for the Orchards Coven. You will never feel the wild earth under your feet again. Ever. You are fucked." I succinctly outlined her present legal situation.

She burst into tears. "It wasn't supposed to be like this!" She sobbed, "We couldn't get the spell right, but we're so close!"

"What was wrong with the spell?" I questioned. "How did you get to this point?"

"The pituitary gland in the spell is supposed to fix the production, storage and release of ADH between the hypothalamus, pituitary gland and the kidneys," Mindy explained, with strong conviction. "Through process of elimination we narrowed it down. The Were female adolescent pituitary gland at rest is it! It must be! You don't understand how important she is!" Mindy appeared maniacal in her belief. "We have to save her!"

"How did you develop the spell?" I wanted to focus on the magic. She would disclose their actions while modifying and experimenting with the configuration of the spell.

"We researched all kinds of healing spells from all types of magic. Ancient and new. Finally, we found a spell book with spells using Were organs. The Were are innately magical." Mindy explained the rational for all her actions. "We believe the ability of the Were to heal quickly will heal Kayla."

I mulled this over. "Will she be infected with Were-ism?"

Shaking her head, Mindy explained, "No. The pituitary gland is alive for the spell, imbuing the magics we need. The spell uses the life. When we cast it, the magic remains, but not the life."

I tilted my head to the side, weighing her information. The mechan- ics behind the magic sounded plausible. "How did you develop the spell?"

"It's a three tier spell. Very complex."

"Well, it's a good thing I'm a classically trained elemental witch with Shamanic foundation of both the North American Nez Perce and the South American Aztec with a Persian background. And I'm a Were. So, explain it to me." I challenged her.

"The book contained a spell for healing multiple sclerosis. It called for a pituitary gland of a young male Were." Mindy explained further. "Since MS and diabetes are both auto-immune diseases, we used it as a starting point. When we tested the spell

113

on Kayla it showed some improvement, but not enough."

"How did you acquire the pituitary gland?" I asked nonchalantly. She shrugged her shoulders. "Scott found a homeless boy in Spokane."

Bingo. We got a name. Finn pulled out his cell and started texting. I swallowed my disgust with Mindy's unrepentant tone. "What was the next variation of the spell you tried?" I knew if I kept her talking about the magic she'd disclose important facts about the kidnappings, murders and hopefully, other witches.

"We tried a female pituitary gland. This time, the results proved promising." Eagerly, Mindy described the breakthrough. "She began producing ADH. Prior to this, her body couldn't."

"What is ADH?" I inquired, rubbing the back of my neck.

"Anti-diuretic hormone. Diabetes Insipidus is the body's inability to create ADH, store and/or properly manage the hormone to regulate the body's water supply. The result is the danger of dehydration," Mindy sighed heavily. "The last few months, Kayla's disease process progressed, requiring IV fluids almost daily. All the best doctors in the world failed to heal her." I sympathized for the teen. It must be very difficult for her family, to watch her suffer on a daily basis. But the parents of the missing girls, and boy, also suffered terribly. "Where did you find the female pituitary gland?"

Totally unaffected, "Scott and I found a girl in Missoula."

Covering my shock at her complete lack of empathy or understanding for her victims, "What variation did you try next?"

"We noticed in the book the chemical make-up of the Were seemed highly significant. We needed to control the emotional state of the Were prior to harvest. We surmised the first female was frightened, terrified. The second one we administered antidepressants, to make her happy." Shaking her head, "That proved an abysmal failure, probably related to the drugs."

I raised an eyebrow. Ya think? Drugs and magic do not mix. "Where did you find the third one?" I hated to ignore the humanity, but she pro- vided facts we desperately needed to learn regarding the kidnappings and murders. And the others involved.

"Coeur de Alene. The fourth, Scott and I found in Spokane. We tricked her into believing we'd release her. With elation, Kayla showed more promise in producing ADH in the hypothalamus and storing it in the pituitary gland." Quite animated, Mindy continued, "Not only did she produce ADH but she also stored it! This was a monumental break-through! Now, if we could get her to regulate the ADH!"

"Fantastic!" Swallowing the bile rising in my throat, "What was your next step?" I asked.

"With the fifth one, we found a girl in Sandpoint. We harvested her pituitary gland at rest, while she slept. Kayla produced and stored ADH!"

Sitting back, "But when it came to the kidneys regulating the ADH and releasing it when needed, it worked sporadically. Can I get a pop?"

Finn jumped up, "Of course! What kind do you like?"

"Dr. Pepper, please." Finn nodded and left the room. "We are so close! Even though she was at rest, we think too much adrenaline remained in her system. The sixth one, Reynolds acquired, but it was destroyed when the police raided his home." Elated, "We are so close! We can make her well."

"Tell me about Carrie." I questioned.

She looked at me quizzically. "Carrie? Who's Carrie?"

"The little girl we found you with in the barn, who'd been kidnapped last night," I clarified for her.

"Oh, her. I didn't know her name. Chaz and Kayla secretly dated for months. They're in love. Like a modern day Romeo and Juliet. Well, sorta." Mindy shrugged, and then continued. "Chaz realized she had deteriorated significantly. He asked if he could help. I gave him the short version of what we needed, a young female Were.

"I told him Mr. Clark would initiate any witches who helped heal Kayla. Chaz said he had a couple friends who would help.

"They called me when they grabbed her and I met them at the barn. I tested her adrenaline level but it was too high. So, I monitored her." She rolled her eyes, "'Til you showed up."

"Explain what happened at the barn." I asked as I sat back in my seat. It was difficult for me to not reach across the table and smack her for her blase attitude towards the Were children she treated as lab rats.

She sighed, shaking her head. "I vaguely remember seeing you and the other witch appear. Then, I was out. I came to when Chaz touched his anklet to me. I hit two people with sleep spells and created dirt in the mouth of the officer." She shrugged.

"What did you think would happen when you cast the dirt spell?" I questioned nonchalantly.

"I hadn't tried it before but I hoped it would suffocate him and it did," She sounded pleased with herself. This woman was a sociopath. Or just fucking nuts.

I needed to keep her talking. "What is the process for harvesting the pituitary gland?" I asked as Malachi brought the Dr. Pepper in for Mindy a tea for me and a Mountain Dew for Swanson, then sat down in Finn's chair.

"Well, the book described specifically how to harvest. First, the specimen must be in the right emotional state and with the appropriate chemical makeup. Then, you cast a hypnotize spell to render the specimen unaware. Quickly, the top of the skull must be cut off. A saws-all work best." Malachi looked at her, morbidly in shock as she described the process. "Find the pituitary gland. Immediately wrap it in mint leaves and boil in pristine mountain water in a copper untainted pot by a low heat magical fire. The low heat loosens and pulls the essence from the pituitary gland into the mountain's essence." Malachi stood up and left the room, looking green around the gills.

"Okay, after you," I hesitated, "'acquire' the pituitary gland, what happens next?"

"Well, the pituitary gland must be preserved with a spell during harvest. Want to hear it?" She asked, eagerly. "I wrote it!"

I smiled and encouraged her, nodding. "Of course!"

"Young she Were
just at puberty
thy rested
thy calm
pituitary gland enrapt en mint
enhance preserve heal
mountains sustain
the essence in water
preserved in mint"

She finished in a soft chant. I considered the process, the

spell, the chant. Seemed plausible. If you possessed the magical ability. "I'm impressed! What happens next?"

"We're ready for the first tier of the spell. It requires dandelions, mashed garlic, wild carrot, and green tea leaves. Mash the garlic in a wooden bowl. Then, add wild carrot, mashing it into the garlic. Pour fresh mountain water into the mash. Add the green tea leaves and the fresh dandelion flowers. The tea leaves and dandelions float on top of the mash mixture. Use a low heat to allow the ingredients to blend. Leave in the wooden bowl. The witch maintains the low level heat at just the right temperature, perfectly curing the potion."

For a witch of Mindy's caliber this seemed simple. All the ingredients proved forgiving to work with. "What happens next?"

"The second tier requires more finesse. This is what I've worked on. Heat ravensara oil slowly. Add cat's claw to the oil. Carefully cut up, releasing the energy into the oil, then add noni. It too, is cut up, releasing its energy into the oil. Prepare very slowly to assimilate the healing properties into the oil. To help bind the oil, add Kayla's essence. I experimented with different ingredients to include her true essence."

"Wow! What worked the best?" I asked.

"Her blood. When binding her essence to the oil, I came up with a binding spell.

"Plant to essence

oil to essence

child to essence

essence to essence to essence to oil"

"Okay. Then what?" The second tier sounded probable.

"We mix the pituitary gland, the oil and the tea together and she ingests it! It's that simple! We are so close to a cure!" She clapped her hands, excitedly.

"Who's doing the final spell?" I wondered. Obviously, someone else performed the third tier. "Scott is. We've worked on it for months!" She smiled happily, lunacy clearly showing.

Playing out a hunch, "What types of magic are you using?"

"Oh, it's part Wiccan and part Elemental magic." She

sighed dramatically, "I'm sorry, but I really must go. We need to work on the final spell to heal Kayla."

"A few more questions." I kept her talking. The evil book was druidic. She didn't know about the druidic aspect of the magical working. The third tier needed way more work. Mindy wasn't privy to the whole spell. Sounded like Mindy was a lackey too. "Who else worked on the spell with you and Scott?"

She shook her head. "Good help really is hard to find. We realized early on we needed a lower level witch to do the first steps of the spell. We couldn't work within the coven because Scott said they wouldn't ap- prove of some of the," she hesitated, "tactics we used. I came up with the idea of using witches who weren't in a coven but desperately wanted to be! Unfortunately, there's a reason why they aren't initiates. Dwayne was just an idiot. The boys worked hard and finished their part. We didn't count on law enforcement," she sighed heavily. "I apologize. But, I need to go. I'm sure Scott's wondering where I am and we have lots to prepare, to ready the spell."

"What's your relationship with Scott?" I asked, stalling.

"Well, actually," she smiled brightly, "we're engaged! We worked so close together these past few months. We fell in love!"

Huh. Congratulations? *Nothing like falling in love while terrorizing and mutilating children.* I thought to myself. "When's the date?" I returned her smile.

She looked up towards the ceiling. "Oh, we didn't set a date yet. We want Kayla to be our flower girl! She's going to be so beautiful! But I do need to go. Can we continue this later?"

I looked at Swanson. "Mindy, the only place you're going is jail." She looked stunned, perplexed, bewildered. "For what?"

"Uh, kidnapping and murdering numerous Were children, murder of a police officer?" I threw back at her.

She laughed, waving her hand. "It was for Kayla."

"Yeah, we got that. You are under arrest for the kidnapping and murder of five children and the murder of a police officer." Swanson clarified for her.

She looked at us like we were the crazy ones. "Call Mr. Clark. He'll straighten this out." Mindy smiled confidently.

"Believe me, we'll be talking to the Clarks soon enough," Detective Swanson stated as he stood up. "Stand up. You're heading to booking, then a jail cell."

118

Dumbfounded, she stood up. I opened the door and a uniformed officer waited for her.

Swanson handed her off, motioning me to follow him. We returned to the conference room we met in before. Malachi, Ryan, Dylan, Karen and Finn sat around the table, clapping.

"Wow! Very impressive, Shyenne. How did you get her to spill her guts like that?" Karen asked.

"Lower level witches always want to impress a higher level witch. Just fed her ego," I remarked, taking a seat.

"Very good job. What is your impression of the situation? The magic, the spell?" Swanson asked.

"She isn't as knowledgeable as she thinks. It isn't just Wiccan and Elemental magic they're using. There's more occurring in the higher tiered spell than she knows. What she expressed, isn't enough. I'd like to see Scott's level."

Finn tapped on his iPad, "Level three. I don't think he could cast the upper tier part unless his level is downplayed like yours."

"Well, we need to bring Scott in," Swanson remarked. "The Clarks gotta know by now this is unraveling."

"Why not ask them to bring Scott in? I vote we avoid a full blown magic shootout, if possible," Karen suggested.

Everyone nodded in agreement. Swanson pulled up data from his iPad, then picked up the phone, dialing Scott Clark's residence, placing the phone on speaker. A female voice answered after two rings. "Clark residence."

"This is Lieutenant Swanson of the Nez Perce County Sheriff's Department. Is Scott Clark available?"

The female hesitated, then said, "Just a moment." Her hand obviously covered the phone.

After a few moments, a male voice came on the line. "This is Scott Clark." Anxiety colored his voice.

"This is Lieutenant Swanson of the Nez Perce County Sheriff's Department. We need to speak with you in regards to an investigation. We would like for you to come down to the Sheriff's Department for questioning."

He hesitated, then asked, "Regarding?"

"We'll discuss it when you arrive." Swanson informed him.

The phone went very quiet for several moments. "I need to contact my attorney. He'll make arrangements with you."

"Alright. This needs to be addressed immediately. We appreciate you cooperation in this matter,"Swanson said as the call ended. "I think I'll talk with Mindy and get specific details regarding the kidnapping and murders of the children. I don't think we need Shyenne. It's straightforward police work."

"Thanks! I don't know if I could sit through much more" I shivered. "Since you two teleport everywhere, pick up dinner and we'll meet you at the house," Ryan said, standing up. We followed suit.

13

MALACHI RELAXED ON the bed. He opened his mind and I entered. We went to the bound area. *"So, you snipped a little there and I became irresistible to women. Let's snip more!"*

I laughed. *"We might as well, since we know the effect,"* I cut several strands, then studied the center. One area was heavily bound. More strings seemed focused in that spot. I snipped three tendrils. *"Okay, lets see what happens next!"*

The next morning, Malachi appeared smokin' hot! Luckily, he sated me completely last night. Interesting his magic consisted of charisma, sexuality, outrageous hotness. We noticed nothing else.

I opened the French door, heading outside to perform my morning salutation. Malachi entered the room. "Hold it a sec! I want to join you."

I raised my eyebrows. "Okaaay." We walked through the doors out into the yard. I knelt down, facing the rising sun.

Malachi followed suit. "Explain the steps to me."

Nodding, "We pay tribute to Father Sun, for rising another day." I moved into child's pose, spreading my knees wide as my breasts touched the ground, and kissed the earth. Malachi followed. "Now, we pay tribute to Mother Earth, for all life. Thank you, Mother, for the water we drink, the scents of the wild, the ground we walk on, the air we breathe, the beauty we see."

Malachi repeated after me.

"Next, down dog yoga pose, arching my back, straightening my arms, curling my toes and pushing up with my legs." Malachi copied my moves. I then walked my hands towards my feet. Inhaling the aromas of the river, I rolled up, circling my arms at my side, above my head, lowering them down to my heart, in prayer pose. "This represents the sun rising," I explained. "Thank you, Father Sky, for the sun that rises, the moon that sets, the stars that guide us, the rain that falls from your clouds. Thank you for feeding Mother Earth with your sun and your rain."

Repeating after me, Malachi thanked Father Sun.

"Next, we honor our parents, we respect others around us, we continue to better ourselves, every day," explaining the next step. "I will honor my mother and father by treating both with great respect. I will treat my fellow humans with love and kindness. I will continue to learn, exude patience and understanding each day as I walk through life."

Malachi repeated my words.

"The next part requests Father Sky to recognize all the goodness we do each day for when our sun no longer rises," I explained, turning my head to look at Malachi. "Let me keep this day so when I am called I can come to you, Father, with clean hands and straight eyes. So that when my life fades as the fading sunset, my spirit can come to you without shame." Malachi nodded as he recited this part of the salutation. "Lastly, we recognize we will return to Mother Earth. Let my body feed you, Mother Earth, as I continue as a small part in the cycle of life."

I raised my right hand, created water and let it rain down on Mother Earth. Malachi followed suit, with a small amount of water falling. "What the hell? I can create water? Awesome!" Astounded, Malachi exclaimed loudly.

I was surprised, too. Another piece of magic let loose? Maybe a result of what we cut? "Cool. Now we're ready for our day and whatever it may bring." Malachi smiled at me.

"Better get going. Dad'll be pissed if we're too late getting to work." When we 'ported to the office, Rosie waited, unable to enter.

Malachi sucked in a deep breath. "Holy shit! I see the spell! I see the magic! I can, I can... it's... Wow! It's so beautiful!"

Malachi saw magic. Characteristically, only a higher level witch or someone who studied magic for many, many, many years developed the skill. Hmmm.

I allowed Rosie access as we entered through the foyer. I realized I never checked her aura. Waves of pink with red pearly looking things.

Magic level one, maybe two. Her magic centered around fire.

Envy and jealousy colored her aura, but nothing else of real concern. I wonder why she couldn't enter the ward?

After making the appropriate morning beverages, Malachi and I went into his office. I started reading while he picked up his guitar and strummed. After about half an hour, his dad came in.

"Swanson said the Clarks are stalling. They hired an attorney for Mindy, but she confessed everything, every detail about each kidnapping and murder." Ryan walked into the office and stood in front of the picture window. "Swanson is concerned she isn't quite sane. She seems to think her actions are justified since it's for Kayla. She doesn't seem to understand what she did was wrong, let alone a crime. For today, we're in a hold- ing pattern until the attorney and district attorney reach an agreement. Swanson does want you, Shyenne, present when he meets with the Clarks. You impressed him in the interrogation."

"What about Scott Clark?" I asked, closing my book.

"He totally lawyered up. We can't get near him, yet. The county attorney needs more than Mindy's word, at this point. Apparently, alibis place him in other locations at the times of disappearances. So, what are you doing today?"

I looked at Malachi. He strummed a few chords on his guitar. "I'm rehearsing with Glitzen. What about you, Shy?"

"I think I'll go on a run. I found a neat place I want to explore further." I stretched my arms above my head.

Ryan nodded, "Okay. I'll call if I hear anything more, but I think we're good for today."

14

I WANTED TO explore the land around the lodge better. I 'ported to the site, changed to a bobcat, and took off running on the canyon trail. Scenting mountain goats and sheep, I followed a barely visible trail. The tantalizing smell of rodents and vermin assaulted my senses, but I wanted to explore. I ran for a little while before smelling sulfur. In this part of the country, sulfur typically meant a natural hot spring! I veered off the trail to locate the source. Jumping from rock to rock, I scaled the canyon wall, exhilarated! The sun gazed down upon me. The sweet aroma of the Salmon river and forest enveloped me. I loved breathing the fresh mountain air. Virtually, no hint of man. The sulfur smell assaulted my senses. Rounding a rocky corner, I saw a small waterfall emptying into a rock pool. Water trickled from numerous sources. I walked over to the pool and stuck a paw in. It was the perfect temperature!

Climbing the rocks, I searched around the hot springs. I found petroglyph stained on a rock protected from the elements. Black, red and blue drawings depicted the hot springs, hunting of deer and goats, fishing the river, canoes heading down stream. A written diary of sorts, detailed the importance of the area to my native people.

The Nez Perce traveled downriver by canoes, made from fallen trees. This spot was a ceremonial site, revered by Indians. In the protected alcove lay remains of flowers, leather pouches, arrow heads, a deer antler, a bone knife, fishhook carved from granite. The leather pouches held talismans offered to the hot springs, as gifts. The Nez Perce left items symbolizing their importance in their lives and continued success in these areas by gift- ing this sacred place. I bit off one of my claws and left it in the alcove, honoring my ancestors. I hopped along the rocks above the hot springs. Something "pulled" me right. I followed the feeling as it grew stronger. Trees held charms, talismans, satchels. A burial ground. I laid my belly on the earth, submissively, resting my head on my paws.

I honor those who came before me, providing me with life, tradition and respect. I hope these ancestors were able to come to Father with clean hands and straight eyes, when life faded as the fading sunset. I hope these spirits came to you without shame. Let these bodies feed you, Mother Earth, continuing as a small part in the cycle of life.

After paying homage, I skirted the perimeter, finding a trail leading away from the springs. Heavily used at some point, now, overgrown. The trail continued on the back side of the canyon, blocking the view of the river. I loped along, turning a corner and found a secret garden!

Fruit trees lined a path with vegetables growing wildly. At one time, someone cared for this garden. A roof poked through the trees. Weeds mixed in with the vegetables while the fruit trees desperately needed pruning and trimming. I walked down the canyon wall along the path, passing a small man made cavern. It was big enough for me as a cat to enter, but a tight fit for my human form. Continuing down the path, I passed a second man-made cavern with a bigger opening. The old odor of animal blood permeated.

Once I hit the canyon floor, I identified all the vegetables. Herbal plants mixed in with the vegetables. I was surprised at some of the herbs. Many originated from Asia and China. Some I failed to identify. *How did they get here?* I changed to human form to gather herbs.

Opening a portal, I pulled out a pair of shorts and a tee shirt. I also grabbed a sharp knife and a handful of glass bottles to store herbs. I set out bottles and started walking through the garden. On second thought, I reopened my portal, removing a book identifying herbs. As an earth witch, I pushed weeds out of the garden, I opened it up to more sunshine. As I worked I felt as if I was watched. I sniffed the air but noticed nothing. I pruned the trees and cleared the pathway, revealing a very old log cabin. Part of the roof caved in, but the stacked log walls and most of the mud mixture insulation was intact. Vines climbed the logs. My people didn't build the house. Maybe gold miners? The Salmon River was infamous for veins of gold running

125

through the rock. Many miners hoped and dreamed of finding the mother lode. Some did, most didn't.

Again, the sense of being watched came over me. I swear, I felt a sigh on my neck from the wind. I opened my mind softly and "searched" for something. I whispered, "Hello?"

"Hello, you hear me?" a male Chinese accent responded.

"Yes, I feel your presence," Unsure what I encountered, my belief is to be welcoming until you need to defend. "My name is Shyenne."

"I am Jiang Gan," the breeze whispered in my ear. "Did you change from a bobcat to a woman?"

"Yes, I'm a Were bobcat and a witch,"I hesitated but he asked me first. "What are you?"

There was a slight pause, "I think I'm a gui, a ghost."

Huh. I never met a ghost before. "Is this your home and garden?" "Yes, it is. Thank you for weeding, trimming and pruning. I'm not able to, in this form." Gratefulness colored his tone.

"Would you mind if I pick herbs? You grew some rare varieties!" "Yes, of course. Take anything you like."

I asked Jiang to identify plants I didn't recognize. "How did you come to this place, here on the river?"

"I was born on Hong Kong Island in December of 1840, during the First Opium War. In January 1841, the British claimed Hong Kong as a colony. As fishermen, my family, lived on the island, earning a meager liv- ing from what we caught. When the British "claimed" Hong Kong, they "claimed" our home as well. We moved to different islands, but the British trade organizations and others pushed us out, wanting to exploit Eastern trade goods. Traders became richer, while the Chinese, poorer.

"I grew up working on the wharf, hearing stories of mountains of gold in America. I worked any job I found: cleaning fish, unloading and loading trade goods, ship repairs, ship cleaning, anything to put food on our table. Fed up with barely making enough to feed my parents and my younger sister, I decided to try my luck in America. I hired on with a ship sailing for California, at age seventeen, during the Second Opium War.

"The British perpetrated the Opium Wars to "equalize" trade between the East and the West. The East provided tea, spices, silk and many other trade goods sought by the West. The West offered less valuable items. However, opium quickly became popular to the East. With the Chinese addicted to opium, trade between the East and West equalized.

"I hired on a Chinese ship, filled with Eastern goods, as a cabin boy. But through our journey, I proved my worth and loyalty, receiving field promotions due to scurvy, men overboard, and the occasional pirate attack. "Once I reached San Francisco, I was completely overwhelmed. I never dreamed society could be so different! Horses pulled carriages, taxis and hauled riders. Houses painted in stark colors. Men wore dull, colorless clothing. Women dressed in ridiculously puffed dresses. And the food! It took a month to acclimate to the variety of foods!

"City life proved too much for me. I decided to head East. I heard many stories of gold in the territories of Washington, Idaho and Montana. Many Chinese traveled to Idaho trying their luck mining. I hired on a wagon train traveling to Idaho. When I reached Lewiston and Clarkston at the junction of the Salmon, Snake and Clearwater Rivers, the bustle of activity surprised me.

"Between shipping, mining, farming and ranching, the two cities flourished. Many Chinese worked and settled here, building lives. But I wanted to find my riches in the gold mines.

"After the law of 1864 passed taxing Chinese miners, I decided to leave Lewiston and the growing discontent between Americans and Chinese. I desired a quieter, less populated existence. Carrying sparse necessities needed to mine on the Salmon, I hiked upriver to the confluence of the Salmon and the Snake. The Salmon River canyon proved less hospitable, meaning less people. I took a shovel, ax, rope, flint, knife, fruit and veg- etable seeds, hammer, pick ax, fishing hooks, string and the clothes on my back. I planned to live off the land.

"I hiked for three weeks, traversing the canyon walls, searching for gold. I finally came to a cave naturally built into the rock wall about two hundred feet above the river. Ribbons of quartz scored the rock. A gorge cut through the canyon wall, leaving a small acre of land, perfect for a garden. A creek flowed along the gorge, offering fresh spring water. As I explored the area thoroughly, I found the remnants of an old cabin. Some of the logs needed shoring up and cracks remudded. The roof required repair. But a fireplace and chimney proved to be in good working order. Dust and rodents indicated the vacancy of cabin. A table, a chair and a bed adorned the interior. This was more than I hoped for! Better than my home in China! As I scoured the area, I found a pot, some utensils, old cans, chisels, nails and other items, left behind by the previous occupant.

"I spent the summer repairing the cabin and planting a garden, readying for winter. I filled in the cracks with a clay/mud mixture. I tended my garden and stacked multitudes of wood, for heat during the winter. I built snare traps for beaver, rabbits and other small furry creatures, for meat and fur. Occasionally, a long boat floated by, en route to Lewiston. I stayed out of sight, not wanting to draw attention to myself. My cabin wasn't visible from the river unless the passengers looked back after passing. Typically, passengers gazed ahead with trepidation, fearing what the river would do next.

"By fall, I had a cozy cabin and started harvesting my garden. I stored produce in the cave. With shelter and food, I focused on mining for gold! Using a torch to light the cavern, I identified promising areas. Chisel marks indicated where the last miner chipped away rock.

"I spent the next three years, mining the cavern. I packed away each fleck and nugget I found. I had no human contact during that time. I spent my days caring for my home, tending my garden, gathering firewood and of course, mining!

"One day, in mid-June, I heard human voices! From the river? I cau- tiously hiked down the gorge. The river flowed high from spring runoff. The Salmon River served as an important route for trade purposes from the cities of Salmon and Leesburg. Gold mines dotted the valleys and drainages along the river.

"I crept to a lookout point above the shoreline. All sorts of debris littered the river: boards, trade goods, oars, clothes, and people. The long boat crashed on its way downriver. I jumped from rock to rock, reaching the bank. Two men floated near, along with supplies. A whirlpool caught a man with bright red hair. It would circle him around from the current, to shore and then back out. The second man, wearing a blue plaid shirt, floated close to the bank. He wouldn't float back out.

"I grabbed the red haired man caught in the whirlpool. Dragging by his coat, I hauled him to shore and then grasped the man in plaid, pulling him in. I picked up supplies. Long boards, crates, sacks, boxes, rope. Red hair coughed, the other gasped for air. I spotted a third man and a fourth, upriver from me. I knew the current of the river would wash them close before it sucked them back out into the middle.

"As the blond hit the whirlpool, I stood in waist deep water and reached out to catch him. Barely able to grasp his arm, I pulled him towards me and noticed a deep gash on his head, which bled profusely. The man in plaid was standing. He raced into the water and caught him as I swung him towards shore. I reached out to the last man, just catching him. Suddenly, I lost my footing and the whirlpool pulled me in. The plaid man reached out, grasping my hand, pulling me and the floating man in. Plaid man and I landed some of the supplies.

"When we saw no more debris, we waded to shore. All the men were alive, for better or worse. I looked at the remnants scattered about. A number of long boards, several crates of supplies, a couple of sacks, and rope. Not enough to build another boat."

"I am Jiang Gan," I bowed to the men, introducing myself.

"I'm Joe Miller, Donald McAmes, Robert Potter, and Christopher McAmes," said the plaid shirt pointing to the red head, blue shirt and bleeding head, respectively. "Thank you. You probably saved our lives. What are you doing here?" He seemed bewildered, looking at the stretch of shoreline where we stood.

Hesitantly, "My cabin is back over the rocks. Is there another boat coming behind you?" I asked.

"Not for a few days," Joe stated.

"Let's take a look at what supplies you recovered." Donald and Robert started towards crates. Christopher tried to stand, then fell back down. I reached out to steady him. The deep gash on his head still bled.

"You suffered a concussion. I can prepare a bandage for you," I looked from Christopher to the other men. They appeared exhausted. "Would you like some tea, rest for a bit?"

"The men gratefully accepted my hospitality. Donald and Robert assisted Christopher over the rocks, to my cabin. I led the way with the three men following and Joe at the rear. I kept my pace slow. After a few minutes we topped the rocks and viewed my cabin below. One of the men exclaimed in relief. We made our way down. I picked up a wooden chair from the porch to bring inside. I only had one chair and a bed.

"My spartan existence was quite apparent to the men. I

picked up three cups and poured tea, then handed one to each man. In a corner, many herbs hung drying. I made a poultice out of comfey and aloe. Christopher leaned against the wall, sitting on the bed. I handed him the poultice. "Put this on your wound. It eases pain and speeds healing."

He looked at me, skeptically, then placed it on his head. The other men sipped their tea. "This is very good!" Joe said surprised. "Do you live here by yourself?"

Nodding my head, I replied, "Yes I do."

"How long have you been here?" Donald questioned. "About three years." I responded.

"How do you survive?" Joe ask, gingerly sipping tea. I smiled, "I hunt, fish and plant a small garden." "Do you mine for gold?" Donald asked.

"I pan a little. But I stay busy with my garden and fishing."

I knew better than to say anything about gold. The white man bore prejudice towards Chinese miners.

Joe and Donald exchanged a look. "Any neighbors around here?"

"Not close by. Boats come through frequently." I replied nervously. "How is your head, Christopher?" I asked, taking the focus off me.

"Actually, it already feels better." He sounded surprised.

"Yes, the poultice is very effective and quick acting. I'll pick vegetables for dinner tonight." I moved towards the door.

Donald stood up, "Here, I'll help you," he said, following me. I nodded. We walked out the door, off the porch and started up the trail lined with cherries, nectarines and plum trees. The rock walls of the canyon heated this area, allowing for a longer growing season. My fruit trees and garden flourished, providing abundantly. In the garden, squash, corn, beans, peas, potatoes, tomatoes, lettuce, chives and an assortment of herbs grew.

"I'm impressed! You have quite the set up here. What a wonderful garden." Donald expressed, looking at the results of my hard work. At the garden, I picked five ears of corn, lettuce, tomatoes, chives and several different herbs. "Here, I'll carry some of this for you," he offered with outstretched arms. I handed him the vegetables. "I store my meat in the cave. It's cool enough to keep meat for quite some time." I nodded towards the canyon wall to the right, with a trail leading around my garden and along the wall.

"I'll follow you." Donald said.

I nodded and started up the trail. It wound up the rock wall and narrowed in places. I was used to the trail, but took it slowly, for Donald's sake. Loose rock dotted the path. I heard Donald stumble along behind me, as we made our way up. A narrow gorge cut through, with a small stream gurgling down to the garden. We jumped across, then an opening appeared in the canyon. I kept a piece of flint in a sheltered crevice along with a torch. I lit the torch. The opening was about four feet high, three feet wide.

With the light of the torch, the cave went back into the mountain and around a corner. As we rounded the bend, a small deer I killed hung from the ceiling. I placed the torch in a crevice and pulled a sharp blade from another crevice near the deer. I cut off four pieces of steak from the back strap. The best cut. Holding the steaks in one hand, I picked up the torch to lead us out. In the sunshine, I extinguished the torch and returned.

"You have quite the homestead here. Obviously, you put a lot of work into it!" Donald exclaimed as we made our way back down the trail. "Did you plant the fruit trees?"

I shook my head. "No, the trees were already here. The cabin barely stood when I found it. Some of the logs rotted or fell. The roof was falling in. I shored up the cabin before winter."

We walked around my garden and followed the trail back to the cabin. During the summer, it was too hot to cook inside the cabin, so I built a fire in the ring outside. I laid the steaks into my frying pan. Leaving the husk on the corn, I placed it on a flat rock near the flame, heating the corn slowly. I weaved several plates and bowls from willow sticks my first winter here. I tore up the lettuce, chives and herbs for a summer salad. Using a sharp blade, I cut tomatoes into wedges. Back at the fire, I flipped the corn, added herbs to the steaks and started frying them. The men came out and watched as I prepared our meal.

"At Shoup and Leesburg, there's lots of gold mining going on. Is there any gold up in these parts?" Joe asked.

I sighed softly. "I haven't found much, but I haven't looked too much. I work on the cabin, my garden and preparing for winter. I focus on survival." I served dinner on weaved plates.

"The steak is wonderfully tender! It melts in your mouth!" Christopher exclaimed, juices, running down his chin and fingers.

131

"Wait 'til you taste the corn! Sweet as can be!" Joe moaned, nibbling his ear.

"If you gotta get shipwrecked, this is the place to do it!" Christopher mentioned, chewing another bite of his steak.

Donald nodded as he ate his meat.

"I'm not much for salad, but the flavors! Incredible! Thank you, Jiang for your hospitality! Wonderful meal!" Joe exclaimed through a mouthful of food.

After we ate, we sat around the fire, watching the sun set over the canyon walls. "There's another boat headed down in two days. We must catch it to reach Lewiston." Joe mentioned, stirring the fire.

"One of us needs to stay down and watch for it." Donald replied as he laid back on the ground, with his feet to the fire.

"Up river, around this canyon," pointing to the left, "is an inlet where you can catch their attention." Jiang mentioned.

"It sounds perfect!"

"I'll show you the trail to the inlet. I fish there frequently off a big rock into a deep hole."

I gave Christopher my bed that night. The other three men and I slept out around the fire.

The next morning, I made a breakfast of fresh fruit and deer steak. Then, I showed them the path to the inlet. Christopher decided to sit there, waiting for the next boat. His head ached but the poultice reduced his pain and his eyesight cleared. Joe and Donald organized the remaining supplies. Then, Joe hiked downriver to see if any other supplies washed ashore.

Ordinarily, I worked the gold mine. I didn't want the men to know about my gold, afraid they favored the prejudice directed against the Chinese. I weeded my garden and gathered seeds to dry for planting next spring.

"The cavern, where you hang meat, did you carve that out?" Donald asked, walking up behind me.

Startled by his sudden appearance, I hesitated to answer. "No, it was already here. I don't know what happened to the first homesteader. I found the place deserted."

"I bet there's gold," Donald surmised, rubbing his chin.

I didn't want them to think I found gold. "My main concern is survival. I work very hard to live here."

"Obviously, a miner settled before you. So, there's gotta be gold." He insisted, puffing out his chest, almost as if he wanted to intimidate me. He stood over a head taller than me.

"No one lived here when I arrived. I don't know who came before me or what happened. I just want to live in peace," I insisted, as I pulled weeds from my herbs.

"Bull! Where is the gold? I know you have some!" Picking up a rock the size of his hand, he held it menacingly towards me.

Completely bewildered by the sudden change in his attitude, "Please, Donald. I am a simple farmer! This garden! The fruit trees! My herbs! This is my focus! I have no use for gold!"

He walked towards me with the rock, holding it menacingly. "Where is it? Where is your gold?" he yelled at me.

I jumped to my feet and backed away from him with my hands spread out in front of me. "Please, Donald! I offered hospitality to you and your friends after your misfortune! I mean you no harm!"

"Tell me where the gold is!" He moved towards me, his long legs quickly eating up the difference in space between us.

I tried to think fast, what could I do to assuage his greed? I tripped over a rock and fell back. He jumped on top of me, easily holding me down with his body weight. He raised the rock above my head.

"I remember hearing a scream. I think it was me. Then, blackness. Now, I'm here, this. Whatever 'this' is." Jiang finished his tale.

I mulled over his story. "I've heard sometimes, a person can't move on due to unfinished business. Is there something you wanted to do, needed to complete?" I asked, sitting under a cherry tree, eating a handful of cherries.

Jiang was silent for a moment. "I want to go home, to China." "How do we transport you," I hesitated, "in this form?"

"In Chinese culture, we believe in cremation. We kept ashes in urns. Any returning Chinese carried urns, taking us to our homeland." The spirit of Jiang answered, a breath on the breeze.

"Have you been cremated?" I tried to be respectful, non-offensive, but I didn't know the proper etiquette of talking to a ghost regarding his corporeal body.

"My bones are scattered all around. When Donald killed me, he left my body here, in my garden." Jiang's response enveloped me, like the breeze hugged me.

I'm not an expert on ghosts, apparitions, spirits. In fact, Jiang was my first ghost. Thinking for a moment, "If I gather your bones and return them to China, would that work?"

The breeze around me sighed, almost giddy, wrapping around me. "Home! To China! If only I could reunite with my family, ancestors and descendants."

I bobbed my head standing. I imagined the garden when Jiang cared for it. Vegetables grew with weeds intertwined with the plants. "Where were you attacked?"

The breeze flowed into the garden, where I smelled cilantro, chives, and other herbs. Pieces of small bones lay between plants. I gathered them, circling around the spot, picking up bones as I discovered them. I made a pile under the cherry tree and continued searching, wider and wider circles. I came to the head of the trail leading up the canyon, to the cavern. A huckleberry bush scented the breeze. Glancing over, I saw white bleached bone, his skull. Gently picking it up, I witnessed the evidence of his murder, a severe crack over the right eye socket.

I carried it to the cherry tree, placing it with the rest. Arms, rib cage, pelvis and legs. Fingers, toes and other small bones were mostly present. I sighed softly. "I think I found..." I didn't know what to call him, the bones. Entering the cabin through a door barely hanging, I looked for something to carry the bones. The roof partially caved in. Remnants of his bed, the table, the fireplace. A large bowl weaved from willows sat on the table.

I grabbed it, quickly, worried about the roof falling in.

Carefully, I gathered the bones into the bowl, starting with the legs, finishing with the skull. "Jiang?" I felt the breeze touch me, softly. "Are you ready?" I picked up the basket.

"Yes" the breeze whispered.

"Imagine where you want to go. Focus on where your ancestors lie," I said, opening my mind to Jiang. I let him build the image in my mind. I saw a manicured lawn, concrete mausoleums lined up. Rows upon rows. I dug my bare toes deep into the Idaho soil, my molecules melting, melding, flowing through the dirt. I held the image Jiang gave me. We moved along the astral plane. Slowly, I reformed, my toes digging into the soil. So dif- ferent than the soil I left. Strange scents traveled through the air. I opened my eyes and stood in front of a white cement mausoleum. The name "Gan" etched in English and in Chinese characters. Many names and dates were depicted in the stone.

"Jiang?" I felt the air weep with happiness. Several sighs.

"I am home," he whispered. "Thank you. How did you do

that?

Amazement and wonder, colored his voice. "Are you a wupo?"

"If that means witch, than yes. And keep in mind, you're a ghost," I responded, "or something. I can put your name and date on the mausoleum, if you like. Your descendants will know you returned home," I offered as I set the wicker basket down next to the mausoleum. "What date do you want?"

"Summer of 1867. Use these characters here, I was named for my grandfather." Jiang responded softly.

I found a blank space on the wall and used a simple spell to move the molecules of the earth in the cement. Once finished, "Do you want me to put you inside the mausoleum?" I didn't like the idea, but I'd come this far. The shit I get myself into.

"Please. Thank you." The breezed settled around me. "Before you do, let me repay your generosity. I want to give you three things. My garden, my orchard, my home, the first thing I want to give you. Care for it as I would. Follow the trail past the garden and up around the canyon wall, across the creek and into the first cavern. Go back into the cavern just past the turn on the right wall, feel along the wall, there's a nook. Inside the nook is a book, "Divine Husbandman's Classic of the Materia Medica. Many of the herbs in this book, I grow in my garden. And finally, for bringing me home, go past the first cavern. Along the trail, pass two more caverns. Keep going. At the fourth cavern, enter and go down until it forks off into three paths. Take the left path. Continue down until it forks again. Take the left path. About four steps down a hollowed out area lays behind the bleeding rock wall. Hidden in the hole, is my gold. It is now yours."

"I'm glad I returned you home. Thank you," I replied, excited about the book. "Ready?"

"Yes, I'm ready to join my ancestors." The breeze sighed and hugged me, then settled into the wicker basket. I picked it up and slowly melted into the soil. I moved us under the mausoleum, then stretched the basket molecules above and pushed it up until it settled on the floor inside. As I felt the basket and bones take shape, I pulled me back down. I really didn't want to go inside a mausoleum.

Instead, I returned to Jiang's homestead. I located the book easily enough. It was in English. The English effect on Hong Kong. I thumbed through it. It was incredible! A book of healing through Chinese medicine. Pictures of herbs helped me identify the plants in the garden I failed to recognize. I opened a portal and put the book inside my library.

Following Jiang's directions to the cavern, I cast a simple light spell, as I entered. The cavern wasn't very tall or wide, but I walked almost upright. It took a while to find the well camouflaged nook. If I didn't know where it lay, I wouldn't have found it. I shined my light in the nook that was as tall and wide as my head and went as far back as my arm reached. I found as many sacks of gold as I had fingers.

I 'ported to the top of the rock canyon, took out my cell phone. I boosted the signal and dialed a number. "How many bags of gold does it take to buy a lodge?" I asked.

15

I TELEPORTED BACK to Malachi's house. After my afternoon with Jiang, I felt exhausted. When I walked into the living room through the French doors, Ryan and Malachi stood toe to toe, yelling. I stopped at the door.

"Are you out of your fucking mind? You can't run off and join a band! We are in middle of a case! A major case. The biggest case we've ever had!" Ryan yelled, almost frantic.

Malachi ran a hand through his hair. "But Dad! This is my chance! Going on tour, with Celestial Beings will sky rocket my career! Playing on Freemont Street in Vegas!" Malachi took a shaky breath, "This is my dream, Dad. My dream."

Ryan's face showed his indecision, between supporting his son and his business.

"What if I bring in a witch the same caliber as me?" I offered. Both men looked at me. Malachi's eyes filled with hope as he glanced at his dad. Ryan looked at me, weighing my offer.

"Who is it? What are the magic abilities?" He questioned.

"Water primary, earth secondary, classified as an idealist." I answered, baiting the hook. "She's the same level I am, three point five, in the Nez Perce Coven."

"What's an idealist?" Dylan asked.

"She literally sees every nuance of magic. She picks apart the threads of a spell. Extremely detailed in her magic." I described, as I sat down on the couch. Ryan was torn between letting Malachi go and acquiring another witch.

He breathed deeply and said, "Are you sure she'll come?"

I picked up my phone, pressed a button, "Call Shay." Her ring-back tone played *Drift Away*. I love that song.

"Hey, calling again, so soon? Find a pile of silver?"

137

"Wanna job?" I asked, laughing.

"Doing what? With you?" She asked.

I smiled and answered her, "Yes."

"I'll come right now. Go find a pine tree. I can't wait to get the fuck out of here," Relief flood her voice. I nodded at Ryan and Malachi, ending the call, getting up from the couch.

"She'll be here in a moment." I opened the French doors and walked towards the large pine tree. Grinding my feet through the grass, into the dirt, I touched the rough bark. Closing my eyes, I "found" my sister. Our minds intertwined and I pulled her to me. When I opened my eyes, Shaylenne stood in front of me and slowly opened hers, her feet planted solidly in the grass, her hand next to mine. She wrapped her arms around me, hugging me.

"Thank you," she whispered.

Though identical, we perpetrated differences between us. My eyes tended to be greener, hers, bluer. I kept my hair copper, gold and blond. Hers, blond, gold and copper. Shay wore a pair of navy shorts and a white polo shirt. She carried a pair of flat shoes. Placing the shoes on the ground, she stepped into them. We walked into the living room. The Delrikkio men stood awestruck as we entered.

"You met my sister, Shaylenne. Will she do?" I asked. Ryan looked to Malachi.

Malachi studied her aura, then turned to his dad. "She's everything Shy said, and more. She's totally got me outclassed, out magicked, whatever the term is." He smiled, almost giddy, jumping across the room, picked me up, and swung me around. "Thank you, thank you, thank you! I'm going on tour!!!"

Ryan resigned, nodded his head once. "Go. We got this."

Malachi jumped, whooped and took off upstairs. "I gotta pack!" Halfway up, he stopped and looked back at me. "Shy, can you take me where I need to go?"

I shrugged my shoulders and nodded.

Ryan walked over to Shay, holding out his hand, "Ryan Delrikkio, 3- D Investigations. Let's bring you up to speed."

"While I'm catching up, Shy, will you call Bane and tell him what's happening? Please?" Worry clouded her eyes.

I nodded. "Do you want me to do it as you or me?"

"Bane will know pretty quick it's you, I'm sure. But take my phone in case Jadan tries to badger me." She held out her phone and I put it in my back pocket.

On my phone, I pushed a button and then said, "Call Bane". *We Will Rock You* played briefly before Bane answered. I walked outside. "Hey, what's up? Are you the reason why Shay disappeared?" Bane questioned.

"Yeah. Ryan hired her. He needed another witch."

Bane took a deep breath, I heard the sliding glass door open as he stepped outside, the Clearwater River roared in the background. He slowly let the breath out. But said nothing. After a couple short breaths, "You take care of her. You watch over her. You protect her," He emphasized "you" each time.

"She's safer with me than she is in Grandpa's house," I stated matter of fact.

He breathed in and out again. "I know she is."

"I would never let anyone hurt her, Bane. You know that." I matched his softer tone.

"I do know that. I'm so use to watching over you two. It scares me, you being out there without us." Bane shared.

I took a page out of his book and took a deep breath then let it out. "We'll be ok."

"I'll deal with Jadan and Grandpa. Be safe. I love you."

"I love you, too. We'll be fine, I promise." I said, with a smile. That went better than I hoped. But Bane always saw the bigger picture. The bottom line was Grandpa hated us. His prejudice ran deep into his soul. I had no doubt given any opportunity, he'd kill us. It's been nice not worrying all the time, here in Lewiston.

I walked back inside the house. I nodded at Shay. She sat on the couch, with Ryan and Dylan on each side of her, sharing their notes. *Bane's taking care of Jadan and Grandpa.*

Shay breathed a sigh of relief, *Oh, good. Thanks. I'm going to talk to Malachi. You okay?*

Yes, I am.

I went upstairs and found Malachi in his bedroom. He tore his closet and drawers apart. It looked like a hurricane entered his room. I raised an eyebrow, then asked, "Need help?"

"I can't find my blue leather pants, lace-up black leather pants, my navy suede vest or my plum suede long sleeve shirt!"

I looked around the disaster area and searched the pile of leather pants. I found the plum suede shirt and vest under the pants and tossed them in the suitcase. I went into the closet and found the two pairs of pants hanging up in the corner. "Anything else?" I asked as I folded the pants and put them in the partially packed suitcase. Malachi radiated excitement, nervousness and a little bit of fear. He stood at an end table sorting through a jewelry box. He held a couple necklaces in one hand and picked with the other.

"I think I almost got it. I just need clothes for a couple days 'til wardrobe figures me out. The lead guitarist od'ed and I got called to finish the tour." He ran a shaky hand through his hair, and half turned to me. "Shy, I'm not leaving you. I hope you know that. This the chance of a lifetime for me. My big break! I might never get an opportunity like this again."

I smiled, "I totally get it. I'll be fine." I folded a couple of shirts and put them in his suitcase. "Go follow your dream."

He put the necklaces in a zipper pocket on the suitcase. He turned to me, wrapping his arms around me, kissing me senseless.

When I regained my senses, we lay naked and tangled up on the bed. "What the fuck happened?" I asked, totally confused.

He laughed as he rolled over towards me and pulled back into his arms, "The last thing I remember I kissed you."

Hey, you guys want dinner? Shay 'pathed to me.

"Shay is asking if we want dinner?" I passed on to Malachi.

"Yeah, I'm starving, all of a sudden. Do you remember anything between the kiss and nakedness orgasming?" Malachi asked, slightly confused.

"Honestly, no." I pathed to Shay, *Dinner sounds awesome. Then get down here.*

"We need to get downstairs if we want dinner."

Malachi sighed. "Okay. Should we dress first?" He laughed.

"Uh, yeah." I climbed out of bed, looking for my clothes. My shorts landed over by the French doors, my bra, by the bathroom and my top, halfway between the two. Shredded, my black lace thong lay at the foot of the bed. Malachi's clothes ended up scattered and tattered, too. We glanced at each other.

"Don't look at me! I'm not sure what the hell happened!" Malachi pulled on his pants as I put on my shorts, bra and t-shirt.

140

I smiled, shaking my head.

Malachi opened the bedroom door and placed an arm around my waist, kissing me on top of the head. As we headed downstairs, the smell of pizza wafted towards us.

"Where did you put the book?" Shaylenne asked as I reached the bottom of the stairs.

"It's in the book case, bottom shelf, right hand side," I replied. She opened a portal and reached in to get it, then hesitated. Wide eyed, she looked at me.

"I'll grab it." I reached in picking it up. Sitting cross legged on the couch next to her, I placed the book on my lap and started to open it.

Placing a hand on mine, "Wait a sec. Let me study the cover. There are runes on it." Shaylenne leaned over my shoulder. I looked at her quizzically, then at the cover. Interested in the aura, I hadn't noticed the runes.

"Want me to grab that one book on runes?" I asked.

"I thought the same thing. I want to check into several of our books. I'll peruse the library." Shay said, standing up and moving to the French doors. Outside, she melted into the earth.

"Wow. That is too cool. She can teleport, too!" Dylan said, amazed.

"We had to learn, to survive," I explained.

Ryan stood up and walked over to the bookcase, pulling out a book. "I have a book on runes, as well." He sat down on the other side of me, looking at the cover. Shay unmelded from the earth, carrying a couple books. She opened the door and entered.

"I found two which may prove useful. I grabbed your notebook, too." Shay sat down next to me, opening the first book and handing me my notebook. I turned to a new page.

Shay pointed to a rune, keeping her finger inches from the cover. "This I recognize. It translates as Were Human Animal." I started to copy the rune into my notebook. "No! Don't draw it! Who knows what would happen if you drew it! Put down number one and then, "Were Human Animal". This one, looks familiar, but I don't know." She opened up a book and paged through.

"That one." I put my finger on the page, to stop her from turning it. "It's similar, but different. The squiggly lines are the same. These dots are congruent to the rune with these dots. So, the dots link this one to that one." We read the description.

Healing. "Healing through this rune. Hmm. What's this one?" I asked pointing to the most complex drawing.

"I don't know, but this rune means subjugation." Ryan said, pointing at the rune with what looked like two figures, comparing it to one in his book.

"Healing through another," I said. "This last one, is the being the healing is going through. The being responsible for performing the healing."

"Okay. We have two Celtic runes and one," she reached over me to see the front of Ryan's book, "Druidic rune. The one being asked to perform the healing is either a Celt or Druid."

"Try an entity common to both. Since runes appear from both, it only makes sense it's something joining the two or a commonality."

Ryan studied me for a moment, then got up, searching the book shelf, selecting one. "Let's see, *Deities in Medieval Cultures*, looking under 'Celtic and Druidic Deities'."

Malachi handed me a plate with pizza loaded with tons of meat and vegetable toppings. I bit in, careful of the book. It tasted as heavenly as it looked! Shay gingerly took a bite as she studied the cover. Ryan flipped through, scanning for our deity. Dylan stared at Shay.

"Shy, what's this rune?" Shay asked.

I glanced at where she pointed on the cover. It looked like a horizon as the sun dawned. "Light." I answered.

"I thought you might know." She nodded. "Write it down in the notebook."

"I think I found our deity. Her name is Carman, the Celtic Goddess of evil magic." Ryan scratched the back of his neck. "It says here she and her three sons roamed the land creating havoc until the followers of the Goddess Danu imprisoned her and drove her sons across the sea. Along with her," Ryan paused, "bio, there are pictures and drawings of artifacts depicting her. One of them shows the rune on the front of the book, I believe." Ryan studied it closer. "The colors faded but it looks like the same drawing."

"Why does everyone send the evil people to America? Gees!" Dylan exclaimed, throwing his hands in the air before stuffing a bite of pizza in his mouth.

Shay opened a portal to her bedroom at Grandpa's house. She grabbed her laptop and closed the portal. "I'm searching for her online," tapping keys.

"Hey! That's my job!" Dylan grabbed his laptop, woke it up and started searching.

Shaylenne glanced up at him, smiling. "We'll see who's search engine is better," she joked, finishing her pizza while the page loaded.

I glanced between Shay and Dylan, then looked at Malachi. He smiled at the two of them. *Aw, they're so cute!* He 'pathed to me. *I'll need to leave here soon. I know where to go. There's an old palm tree a few blocks from Freemont Street. Have you ever been to Vegas?*

I shook my head. *Just let me know when you want to leave.* I finished the last bite of my pizza.

"Do you ladies need another piece of pizza? You gentlemen?" Malachi asked, jumping up from the couch, heading to the box of pizza, laying on the bar.

"I'll take one," Shay and I answered in unison.

"Wow! In stereo!" Malachi laughed, bringing us each a piece. "Me, too." Ryan and Dylan requested.

"Okaaaay!" Malachi handed pizza out. "Hey, Shy! We need to stop at the office before we head to Vegas. I want to grab my guitar. I'll take it and the green gibson."

"I'm ready whenever you are," I said as I downed my pizza.

He headed towards the stairs. "I'll grab my bag and then be ready in a few minutes."

We materialized on a street filled with people. The sexy moan of a base guitar played over speakers as hundreds of people milled around. Overhead, laughing teenagers zip lined along an LED screen flashing a myriad of geometric shapes and bright colors. Scents of food and alcohol floated on the breeze. Scantily clad street performers tried to attract attention of bystanders while staying within a circle drawn on the side walk. Closed to traffic, many stages spread along Freemont Street.

"The Golden Nugget. We're doin' it old school. I'm meeting the band here some time tonight and we'll play tomorrow night." Malachi breathed deeply. "Here. On Freemont Street!" Malachi spun around in a circle, with his arms spread out. Then he wrapped his arms around me, spinning me. I laughed, encircling his neck. "Thank you, Baby." He kissed me, lowering me to the ground.

"Let's check you in. I need to head back soon and get Shay

up to speed," I mentioned.
   He nodded.

16

THE KNOCK AT the door woke us. We shared a spare room, over looking the subdivision the Delrikkio's home was located. "Shyenne? Shaylenne?"

I moaned as Shaylenne sleepily responded, "Yeah?"

"Swanson just called. They received a search warrant on Scott Clark. NPCSD wants us on site within thirty minutes," Ryan said. "Sorry it's in middle of the night."

Shaylenne jumped up. "We'll be ready in a few minutes! Get up, Shy."

I groaned, not wanting to leave the warm comfy bed. I sat up, rubbing my eyes. Shay opened a portal to our closet. She pulled out a pair of navy capris pants and a navy and white striped short sleeve cowl neck top. I reached in, pulling out a pair of Levis and an emerald green t-shirt. Shay raised an eyebrow at me and I ignored her. She grabbed a pair of navy flat canvas shoes while I picked brown slides.

I opened the door and we went downstairs. In the kitchen, Ryan made a cappuccino. "Shay, what do you like?"

She stifled a yawn, answering, "Whatever Shy likes, I like."

"Orange spice tea, it is." He held out a go cup to me and started one for Shay. "Swanson found a judge prejudiced against witches who happily signed the warrant. He wants us to aid in the search." He handed a go cup to Shay. Sighing, "We should hit the road. It'll take about twenty minutes to drive there."

Shay sipped her tea, "Why don't we just teleport?"

I nodded vigorously. "I second the motion."

"I do, too! I do, too!" Dylan exclaimed as he walked in, pulling a t shirt over his head, grabbing his coffee. "I call Shay!" We both laughed at his enthusiasm.

Ryan looked at her and then me. "Do you know where we are headed?" I asked, sipping my tea. Both nodded. "Okay. We can 'port there. We'd much rather than drive."

Arriving about a block away from the house, we scanned the neigh- borhood, protection wards guarded many of the homes lining the street. It appeared several members within the Coven lived here. I pinpointed the Coven leader's house. Numerous protection wards cast by different witches guarded the home, as well as wards against ill intent.

"That's an interesting over indulgence of protection wards." Shaylenne observed.

"Will you be able to enter the premises?" Dylan asked.

I nodded and Shaylenne answered, "Yes. We mean no harm to anyone inside." Coven etiquette did state we shouldn't enter without the permis- sion of the home owner. I guess in this situation, with a search warrant in hand, it would be okay.

Two squad cars and an unmarked car pulled onto the street, heading to the home. Ryan nodded. "Let's go!"

We walked over to a two story house with a large porch. A bar with several stools around it stood in a corner, along with a couple easy chairs and a side table. Swanson and Finn climbed out of the unmarked car, while Karen and three uniformed officers exited the marked cars. One of the officers jumped when we walked up behind them.

"Where did you come from?" Swanson asked, surprised by our appearance. "Shyenne, do you have a doppelganger or did you multiply?"

"We teleported! It's really the only way to travel!" Dylan laughed. "This is Shaylenne, Shy's twin. How do we do this?"

"We knock on the door," Swanson replied as he knocked and an- nounced, "Nez Perce County Sheriff's Department!

After a few moments, the door opened and a tall thin man with rumpled brown hair appeared in blue plaid pajamas. He startled when he saw the officers.

"Scott Clark? This is a search warrant. Stand aside," Detective Swanson stated, handing the search warrant to him, as he pushed him out of the way, gaining entrance into the home.

Scott blinked his eyes hard and shook his head. Obviously stunned, he tried to determine what to do next. Finn, two of the officers and Ryan entered the home.

"Wait a minute! You can't do this! I'm calling my father!"

146

Scott's voice raised as more people poured into the entry way.

"Call your father. Call your attorney. We're starting our search." Swanson stated matter of fact. "Finn and Ryan, start down here. Shyenne and Karen, upstairs, Shaylenne and Dylan, basement."

"No. Shaylenne stays with me." I contradicted his order. Scott's attention turned to Shaylenne and me. The anger in his face changed almost to fear.

Swanson looked at me. "It'll be a lot faster and efficient if you two split up." Irritation clouded his voice.

"Yeah, and if something happens to Shaylenne the ramifications I'll suffer make these people look like little kids. No. She stays with me while we're here," I stated with my hands on my hips.

Scott grabbed a phone and quickly dialed a number. "The sheriff's department is here with a search warrant! What do I do?"

Due to my bobcat hearing, I overheard the other side of the conversation. "Son of a bitch! Try and stall! I'll get Oscar. I'm coming over right now. How in the hell did we not know about this?" The male voice sounded older, concerned, frantic. "Do not share anything, offer anything, show them anything. I'll be there in a moment."

Scott nodded and hung up the phone. "We request you wait until our attorney arrives. My father is concerned about the legality of the search warrant." Scott squared his shoulders and tried to exude confidence. But his pheromones oozed fear.

"The county attorney drew up the search warrant based on informa- tion provided during interrogation naming you as an active participant in the abduction and murder of five children." Swanson summarized, looking Scott squarely in the eye. Scott started thumbing through the warrant. "Judge Navarro signed the warrant. We are serving the warrant and performing the search."

The front door opened. "I am Richard Clark, leader of the Orchards Coven. What the hell is going on here?" An older version similar to Scott walked through the door, attempting to appear in control. I smelled fear emanating from him. These two were hiding something.

Scott's relief was clearly evident at his father's presence. He walked over to him and handed him the search warrant.

"There's the warrant. We are starting our search. Brown, Taylor, you stand guard with these two. Do not allow them out of this room or to touch anything."

Richard quickly scanned all of the people in the great room. He immediately zeroed in on Shaylenne and I. Then, Finn.

"Who are you? Introduce yourselves." Richard commanded us, finding some solace in his position as a coven leader.

I nodded and acquiesced. "I am Shyenne de la Angelino of the Nez Perce Coven, level three point five, earth primary, water secondary, classified as a catalyst."

Shaylenne followed suit. "I am Shaylenne de la Angelino of the Nez Perce Coven, level three point five, water primary, earth secondary, classified as an idealist."

"I am Finn Fielding of the Snake River Coven, level three."

Color drained out of Richard's face, Scott inhaled sharply. "Is anyone else here?" Swanson asked, as the men stared at Shay and me.

Shay took a step behind me and I stood squarely in front of her. Scott shook his head. Swanson indicated to start searching. Shay and I went upstairs. The search revealed nothing. A few magical items made by members of the Clark family. Same thing with the ground floor and the basement, nothing.

Not even a magic room, his altar.

We met in the great room. I started thinking about the dimensions of the upstairs and the ground floor in comparison to the basement. The basement seemed... off. I went back to the third floor and walked full length and width. Downstairs, on the second floor, I did the same.

"What are you doing?" Ryan asked.

"The dimensions aren't right." I measured in my mind, trying to figure out what was off. Richard and Scott glanced at each other.

"This is ridiculous! You searched my entire home, in middle of the night! Oscar! Can't you do something? I demand you leave my home!" Scott yelled.

I felt a push behind his command. At the same time, Shay and I formed a barrier covering everyone, except one of the officers and Karen. Both immediately exited the house. Oscar must have arrived while we searched upstairs.

Shay, get behind me! I 'pathed as I moved to the center of the room, directly facing Richard and Scott, protecting those behind me. Shay grounded herself and tethered to me.

"Swanson, Del Rikkios, go outside now," Finn said quietly. I heard the door shut as they left.

"Scott! Stop. We must comply and cooperate with law enforcement. You have nothing to hide," Oscar attempted to reason with Scott while trying to figure out the safest exit.

"Richard Clark, Leader of the Orchards Coven. Scott Clark, member of the Orchards Coven. We mean you no harm or disrespect. Please allow us to finish our work," I asked, softly, trying to ease tension. I locked eyes with Richard, hoping he could control Scott. I tried to track Scott peripherally.

Scott glanced to his father, his father met his gaze. Richard shook his head. Shit. Scott formed a fireball. Immediately, I formed two water balls, one in each hand, pulling on Shaylenne's magic. My water balls expanded as they crashed into the fireball, nullifying all the spells. Again, Scott formed a fireball, and again, I sent water balls, squelching the fireballs. Behind them, stood a large fish tank. Sorry fish. I started a tidal wave from the tank, hitting them from behind, soaking them and knocking Scott off his feet. Immediately, Finn jumped on him, zip tying his wrists with the magic ties. I crouched and leapt at Richard, taking him out at the knees.

"Swanson!" I kept my knee in his back and my hand held his neck immobile. Swanson, a uniform, Ryan and Dylan ran back into the room. Swanson pulled zip ties out of his side pocket. Once secured, I climbed off him and looked to Shay. Breathing hard, but fine. I high fived her, held her hand and kissed it.

Finn and I searched them for talismans and any other magic items, placing them magic void bags. Dylan, Ryan and the rest of the officers returned to the house.

"Sooo, I'm guessing something's up with the dimensions." Dylan observed. "You're good at this, Shy. Lead the way."

"The basement." I turned with Shay and headed towards the kitchen. The basement entrance was across from the back door. Dylan followed behind us. The light switch was at the top of the stairs. I flicked it on as I opened the door, leading down narrow, solid pine timber steps. We entered a man cave. A large screen tv dominated one wall while a granite top bar stood in the corner with barstools around. Beer taps peered over the bar. numerous bottles of whiskey, rum, and scotch lined a shelf. Leather easy chairs spread throughout the room. Multi-colored textured rose up most of the wall with a small ledge running

149

near the ceiling.

I walked the length and width of the room. Yep. Something was off. The width wasn't right. The east wall. I leaned back half way across the room against the west wall and surveyed it. It took me a while before I found it. Knee high, not quite half way up the wall, a crack ran along the texture. Camouflaged by the texture and color mix, it was almost impossible to see. The opening appeared to be very small. A tight squeeze. I fiddled with the wall and finally found the trigger, opening the door.

"Awesome!" Dylan exclaimed. The opening led to darkness. I couldn't see anything inside. Using a pine cone petal, I cast a light spell. Light flooded the room. I duck-walked in, then stood up. I twirled all the way around.

"Oh, shit." Shay rarely cussed. The experimentation occurred here. The room reeked of stale blood, terror and death. At times like this, I hated my extra perceptive cat senses. Small glass bottles holding a variety of spell components lined the short wall. An altar stood close to the bottles, allowing a witch to reach components and pivot to the altar.

A stainless steel work table stood opposite the entrance. It tilted to one corner with a reservoir all around the table, catching and draining liquids to one spot and into a tub. An empty cage stood in the corner. Barely large enough to hold a person.

A book case stood against the all we entered. Shay performed a light spell on a pine cone petal, handing it to Dylan and lit one for herself. She walked over to study the spell components while Dylan perused book titles. I walked to the wall holding the cage. He built shackles into the wall to bind wrists and ankles. I swallowed my vomit as I looked from the cage to Shay. Taking a deep breath, and quickly exhaling, I realized this wasn't all. The dimensions were still off.

I studied the wall from the edge of the cage to the corner. This doorway was easier to see. A small ring dangled from the concrete. I pulled on it and the door swung towards me. I held the petal in the room, illuminating it. I heard a whimper. Shay and Dylan turned to me.

"Go tell Swanson we need an ambulance. Now." I said quietly. Dylan quickly exited the room through the small doorway.

She was a werewolf. The woman lay curled in the fetal position in a cage, on a sleeping bag. A bucket stood in the corner. By the smell, obviously used as a toilet. Scott provided her a jug of water, a box of crackers, an orange and a McDonald's bag. Matted, unwashed hair concealed her face. She wore a dirty, tattered green cotton dress. Her gaunt face turned to me, in fear.

"I'll free you. Do you know where the key is?" I asked. She looked at me, almost dazed.

She shook her head. In a shaky, deep voice, "He keeps it." I 'ported into the cage, wrapped my arms around her, and 'ported out. Obviously shocked, she reached up, touching my face. "You're real? You're here?"

"Yeah. Let's get you up out of this hell hole," I put an arm around her waist to support her. I helped her into the first room. She looked at Shay, then me, back to Shay, back to me. "We're twins. Her name is Shaylenne. I'm Shyenne. What's your name?" I asked gently.

She hesitated, "Rhiannon."

"Queen of fairies," Shay came to her other side and assisted her to walk to the entry way. "Let's 'port upstairs." I agreed. We arrived in the great room. The room buzzed with activity. Rhiannon cried out, shrinking back. Shay wrapped her arms around Rhiannon, protecting her.

I took a defensive stance, holding my arms out. "Stay back. She's pretty traumatized."

Swanson walked to us slowly, "The ambulance is en route. Do you want to go outside, breathe fresh air?"

Rhiannon cowered under Shay, nodding. Everyone stood back as Shay walked her to the porch. Dylan accompanied them.

I took a deep breath and exhaled slowly. "We found the room where they caged the Weres, killed and dissected them. He kept her in another room, in a cage." I swallowed the lump in my throat. "With a jug of water, box of crackers and a bucket to use for a toilet. He stocked all kinds of spell components and spell books." I focused on breathing for a couple moments. "Do you have a magical crime scene unit? The spell books and components need to be handled carefully or may be dangerous."

"She isn't joking." Ryan said, as the ambulance pulled into the driveway.

"Yes we do. It's you." Swanson said, pulling his cell phone out of his pocket. "This is Swanson. You won't believe this. We found a woman in a cage in Clark's basement. She's headed to the hospital now. She looks malnourished. Obviously, he kept her imprisoned for a while."

I'm going to the hospital with Rhiannon. Shay 'pathed to me.

Okay. "Shay's riding with her to the hospital." Swanson nodded. I continued quietly. "A regular crime scene unit can deal with the cage room."

I opened a portal to my closet. I kept a bottle of emergency rum. I poured a double shot, swallowed it, then closed the portal.

"Huh. That was weird." One of the officer's remarked.

"Sorry. Her situation was the worst thing I ever saw." I looked down, took a couple of breaths and looked up at Finn. "Wanna check it out?"

He nodded, grabbing his crime scene bag. I led the way downstairs, to the entrance into the room. I didn't want to call the room an altar room or magic room. It didn't deserve that distinction. I duck-walked inside, moving as Finn followed. He surveyed the room, noting the table, altar, components and books.

"I'll check out the books, unless you want to," I offered, moving to the bookcase.

"Sounds good. I'm curious about the components," Finn walked over to the shelf lined with bottles.

I scanned the bookcase first, looking for oily, ugly, nasty auras. None. Good. Several books looked like personal spell books. I pulled one out, scanning it. He dated the page. It detailed the first experiment, confirming Mindy's account, with specifics as to handling the components. I thumbed through the book. It explained the first three attempts of creating the heal- ing spell for Kayla. It described in detail the treatment of each victim up to and after death. I was nauseous.

Swanson stuck his head in the room and rotated his torso sideways to fit into the room. "Wow. How goes it? Finding anything?"

"All sorts of components. I never even heard of some of these! Some are impossible to find! Some are definitely controlled and downright illegal. And some of these should be controlled and downright illegal." Finn shook his head as he researched an item on his phone. "What about you? Finding anything interesting?"

I hesitated. "Yeah. Detailed account of the first three experiments with the Weres."

"I'll take that." Swanson stood upright in the room, glancing around. "Holy shit! This is out of a horror movie!"

"I'd love to hand the book over to you," I held it out to him and took a similar book off the shelf. Opening it, it started where the last left off. "This one's for you, too. Volume two." I handed it off to him. I picked up the next book and perused it's contents.

17

AFTER A COUPLE hours of reading through magic books, "I need a break," I announced as I headed to the doorway.

Finn nodded.

I crawled through the doorway and made my way upstairs, then out the front door. I sat down on the steps. It was mid morning. I lost track of time in the dungeon. A couple uniform officers stood around, guarding the entrance to the house. "Want a coke?" One of the boys in blue offered me. Gratefully, I nodded my head. "Thank you." He went to his patrol vehicle and grabbed a coke out of the small cooler on the floor of the front seat. I smiled as he handed it to me. "You come prepared!"

"Yep, I've been on the force for thirteen years. I learned to keep cold caffeine drinks and emergency food in my patrol car," He smiled at me as I popped the top. His name tag said "Wilson".

I gazed up and down the street. Next door, an older woman assisted a teenage girl out the door and down the steps. Suddenly, the girl collapsed. Reflexively, I 'ported to her side and caught her before she fell down the steps. I helped the older woman move her back to a chair. Gently, we sat her in a blue deck chair.

The girl looked up at me, "Thank you." She had the deepest blue eyes I ever saw. I became aware of the magic emanating from both of them. I sat back on my haunches and took in the younger girl's being. The force of her magic projected outward. Her blue eyes reminded me of the Idaho sky during a thunderstorm. I was transfixed. Her aura was awe inspiring. More like an ocean, or a stormy sky, or the northern lights. Blues, greens, lavender, melted together in waves. I understood Mindy's devotion. I couldn't identify her magic. Not elemental, druidic or wiccan. I saw the sickness in her, too. It almost overwhelmed her. I held out my hand and she took it. I pushed positive energy into her, enveloping and melting away as much of her sickness and pain as I could. "Be well."

I stood up and backed away from her. I glanced at her face. Her color returned, her breathing softened, relieved. "Thank you."

Tears fell from her mother's eyes. "I'm Mary Clark, council member of the Orchards Coven. This is my daughter, Kayla Clark, of the Orchards coven."

I nodded, and as custom required, "I'm Shyenne de la Angelino of the Nez Perce Coven." Mary was an air witch.

Mary raised her eyebrows in surprise. "I wasn't aware the Nez Perce Coven practiced."

I nodded. "My generation has come of age. There are six of us plus my uncle Alberto. As we venture out into the world, he decided we needed to be declared."

"de la Angelino? of the Clearwater Pride?" She questioned.

"Yes. My Grandfather and I don't get along. He doesn't claim me if he doesn't have to." Shrugging, I hated discussing our family's dirty laundry.

"Your mother was Maria." Mary stated. Again I nodded. "Why are you here?"

"I work for 3-D Investigations. I'm assisting with the search warrant," I explained.

Mary's attitude went from sweet and motherly to a ferocious bear. "That is absolutely insane! My son did nothing that would remotely be considered illegal!"

Great. Why did I have to be the one to mention the lady locked in a cage in her son's very own evil laboratory? "Ma'am, I recommend you contact your attorney. Your son is in a lot of trouble. We found a Were woman locked in a cage in your son's basement with handwritten journals documenting his attempts to create a spell using different parts of the body of a Were female. I personally found the woman." Shock filled her eyes. Her breathing came in short gasps. Tears rolled down her cheeks. I took her arm and sat her in a chair next to her daughter. "I'm so sorry."

"It's for me. He's trying to find a way to heal me." Kayla said softly, choking down tears.

Mary bit back a sob. "Oh my god. It's that damn book!"

155

"What book?" I asked, already knowing the answer.

"Richard found a book passed from a druidic circle. He paid handsomely for it, hoping it might hold a cure. The book contained spells for healing. But it required illegal, unethical spell components." She sighed heavily, wiping tears from her eyes.

"What sort of spell components?" I asked gently.

"Were." She answered.

I furrowed my brow. "Who knew about the book?"

"Richard, Scott, Mindy, myself. No one else. Our coven would never condone the use of ... those type of components." Hesitating, "Where is my son and husband?"

"Scott's under arrest. I'm not sure if your husband is or not. Scott attacked us magically. My sister and I incapacitated them long enough to zip tie them." I explained. "Would other members of your coven help Scott?"

She thought for a moment, then shook her head. "No one in our coven. We researched many different magical practices but stayed away from anything calling for any type of sacrifice."

"A number of people hang around Scott, hoping to be invited into the coven. Being a handsome man, women flock to him." Kayla spoke softly. "Most have fairly negligible magical abilities."

"I need to take Kayla to the hospital for IV treatments." Mary wiped her tears, kicking back into mother-mode.

"If you want to get your car and pull it up to the curb, I'll help Kayla walk to it," I offered. Mary nodded and went down the stairs, heading towards the garage.

Kayla curled into a ball, hugging her knees in the chair, silently weeping with her head laid to the side. "How much trouble are they in?" Kayla asked, looking up at me.

"Scott and Mindy are in a lot of trouble. I don't know about your father." I answered honestly. Mary backed the car out of the garage and to the curb. I held a hand out, helping Kayla stand.

"I'm feeling a lot stronger after your touch. Thank you." Kayla said, holding on to my arm but bearing her own weight.

"I wish I could do more. Your aura is so beautiful. If you need me, please don't hesitate to call." I opened the car door and helped her inside. I handed her a business card from my back pocket. "Take care." I closed the door as Kayla and I locked eyes until her mother drove away.

Back to the evil laboratory. Sigh.

Shay helped Rhiannon out of the wheelchair, outside the hospital. "Let's take her to the lodge. She will feel safe there." I nodded in agree- ment and we walked over to a pine tree. We emerged next to the front door.

"If you want to change and run, feel free." I suggested as I walked to the front door. Rhiannon looked at me, changed to a wolf and took off. Running with forest on one side and the river on the other, would begin healing her soul.

Shay walked over to the Realtor sign, took a pamphlet and started reading it. She raised an eyebrow and glanced at me. "How much gold do you have?"

I shrugged my shoulders, "A couple small burlap sacks."

"Go get 'em. I'll work on buying this for us." She continued to read the pamphlet. I walked over to a pine tree, 'porting to Ji- ang's garden. I inhaled deeply. Between the fruits, vegetables and herbs, the small homestead had an aroma all it's own. I walked the trail to the mining tunnel, retrieving the sacks of gold.

Back at the lodge, I handed the sacks to Shay. She laughed, shaking her head. "Only you would stumble on six sacks of gold out in the middle of nowhere!"

Our cousin, Lance, yelled down to us from the overhead bal- cony. "This place is awesome!"

Shay said, "I called Lance. He's really smart when it comes to business stuff. Lance come check this out!"

Lance 'ported down to us. "Holy shit! Six sacks of gold?! Do you know what you have here?"

"Six sacks of gold?" I answered hesitantly.

He poured the gold out onto the floor, as he eyed the con- tents, per- forming a detect gold spell. "Son of a bitch!" He looked at me and then Shay, then back to me. "You two are buy- ing a home. Take three of the sacks back to your hidey hole. This is plenty and then some to buy the house. I'm sure I can nego- tiate the price, paying in pure gold." He used a spell, sweeping it back into the sack.

Shay opened a portal and pulled out a backpack. Carefully, she placed them in the backpack, then handed the backpack to Lance. "Okay, Let us know."

He nodded, slinging the backpack over his shoulder, heading down the broken walkway, then turned back towards us. "My fee is a bedroom." "Deal." Shay and I said in unison. I picked up the remaining sacks and returned to Jiang's homestead.

18

SHAY AND I worked at our lodge, repairing years of neglect, when Ryan called. "The Sheriff's Department requests you to accompany them to the Clark home. They received a search warrant for Richard Clark's residence. Richard's involvement needs to be determined. NPCSD believes questioning may be more productive if the two of you are present. Scott lawyered up and refused to speak. Between your information from Mary and Mindy's interrogation, Richard acquired the book and shared it with Scott and Mindy. At this point, we don't know if Richard knew about Scott and Mindy's activities."

"Okay. Give us a little time to prep a few spells. Just in case." I ended the call, turning to Shay, relaying Ryan's message.

"What are you taking?" I asked Shay.

"Since Richard uses fire, a protection bubble with water as the foun- dation. A couple water and ice type spells. What's his wife?" Shay asked, picking up several pine cone petals, readying them to absorb spells.

I thought for a moment, "Air witch. Mesmerized by Kayla's aura, I didn't pay much attention to Mary. She is, however, a high level witch. At least a four. I don't think we need to worry about her. Her heart is solid gold. Same as Kayla."

"What do you think about Richard?" Shay asked, pushing the protection spell into the petal, but not activating it.

Weighing my knowledge of him, I sighed. "I'm not as sure about him. He sought the book and shared it with others. I didn't know if he'd side with his son against us. I don't know if he knew what he'd do. His aura grew darker over time. I see the ripple in his aura indicating the event that changed his outlook on life. I imagine it resulted from Kayla's illness."

I paused a moment. "Do a few power boost spells. I'm cast-

159

ing of- fensive and defensive fighting spells. Hopefully, we don't need them. I really don't want to fight a coven leader." Shay sighed. "If we do engage-," I hesitated.

"We will be just fine," Shay finished.

"You move behind me, ground yourself and stay safe." I scooped upthe pine cones and started picking petals off, taking care not to poke my finger on the ends. I'd activate the spell when needed by poking my finger. My blood activates it. Pine cone petals were the perfect talisman for spells. With the element of earth, it provided more "oomph"and the pokey part made it easy to activate. Especially in a hurry.

I sighed softly. For fighting spells, ice balls, water sword, and hurricane. Defensive spells: wall of ice, blizzard, whirlwind. And a couple healing spells. Just in case. I looked up at Shaylenne. "I'm done. You?"

She nodded. "Yeah. Three boosters, a snow globe, and a couple protection bubbles."

"Sounds good. Before we go, I want to fill my chi at the confluence of the rivers and with the forest." I put the offensive spells in my right pocket and defensive in my left of my shorts.

"Yep. Me too. We need to find the perfect spot and set it up for chi- ing." Shay sorted her spells into boosting and protection.

We spotted a tall pine tree at the edge of the rivers' bank where the Salmon and the Snake joined at the downriver spot from our lodge. We 'ported to the tree, slipping our shoes off. Each of us placed our right hand on the tree, knelt down, placing our left into the river and grounded our bare feet into the black soil. We both breathed deeply, filling our lungs with the crisp mountain air. As we breathed in, the magic entered through our left hand, circled to the right hand where magic from the tree joined, then magic from the earth soared through our legs meeting in the center of our being with the other two magics. The magics circled, mixed, melded into one, filling us. We were ready.

Shay and I 'ported to Ryan's house and from there, to the Clark, with Ryan and Dylan. We arrived several houses away.

An NPCSD SUV pulled up in front of the family home. Swanson drove. He and Finn exited the vehicle as we crossed the street. Swanson shook his head as we joined them on the porch. As he rang the doorbell, "Too good for vehicles these days?"

"I get car sick." I stepped up from behind Ryan.

Swanson laughed. The door opened and Richard looked out at us. I saw him sigh, inwardly. "What do you want?"

"Sir, we have a search warrant," Swanson handed a set of papers to Richard. He looked like he sucker punched him. Hard. Swanson gently pushed past him, opening the door wider for us to enter a foyer which gradually spread into a great room with a staircase curving towards the second floor.

"Wh- wh- what are you looking for?" Richard stuttered as he quickly perused the warrant.

Swanson eyed the layout of the house and the rooms leading off from the entry way. "We will seize all computers, tablets, and spell books deemed pertinent to the investigation. Spells, potions, talismans and other magical devices deemed pertinent. Items thought to be used in the crimes involv- ing kidnapping and killing of Were humans," stated Swanson as prepared a game plan for the search. "Who all is present?"

I kept an eye on Richard. The blood drained out of his face at Swanson's explanation. Something incriminating was in the house. He paused a moment before Swanson's question registered. "Just me, my wife and daughter."

"They need to come down here while we search. Finn start down here. Shyenne, Shaylenne, upstairs please." Swanson looked at each of us in turn, indicating where he wanted us.

At that point, Mary walked into the room from the kitchen, drying her hands on a kitchen towel. "What's going on?" She asked, the color drained from her face.

Swanson looked at her and stated, "We're conducting a search warrant. We need you, your husband and your daughter to remain here while we perform the search. Can you call your daughter down?"

Tears came to Mary's eyes. "Kayla had transfusions today. She is extremely weak. I don't know if we can get her up and back down the stairs."

I watched Richard. I didn't like the look in his eyes. He weighed his options. Without taking my eyes off of him, I said, "Kayla is fine. She won't harm us."

"I thought she was this great, powerful witch." Ryan remarked from the doorway.

I nodded. "She is. But she'd never hurt us." Richard made a

decision regarding his options. And it was a bad one. I stepped forward as Shay stepped back and behind me. I felt her link to me. "Richard, let's talk about this. We all want to help Kayla." The heat left the room, collecting at Richard's right hand.

"Everyone leave." Shay said very quietly. Stepping in front of Swanson, I positioned myself so I faced Richard. Nothing between us. He took a couple steps towards the staircase leading upstairs, away from me.

I sighed. "Please, Mr. Clark, let's work this out. No one needs to get hurt." I saw a water bottle on the entry table, a fish tank up against the wall, a vase with irises. Shay pulled water from the vase.

I stepped out of my flip-flops onto the wood floor. "How old was Kayla when you found out about her illness?"

He looked surprised, shook his head. "She was four. The doctors tested her for everything. Put her through so much." Richard ran a shaking hand through his salt and pepper hair. "Initially, we kept her comfortable through healing spells. But as her condition progressed, the efficacy of our spells weakened."

I shook my head. "It must have broken your hearts. When did you begin researching magical alternatives?" Keeping him talking might be the most effective way of avoiding a battle.

Nodding, "We went to our coven and tried other types of magic. When those failed, we combined magics."

"And when that stopped working?" I softly prompted. *Where is everyone?* I 'pathed Shay.

Finn is behind me in the doorway. Everyone else left. He's holding a fireball. Shay responded.

I know.

Richard sighed deeply. "We researched other magics: Voodoo, Shamanistic, Druidism, Chinese, Egyptian. I guess," he hesitated briefly. "I guess, I became obsessed. I chased any rumor of magic offering hope. While I chased, Mary cared for Kayla. Our coven tried creating spells using mixtures of magics." He cocked his head. "Some worked. Never for very long though. Her illness was too severe. And then I heard about the book."

Bingo. "Book?" I questioned.

He nodded. "I came across a druidic circle in England. They spoke about a woman creating a book of healing using druidic magic and the healing properties of Were creatures. The legend said the woman fled Portugal and the Irish captured and imprisoned her. Her four sons escaped. After searching through Europe, I found the book, paying handsomely for it. It didn't include a specific spell dealing with Kayla's illness. But we found similar ones."

I needed to keep him talking. "What did you do?"

He inhaled deeply. "We began... experimenting." I raised an eyebrow.

Mary sobbed quietly from the kitchen doorway. "The initial spell showed improvement in her condition. As I read the book, I realized an important component in each spell required specific circumstances the Were creature had to experience at the time of harvest."

"Specific circumstances?"

"Yes. For instance, a female adolescent Were at rest, meaning no adrenaline in her system. Through a step by step process, we manipulated the spell for Kayla's benefit. At this point, we know the precise components to heal her, fully."

"Who's "we"?" I knew I was pushing by asking.

He looked at me, processing my question and the ramifications of his answer. For everyone. He weighed his options. Fight or acquiesce. I saw the answer a split moment before he threw the fireball at me. I pulled water from Shay into a frozen wall. The fireball smacked into it, burning through but effectively turning the fireball into a brief spark. Shay and I used water from the fish tank. I formed balls of ice. Shay held hers. He threw several smaller fireballs towards me. My balls of ice intercepted most of the fireballs, nullifying the spell. One slipped by me as I twisted out of the way. Shay ducked. It hit the wall behind her. Finn dove into the entry way. Mary screamed, as the wall caught fire.

Richard created a fire sword as I reached for the ice sword. Shay threw a bevy of icicles, briefly slowing him. She boost me as Richard swung the flaming sword. I parried his attack with my own weapon. He obviously used a sword before, way more experienced than me, quickly advancing, swinging. Retreating, I blocked each flaming arc, but just barely. Without Shay's boost, I wouldn't be able to defend myself. I didn't know how long we could sustain our defense. Already, my magic waned against the onslaught of his. I parried a blow aimed at my head, but failed to block Richard's reverse swing, burning my calf. I screeched in pain, jumping back, but he advanced.

Fuck! We need try something else! I don't think I can maintain this. Between the spell and parrying his attacks, I'm quickly running out of energy! I 'pathed to Shay as Richard swung around me, coming between us, severing our link. He backed me against the stairs. Richard ran towards me with his flaming sword. I swung short movements in front of me, blocking blow after blow. I couldn't keep it up. Wood covered the stairs and the wall. I backed up against the wall, melted into it and reappeared back down by Shay. She immediately linked with me again. As I turned to Richard, he threw a fireball. I formed a snow globe over us, dropping my sword. The fireball smacked the globe, cracking it. Richard laughed, juggling three fireballs.

"Richard! Do not do this!" Mary screamed from the doorway.

Richard glanced at Mary. "No choice, at this point. We're too close to saving Kayla." He walked half the distance to our globe. He threw another fireball. The crack spider webbed. The last two balls would demol- ish our shelter. I contemplated our options. I hated to retreat but I didn't see a choice. Suddenly, Richard dropped to his knees hitting the floor. Immediately, I pulled zip ties out of my pocket, ran over to him and secured his wrists behind his back. I slapped him with a sleep spell, as did Shay. Surveying the scene I searched for other threats. Perched at the top of the stairs, Kayla clung to the banister.

"Is he secure?" She gasped. I nodded. "I couldn't let him hurt you."

Dumbfounded, "Thank you." I winced in pain, awareness of the burn reached my consciousness.

Finn, Ryan, Dylan and Swanson ran back into the house. Finn cast a detect magic spell on Richard.

"He'll remain asleep for a couple hours." Shay stated.

"Shy? Could you help me... down?" Kayla asked softly. Iimmediately 'ported to the top of the staircase, put an arm around her waist, 'porting back. "Thank you," she said. "My father wears a ring on his left middle finger that boosts fire spells, a ring detecting magic, a protection talisman and a healing bracelet."

Mary stood next to Kayla, putting an arm around her waist. Finn glanced at her, removing the magic items and handing them to Kayla. Swanson put a hand out to stop Finn. "We may need those as evidence."

Finn shook his head. "No, we don't. We don't want the responsibility if these magical items disappear, and they will disappear. They're family heirlooms and by rights pass to the children. By custom, these now belong to Kayla."

Swanson raised his eyebrows but didn't argue. Silent tears rolled down Kayla's face while Mary sobbed as Finn handed the items to her. I walked over to Shay. *You okay?*

She nodded. *You?*

My leg hurt where Richard burned me with his sword. I looked at it. Blisters formed on my calf and started to ooze. I needed treatment to stop the festering.

"Fabulous job, Shyenne. He disclosed enough to charge him as a co- conspirator, at the very least, along with Scott and Mindy," Swanson stated. Two uniform officers entered the house.

"Want us to transport him down to the station, Detective?" One of the officers asked.

Swanson nodded. "Thanks. That would be helpful." Mary cried as the officers carried Richard out of their home.

"Shy, you need your leg healed. It will to continue to fester and burn. Want me to call Bane?" Shay pulled her phone out of her back pocket. I nodded.

"Here. I'll heal you," Mary squared her shoulders, wiping away her tears. "I made healing spells specifically for burns." She walked over to me, placing a hand on my shoulder. "May I?"

I hesitated, then nodded. The innate goodness I saw in Kayla's aura came directly from her mother. Mary whispered words of the spell. It sounded liked medieval Irish. The burn began to cool. I exhaled as the pain melted away.

"Thank you. Your kindness is much appreciated. Especially at this difficult time." I met her eyes.

"You gave Kayla relief from her pain when she needed it most," Mary demonstrated an incredible inner strength, fortifying herself for what was to come. "I know what you hope to find in your search. I'll show you where it is. Richard manipulated a spell he found in that retched book. He kept a spell book dealing solely with their experimentations." She started towards the stairs.

"Did you know he used Weres in the spells?" Swanson questioned as he followed her.

She stopped midway up and turned back towards the detective. "No. I assumed he developed a way around using Weres, requiring manipula- tion of the spell. I made it very clear early on I would not support using blood magic or anything harming another being." Shaking her head, her eyes filled with tears. "I, I assumed he found a way around using the Were," hesitating, "body parts."

"What did you think he used?" Finn questioned, following Swanson.

"Were essence. I thought the same effect might be achieved using essence." Mary replied. "Shyenne? Would you mind staying with Kayla? Make sure she's alright?"

I nodded, leading her to the couch to sit. Shaylenne sat next to her. Kayla cried silently. Shay wrapped her right arm around her, holding her hand.

Kayla laid her head on her shoulder. "I'm so sorry! I can't believe all this! Over me!"

I thought about what Mary said. Were essence. Essence held the healing power of the Were. Gathering the essence at the appropriate physical condition may provide the necessary composition. With no Weres harmed in the process. I opened a portal and pulled out a notebook and pen. I sat down on the floor, curling my right leg under me, crossing my left over the right. Opening to a blank page, I wrote down *Were essence*. How to gather the essence? I could go in psionically to that part of the brain. Could I gather my own essence?

"Shy? I can't open the lock on this door. Neither can Mary. You want to try?" Finn questioned from the top of the stairs. I looked questioningly towards Shay.

She nodded. "We're good here."

I opened the portal and threw the notebook and pen back in, then went upstairs.

"Richard placed a protection ward on the box he kept the spell book in." Finn explained. "To keep Mary and Kayla oblivious to their activities." "Yep. There's no way they would condone their activities." The stairs flowed into a circular room with several doors leading off. The door to my left opened into the master bedroom. Finn entered second room. The magic room. Pristinely clean. Burgundy silk covered the altar. An array of colored candles formed a half circle on the altar. To my right, a book shelf covered one wall, filled with magic books and spell books. Mary and Swanson stood at the right end of the altar, with a gold ornate box, guarded by a spell.

"I don't know how to open it," Mary threw her arms out to her sides.

I studied the box. Covered in Celtic runes, I saw no way to open it without using magic. I decided to try to open it using my magic. "*Aperio.*" The box opened revealing a notebook. I looked to Swanson. He nodded.

"That's it. The book he kept his notes in for the spell variations. I only saw it a few times." Mary identified the notebook.

I reached in and picked up the book. Opening it, the first page was dated with handwritten notes. He wrote out the spell, detailing the ingredients, along with the age and activity level of the Were. The notes described Kayla's response. Page after page described each variation, dated, with Kayla's response, and possible variables to try next. I handed the book to Swanson.

I glanced at Mary. She met my eyes. "I can't imagine how difficult this is. Thank you for your assistance."

Mary tried to keep tears from falling from her eyes. "As much as I want to heal my baby, it can't be at the expense of others," shaking her head. She took a deep breath, exhaling forcefully. "We kept remnants of the potions in Kayla's room."

Totally surprised, I raised my eyebrows at Swanson. He swept his arm towards the doorway. "Show us." Swanson requested. Mary nodded, leading us to a door across the hallway from the master bedroom.

We entered a soft green room. The bed had a white tulle drape centered, reaching down with crystal lights of different hues providing illumination. A green suede loveseat recliner faced the bed. On the wall, a flat screen tv hung adjacent to a sliding glass door opening on to the balcony. Chaz's main entry into Kayla's room. Two white night stands sat at each side of her bed. Several medications and two syringes lay on top of one of the night stands. An armoire stood against the same wall as the bed. Mary opened the main cabinet. Inside, a key pad guarded a safe. She punched in the code, opening the door. Stepping to the side, she waved us to the armoire. I looked to Swanson. He nodded to me. Many glass vials of assorted colors lined the top shelf. On the next shelf held prescription bottles. On the bottom, stood syringes and insulin vials.

"Shay is more proficient in identifying components than I am," eying the bottles. I recognized some of the ingredients but others, not so much. Shay studied, picking magic apart and saw each step or ingredient whereas I tended to "make things happen". I returned downstairs. Shay and Kayla sat on the couch, Kayla's head still laid on Shay's shoulder, sobbing quietly. *We found vials of leftover potions. You're better at identifying components than I am.* "They need Shaylenne upstairs. Would you mind if I sit with you, Kayla?" I asked as she raised her tear soaked face from Shay's shoulder.

Wiping the tears from her eyes, she nodded. Shay and I traded places. She climbed the staircase, entering Kayla's room. Kayla laid her head on my shoulder, relaxing. Gently, I eased her pain. She sighed in relief, drifting to sleep. I slipped softly into her mind. I gazed at the center of her magic. Within our coven, psionic magic was common. As children, we entered each other's minds and familiarized ourselves with how magic looked. Her's appeared completely different. Kayla's magic glittered, reminding me of a multi-dimensional snowflake, with sharp points in some areas and holes in others. Breaking my gaze away from her magic, I decided to check out other parts of her mind, looking for the epicenter of her disease. Unsure of what to look for, I meandered softly. The part of the brain I associated with intelligence appeared healthy, as did the emotional and impulse. Physical function showed weakness and a twinge of atrophy. The autonomic functions area seemed okay, other than one spot that looked... black? That couldn't be good. The hormone, insulin, adrenaline section was black and withered, barely alive. I touched it, offering a healing spell. Some of the black, lightened. It seemed like more life returned to the area. Sighing, I backed out of her mind, onto the couch, again. She breathed softer, resting peacefully. Ryan watched me, raising his eyebrows as I opened my eyes. I gave him a wry look. I pondered my observations. I identified the damaged area and the healthy areas. How could she be healed? The unhealthy areas are intricate to... life. The damaged areas couldn't be removed without killing her. Could the areas be healed from within? Psionically? Could a potion be astrally ... administered? A poultice? For that matter, could Were essence be harvested psionically and then transferred to Kayla? I contemplated the possibilities. We had the spell. I needed to call Lance and Uncle Al.

Mary descended the stairs. The anguish in Mary's face abated slightly as she saw Kayla resting comfortably on my shoulder.

Tears filled her eyes, "Your sister is studying the potions now. I must say you two are quite impressive. If you like, I can take Kayla."

I shook my headed, softly. "It's okay, she needs rest. Ryan, could I see Richard's notebook? I can study it while I'm here."

He nodded, handing me the notebook. I opened a portal and grabbed a pad and pen, then closed it. Mary's face lit up with surprise, as I turned to a new page.

"Just go with it, Mrs. Clark," Ryan smiled. "We do." Astonished, she nodded.

I opened Richard's notebook and began reading from the beginning. I documented the results throughout the "experiments", noting details such as dates and identifying information of the Weres. On a separate page, I documented Richard's results, observations suggested alternatives. While I worked, Mary brought me a cup of tea and chocolate chip cookies. I noticed she attempted to read my notes, but since I wrote in Latin, she couldn't.

Finn, Dylan and Ryan continued the search of the home, with Swanson overseeing. Shay brought the bottles of potions downstairs and sat in an easy chair across from me. She studied as I continued my notes.

The sun set low in the sky as the men came downstairs. "Here's Mindy's magic notebook. Compare it with Richard's. See if they corroborate each other." Swanson stated, handing me a pink book with purple violets decorating the cover.

I nodded. "I finished Richard's book. It shouldn't take long to go through hers." I spoke softly trying not to disturb Kayla. But it didn't work. She sat up, rubbing her eyes.

Shaking her head, the realization of what occurred returned. Stuttering, "I'm sorry! I didn't mean to keep you from your work!" She apologized.

"You're fine. You needed the rest and I got a lot done," smiling at her. I stood, stretched and picked up all the notebooks. Shay also stood, opening a portal and grabbed a backpack and several t-shirts. She wrapped each bottle carefully, placing them in the backpack.

"Why don't you all call it a day? Tomorrow focus on analyzing the potions and the spell books. We need to organize the evidence and figure out who did what," Swanson ran a hand through his brown hair, shaking his head, then glanced at me.

"I'll send Scott's books over as well."

Mary came forward, wringing her hands. "What do we do?" Swanson hesitated, "Just take care of your daughter."

19

BACK AT 3-D Investigations, I finished the spell books. They corroborated each other. Mindy's notes tended to provide more of an emotional and physical accounting of Kayla's responses to the spells. It detailed specifically changes in her ADH functions, blood levels and chemical makeup. Scott's notes focused primarily on the Were, physical attributes, age, activity level, chemical balance. What the Were experienced prior to "harvest". He explained in great detail the steps taken to "harvest" the component. It was actually creepy, bordering on a serial killer mentality. Richard's notes pulled the others' observations together, theorizing and hypothesizing options for a favorable outcome.

Along with documenting the corroboration, I tracked what they noted- worked. I needed to talk with Lance and Albert. I gazed out the windows in the library from the overstuffed recliner, watching the waves of the river roll on by as the sun hung low in the sky.

I glanced over at Shay. She sat cross-legged on the couch with the vials in front of her. She moved more than half to one side, as she identified all of the ingredients in those vials. I stood and stretched as she concentrated on a blue potion.

"How ya doin'?" Shay asked, stretching her arms above her head, bending side to side.

"I think I'm done. I made it through everyone's books and they show part of the picture. Their notes corroborate each other's roles in the, the - What the fuck do you call something like this?" at a loss for words.

Shay sighed. "I don't know. The realization of what these monsters did!" She shook her head in disgust. "I understand wanting to help Kayla, but not to this extent!"

I nodded, agreeing. "I also noted what they determined -

worked. I want to talk with Uncle Al and Lance. I think I might be able to help Kayla." I voiced my own thoughts to Shay.

She looked like I slapped her. "How? Who are you going to kill?" Shaylenne responded sharply, putting the vial down forcibly and jumping to her feet.

Shaking my head, "I won't hurt anyone. I think we could obtain Were essence psionically, from me, perform a four tier spell and administer it psionically. Actually go in and heal the areas requiring healing. Richard and Mindy noted specifically what worked. Scott is a serial killer in the making, if he isn't already. "

Raising an eyebrow, Shay weighed what I said. "While Kayla slept, I checked out her," rocking my head, "being. I saw the diseased parts. I just need someone to help retrieve my essence."

Contemplating what I said, Shay said, "Let's go to Uncle Al's. If we can, let's do it."

I smiled, opening a portal, placing the spell books. Shay handed me the potions, as well. We left the library and found the Delrikkios in Ryan's office. "We're calling it a day and heading to our Uncle's house for dinner," I announced from the doorway.

"Alright. Where are you ladies at?" Ryan asked.

"I finished the spell books. Bottom line: they corroborate each other's involvement." I leaned on the door frame.

Shay arched around me. "I made it through four of the potions. I identified all the ingredients and the amounts. I'll make it through the other two tomorrow. Most of the components remain the same. Just a couple changes were added."

Ryan smiled and nodded. "Awesome! You two are fantastic! Have a great night. We'll see you in the morning."

Dylan smiled, and held Shay's gaze for an extra moment, or more. "Good job! Enjoy!"

We ported to our uncle's home in Kooskia, landing in his backyard, on the bank of the Clearwater River. Shay led the way to the French doors leading to the family room. Our cousin, Lance, reclined in a chair with the tv playing 90's rock music, reading a book. He looked over his shoulder and smiled when he saw us. "Hey! Gorgeous Squared! What's up?"

Shay went to the fridge and grabbed two ice teas. "I wanted to run a spell by you and Uncle Al. It's pretty complex." I stated as Shay handed me one of the teas.

Lance raised his eyebrows. "Hmm. Al should be back anytime. He went to town for something. Whatcha got?"

I sat down on the edge of the couch facing Lance. "There's a teenage girl who's really sick from Diabetes Insipidus, the daughter of Richard and Mary Clark, leaders of the Orchards Coven. It progressed to the point where it can't be controlled with medication. She may die, soon. They worked on spells to heal her, but the main ingredient they need," I hesitated, "isn't very accessible. But, I have an idea how we can obtain it."

I piqued Lance's interest. "What's the ingredient?"

"A pituitary gland from a resting female Were adolescent."

Shock colored Lance's face. Deadpan, "You're kidding."

Shaking my head, "No, I'm not."

"And how do you intend to obtain a pituitary gland from a resting female Were adolescent ? Without harming anyone?" He questioned.

"Going in astrally, getting essence from the pituitary gland, leaving it in astral space, then going in astrally and administering that part of the spell." I explained, swallowing my ice tea.

Lance and Shay mulled my idea for several moments. "Can you do that?" Lance asked, scratching his chin. Lance was very gifted psionically. Shay and I presented with "pretty good" skills, while Tristan, Bane and Jadan displayed basic abilities. Psionic magic dealt with mental magic, a lot of it occurred within the astral plane. Telepathy, teleporting and por- tal opening skills were forms of psionics. We all performed those skills inherently.

I shrugged my shoulders. "I don't know. That's why I'm here. I'm asking you." I took a drink of my tea. "What do you think?"

He considered this. With a wry look, "Sounds like, possibly? How would you ... contain the essence?"

"Take a jar in with me?"

Rocking his head back and forth, "It could work, I guess." Lance responded.

With a teasing smile, "Wanna try it?" I knew how to rope my cousin into my plans.

Cautiously, "What's your plan?" Lance asked.

To this point, Shay sat quietly listening to us. "This isn't a good idea. Let's wait 'til Uncle Al returns."

Cajoling, "All we need to do, is go into my mind astrally, look around, see if we can take a little bit of essence and leave it in astral space." I presented my idea simply and fairly rationally.

173

"Oh, well, if that's all we're doing." Lance responded, sarcastically, rolling his eyes. "Have you ever done anything like this?" He set the recliner down and got up to grab a Coke.

I hadn't told anyone about Malachi. "I worked with Malachi. Someone bound his magic. We went in astrally several times, cutting the ties."

"What?! Are you kidding? You can't just do that! You don't know what might happen! There may be a reason why his magic is bound! Shy!" Shay threw her hands up, exasperated.

"He became irresistible to women, created water and can see magic." I shrugged. "Besides, it's his body, his magic. He has a right to it!" Refocusing my attention to Lance, "So, what do you think?" I asked him.

"I'm game. Anything in the pursuit of magic! Want to do it now?" He asked.

"No!" Shay splayed her hands out.

"Yes. Shay, if you don't want to take part, then don't. We're doing it now," I stated, glaring at her. "Lance, let's go together and look around."

"Okay. Lay back in the recliner." I sat down, laying back. "You com- ing?" I asked Shay.

She sighed heavily, nodding. "Someone with common sense should be along. Just in case. Wait a sec! I'll grab a potion jar out of the magic room."

"There's a thought," Lance stated, matter of fact, as he sank to the floor, chuckling.

Shay quickly returned with a small glass jar and stopper. She came and sat on the right side of me, next to Lance. I closed my eyes and the three of us met in astral space and then entered my mind. We moved along a path, near the area where my magic lay. My magic shined an emerald green with blue sparkles. "

We continued, reaching where my Were resided. It possessed a brown, furry feeling. We passed the areas of my mind where intelligence, impulse control, emotion and physical activity were located, reaching the site of the pituitary gland, hormones and organ function.

The three of us gazed at the area. It was a light purple wavy… thing.

Not a solid, liquid or gas. It was… essence. Just what I needed.

Okay, so now that we're here, what do we do? Lance asked. Shay and I looked at him, then back at the spot. Shay took the stopper off the jar glancing at me. *Do I just... scoop it up?*

Sure? Not really an expert, I figured that was all we could do. Shay dunked the jar in the purple wavy essence, scooping some up. It stayed in the jar. We looked at each other and shrugged. Seemed to work.

Now what? Shay questioned, eyeing the contents.

Lance also inspected the essence. *Wow, that's too cool! I just love hanging with Gorgeous Squared! No one else wants to try new stuff!*

Laughing, Shay replied, *Don't include me. I'm just here as a spectator. It's all her,* nodding towards me.

Rolling my eyes, *Let's put this in astral space and go from there.* I took the bottle from Shay. As I touched it, it tingled. *Ready?*

Both nodded. *As much as I like skipping through the pathways of your mind, lets head out. Uncle Al will be home soon.* Lance remarked, turning to leave.

We moved down the path, transitioning to astral space. Astral space. A transparent wavy landscape where solid objects didn't exist. Outlines delineate the essence of matter located on the solid plane. Since solid objects failed to exist, movement from point A to point B was fluid. You just- flowed. Shay and I teleported through the essence of trees. The most efficient way for us, as trees grew everywhere in the physical world and their essence flowed throughout astral plane. I believe the essence providing the basis for astral space originated from trees.

We returned to Uncle Al's. I left the jar in astral space, near his home. Re-entering our bodies, Uncle Al sat in his deep mahogany leather chair, waiting for us. He raised an eyebrow as we found ourselves. Shay and Lance jumped up as I sat forward.

"Whatcha doin'?" He questioned carefully, sipping a double shot of whiskey.

Lance and Shay both looked to me. I rolled my eyes. Cowards. "I developed a theory for a major healing spell. Lance and Shay helped me obtain an ingredient."

"Watcha doin'?" Al asked again, over the rim of his glass.

"We went into my mind and took a jar of essence from my pituitary gland and saved it in the astral plane." Al choked on his drink, leaning forward in his chair. Once he could breathe, he looked at me, sternly.

175

"How about a little more of an explanation? What is your spell? Exactly." Al sat back in his chair, then held up a hand, took a long drink of his glass, got up, refilled it, then sat back down. "Go ahead."

"Richard and Mary Clark, Leaders of the Orchard Coven, have a teenage daughter, dying from Diabetes Insipidus. Her condition is very dire. They tried many spells and narrowed down the components to make the spell work. I thought essence of Were animal might work as an alternative ingredient than what Richard tried. Lance and Shay came in with me to obtain essence." I shrugged my shoulders.

Al just looked at me for a few moments. "What was the alternate ingredient?"

"Female adolescent Were pituitary gland, at rest."

He took another long drink, then asked me, "What's your spell?"

That held promise. "It's actually a four tier spell. The first tier is a cleansing- internally as much as externally. The second tier would be healing: organs, blood. The third tier includes a poultice applied directly to her pituitary gland psionically. The fourth tier consists of a binding spell powered by a double crystal, the heart chi and the sun which keeps the healing spell in effect for - well, forever." I looked at Al. "Whadda think?"

He swirled the scotch around the ice in his glass, as he mulled over my plan. "Wow. Did you work the spells?" He asked as he met my eyes, clearly interested in my theory.

"Yep," nodding, I picked up my notebook. I thumbed through the pages until I found the correct one. Handing it to Al, "I worked off Richard's notes of variations of the spell they tried with growing success."

I stopped talking while Uncle Al read my spells, sipping his whiskey. Al looked askance at me. "Have you spoken with the Clarks about this?" I shook my head. "I didn't know if we could actually obtain essence, store it in the astral plane and transfer it psionically to someone else." Sighing softly, "I didn't want to get their hopes up. Do you think it will work?"

He was quiet for several moments. "You always have a unique out- look on devising other ways to perform a spell." He sipped his whiskey. "It might work. I'd add a circle of seven to perform the first, second and fourth spells. For the third spell, I think the fewer people mucking around in someone's mind, even psionically, is for the best."

I nodded. "Do you think I can approach Mary with my idea? Kayla isn't doing well. She might not have much longer."

"The newspaper said Richard, their son and the nurse are being charged with the kidnapping and murder of five Weres? Did you have something to do with that?" Al asked.

"The police are still figuring everything out, but, yeah." I answered evasively, pretty sure I couldn't share information on an active investigation.

Uncle Al looked at me for several moments. "I'll go with you to speak with her. Let her know our Coven is ready and willing to assist her especially at this time." He sipped his drink. As an afterthought, "Did she have anything to do with the murders?"

I shook my head. "Mary had no knowledge. She came up with the original idea of using essence and assumed they experimented with it."

"Okay. I'll call her and see if we can set something up, if she's inter- ested," Al stood up, "Are you two staying for dinner?" We both nodded. "I'll tell Irene."

I smiled. Having my uncle's approval, especially for something of this magnitude, meant a lot to me. Al tried to be a support for us, but our paternal grandfather, refused to allow much visitation growing up. He didn't approve of the magic world mixing with Weres. Our brothers, Shay and I, discovered our magical abilities on our own and taught each other, early on. What little visitation we had with Al, Lance or Tristan, we sucked up as much magical knowledge as possible. Once we learned to 'port, we came and went from our grandfather's to Al's frequently.

"Let me see your spell, Shy," Lance reached for my pad. I handed it to him. He sat down next to me and Shay sat on the other side of him, leaning in to read it. Nervously, I waited for their opinion. They read through it once, then re-read it.

Finally, I couldn't take it anymore. "So, what do you think? Any obvious issues?"

"Don't tell anyone I said this but it's fabulous! Incredible! It's so intricate," Lance gushed. "The tiers set the spell for maximum effect. I'm curious to see if the cleansing and the binding increase the potency of the actual spell."

Shay nodded. "As much as I hate to say it, this is incredible.

I'm in awe!" She even sounded awestruck.

Throwing up my hands, "Seriously, you guys are surprised?"

"Uh, you never think. You just, do. And it always works. Obviously, you spent a lot of time on this well thought out spell." Lance explained. I raised an eyebrow, shaking my head.

Irene stuck her head in the room. "Dinner is ready. Good to see you girls. Fried chicken, mashed taters and gravy, broccoli with hollandaise sauce and homemade sourdough bread."

My mouth instantly watered. "Yum. Sounds scrumptious!" I jumped up from the couch with Shay and Lance following. Irene served as Uncle Al's long time cook and housekeeper. She worked here for as long as I remembered. The older woman stood shoulder height to me with dark gray curly hair that she set in curlers each night. She wore thick glasses magnifying her blue eyes to match glacial waters. Irene always offered a hug and a cookie any time you needed either.

We entered the dining room and took our places at the table. Irene placed all the food, along with beverages. Al came in and sat at the head of the table. "We have a meeting with Mary at ten o'clock tomorrow morning to discuss your spell."

20

MARY OPENED THE door to Al, Lance, Shay and myself the next morning. "Good morning. Alberto, it's been a long time. Good to see you," extending her right hand to shake.

Uncle Al nodded, and took her hand. "I wish we met under better circumstances."

Tears welled up in Mary's eyes, as she nodded. "Well, I can't wait to hear Shyenne's plan. She provided more relief to Kayla than anyone." She held the door open and we filed in. "Everyone else is already here. Let's go into the dining room." Mary led the way through the great room where Shay and I spent yesterday with Kayla. It opened into a formal dining room with a large mahogany table. I recognized the Kanes' seated at the table.

Uncle Al stopped us as we entered the room. He stepped to the side and announced, "I am Alberto Mendoza, Coven leader, of the Nez Perce Coven. This is Lance Mendoza, Shaylenne de la Angelino and Shyenne de la Angelino, members of the Nez Perce Coven. May we be seated?"

Steve Kane stood and announced, "I am Stephen Kane, Coven leader, of the Orchards Coven. This is Mary Clark and my son, Nathaniel. Yes, you may be seated." Al took the head of the table opposite Steve. Lance sat to his right, with me on his left and Shay beside me. Nate sat at Steve's right and Mary to his left.

A lady took drink orders and then left the room. "I'm very glad to hear the Nez Perce Coven is practicing again. I met Shyenne already. I'm impressed with her skills and abilities."

Al nodded. "Thanks. This generation is coming of age, with significant skills and I decided they need the guidance of a coven as they venture out into the world."

"How many members are in the coven?"

"There are four more. Tristan, my son, and Shy and Shay's two brothers, Jadan and Bane, who are in the hierarchy of the Clearwater Pride." Al took a deep breath and sighed, "And my brother, Andrew."

Steve raised his eyebrows in surprise. "Drew! How is he since-," Steve ended mid sentence.

Al bobbed his head. "He's", he hesitated, "okay. Drew does his own thing. I hear from him sporadically. Your wife?"

"Sarah needs supervision. She has no impulse control or control of her magic," Steve sighed. The maid came in with our drinks. I thanked her. Once she exited, Steve asked, "Mary stated you created a spell to help Kayla?" Skepticism sank in his voice.

Turning to me, Al said, "Shy, explain your spell."

I nodded. "After reading through what Richard, Scott and Mindy tried, recorded and hypothesized, I came up with a multi-tiered spell. The initial spell focuses on cleansing of the aura, essence and soul."

Steve reached his right hand up to halt me. "I'm just going to cut to the chase. How are you going to address the Were body part ingredient of the spell?"

I glanced to Mary. "Mary gave me the idea of using Were essence. We obtained pure essence straight from the pituitary gland." I explained.

"And how did you do that? We want no part of harming another being." Steve forcefully stated, disbelief crossing his face.

"We went in psionically and gathered the essence."

Raising his eyebrows, he sat back in his chair. "Explain your process." We needed to cover more important things rather than this. But, oh well. "Shay, Lance and I astrally traveled into my being. Shay gathered some of my essence and we stored it in astral space, awaiting the spell. I provided the essence, voluntarily. I was not harmed in the process, nor suffered any adverse effects."

Head down, Mary stared into her coffee. At my statement, she raised her head, hope colored her pale features. She raised a shaking hand to her mouth, tears filling her eyes. Steve glanced at her. He coaxed me on. "Okay, start with the first tier."

"As I said, the first step focuses on cleansing of the aura, essence and soul. Next, we heal the secondary effects of her disease: the kidneys, lymph nodes, adrenal glands, heart. We create a poultice and apply it psionically to Kayla's pituitary gland. The last step is a binding, powered by a double crystal, charging from the heart chi and the sun, as a perpetual charm, continually feeding the spell." I described the process.

Quiet this whole time, Nate finally spoke, "I'm not familiar with psionics. Can you actually do that?"

Lance, Shay and I nodded as Al replied, "The Mendoza family has always been very strong with psionic magic. Lance is simply phenomenal, possibly better than myself. He will surpass me in time. Shyenne possesses the unique ability to just," he paused, "DO what she wants. Shaylenne is equal to Shy in ability but she completely picks magic apart, understanding every aspect. The three of them went in and "procured" the essence before I realized what the hell they were doing."

"That's how you teleport, isn't it? You travel astrally." Steve questioned.

All of us nodded. "I think we need a circle of three psionically, then a circle of four to ground them," Al stated.

Steve, Mary and Nate digested this. "I'd go one step further, recom- mending a circle of six outside the four, boosting them, then the three. That kind of directed power may work wonders," Nate offered. After mulling it over, everyone agreed.

"That's seven. Can we find six more?" Mary asked.

"You're not in this alone, Mary. The coven is here for you," Stephen reinforced.

"We can probably get Jadan and Bane. Maybe Tristan, if we can find him," Al offered.

Steve and Mary shared a look. "Sarah, Ana, and Kiki."

"Ana White?" I questioned.

Steve nodded. I shook my head. "She's incarcerated. During Chaz's interrogation, she attempted a magical attack on myself, and two others."

Mary inhaled sharply and Steve had been caught off guard. "I wasn't aware of that!"

"Finn might be willing to help," I suggested.

Al looked questioningly at me. "Who is Finn?"

"He's a level three witch who works for the Nez Perce

County Sheriff's Department," I explained. "He asked for the opportunity to work magic with me." I hesitated a moment, "Sarah? Is she… capable?" I asked, gently.

Nate nodded and Steve answered. "I direct her and Nate channels and grounds her magic." Steve ran a hand through his muddy brown hair. "She is a level four with no ability to control the amount of magic she wields." Nodding towards his son, "Nate intertwines her magic with his, and controls both. We could put Sarah in the second circle with Nate in the third, in control. I can be with Sarah, setting her focus."

"What ingredients will the poultice be made from?" Mary asked, trying to control the hope invading her face and voice.

"Using the ingredients Richard et al worked with, I intend to use a mash of dandelions, garlic, Madagascar periwinkle, eucalyptus, and wild carrots. I want to add psyllium, forming a gelatinous substance. Once in astral space, I'll add the essence with the mixture to form the poultice."

"I developed a very good cleansing spell utilizing green tea," Mary stated as more hope crept into her voice. "Shy, your healings provided more relief than anything else we've tried. Especially, whatever you did yesterday. She experienced so much pain, until you healed her."

Al stated, "Actually, Bane's healing spells prove more potent than even Shy's. Healing seems to be his bailiwick."

"Where should we do it?" Steve asked.

"We are all either earth or water primary and secondary," I answered. "Your coven is a mixture of everything, I noticed."

Steve smiled. "We don't discriminate against anyone. The Kanes' are Wiccan, Mary, air, Kiki, druid."

"Finn is Wiccan."

"Sounds like to optimize the magic, we should perform the ritual outside, near water?" Steve questioned. I thought about our house, but wasn't sure if I wanted to share it yet.

"I offer my house. It's on the Selway River. Isolated." Al offered. "In fact, everyone's welcome to stay there a couple days to ready the spells, accentuate powers, rest up, recuperate."

Sighing softly, "It sounds perfect. I don't mean to be pushy, but time is of the essence. Kayla is fading quickly." Mary ended on a whisper.

Al nodded. "I'll clear my schedule. Lance, track down Tristan. Shay, talk with Jadan and Bane. Shy, gather all the spell components and anything else you think you might need." Hesitating briefly, "Steve, I have a cook and housekeeper, but don't have others to be "support personnel."Are there members of your coven or coven family we can rely on?"

Steve thought for a moment. "My youngest son, Zeke, and I'm sure we can round up a few more."

"I'll bring my cook and housekeeper as well. They're part of our family." Mary stated.

"Dylan and Ryan Delrikkio would love the opportunity to participate and observe," I suggested.

Steve and Al both said in unison, "Yes!"

"It would be a tremendous relief to know Ryan was dealing with all the mundane and distractions while we focus on the ritual,"Mary said, excitement now creeping into edges of hope.

Smiling at Mary, "I'll talk with them and Finn."

"Can we be ready in two days?" Al asked. Everyone looked around the table and no one offered a negative.

Tears flowed down Mary's cheeks. "Thank you. Thank you for doing this for my baby."

Of course, Dylan, Ryan and Finn were thrilled to be involved in the ritual. Ryan immediately called Steve and Al to thank them and see what all he could provide. I globe hopped all over earth, literally, obtaining the freshest, best ingredients possible. I 'ported to Madagascar for the periwinkle, China for the green tea and ginseng, Australia for the eucalyptus. The rest I found closer to home. I ran to the top of the Selway Crags, the headwaters of the Selway River for the mountain water. Silt from the confluence of the Salmon, Snake and Clearwater Rivers.

Frustrated, Shay called me while I harvested cats claw in Peru. "Jadan is being an ass. Can you talk to him? We're home."

Sighing, I 'ported to the lodge. Landing at the porch, I pushed open the front door. Voices drifted from the back. I found Bane and Jadan sitting in old wooden chairs facing the wild forest beyond the rock canyon walls. Shay looked exasperated.

"No fucking way! Why in the hell would we endanger our lives for someone we don't even know?" Groaning inwardly, I turned to face my brother, Jadan. He raised his right hand and pointed a finger at me. "You are not doing this, Shyenne. Neither is Shaylenne. Period."

I cocked an eyebrow. "When was the last time I actually took an order from you?" I pretended to think hard. "Long before I transformed from a kitten."

His chest puffed up, a growl, low in his throat. "Jadan. Quit. Let's hear 'em out." Bane interrupted Jadan's attempt at bullying.

Jadan tightened his jaw, but backed down. *Thank you.* I 'pathed to Bane. "Kayla possesses the most beautiful magic. Her aura is amazing. Just come meet her. After that, if you don't want to do it, we'll understand." I implored.

He rolled his eyes, "Fine." Sighing, "I'll meet her."

I smiled, pulling out my cell phone and found Mary's number. After a few moments, she answered. She was thrilled our brothers wanted to meet Kayla.

We 'ported to Mary's porch. I knocked on the door. Mary opened it with a smile. "Come in, come in," she stated holding the door. "I'm honored to meet you! Can I get you anything?" She ushered us into the great room.

"No, ma'am." Holding out his right hand, "I'm Jadan de la Angelino and my brother, Bane."

"Ma'am," Bane said, inclining his head, shaking her hand.

"My brothers wanted to meet Kayla prior to the ritual," I explained, glancing up the stairs. "Is she in her room?"

Nodding, Mary said, "I'll take you up. I told her you were coming." She led us upstairs and knocked on Kayla's door.

"Come in," she called out. Kayla sat on her love seat, reading. Wearing snoopy pajamas, she stood as we entered.

"Kayla, these are my brothers, Jadan and Bane de la Angelino." I introduced her as my brothers stopped in their tracks. I always suspected Jadan had the ability to see magic and auras. His response proved my theory. My grandfather held a prejudice against magic, Jadan was right to not disclose his.

Bane recovered first. "Kayla, it's a pleasure to meet you. Your aura, it's unlike anything I ever saw. And your magic!"

Jadan blinked a couple times, recovering his manners. "Jadan de la Angelino. We're honored to assist in the ritual for your health."

I smiled and returned to gathering spell components. Shay could deal with them, now.

21

AFTER I FINISHED gathering all the spell components, I went to my uncle's home on the Selway River, a fork emptying into the Clearwater. "Shy. Perfect. Mary and Kayla arrived about an hour ago and are getting set up in their rooms. The Kanes arrived as well. The boys jumped in the pool. Stephen and Sarah are practicing control exercises. The Delrikkios left Lewiston about an hour ago." Al stated as he drank from a glass of ice tea. "How about you?"

"I obtained all the components," I said patting a backpack. "Should we use the area in the garden?"

Nodding, "Your brothers and Tristan should be here soon. If you want to start readying the site, that would be great."

"Okay. I'll grab a glass of ice tea and take a look see." After pouring a glass, I exited through the study.

Zeke and Nate played around in the pool. Zeke spotted me, waved his arm, "Shyenne! Hi! You got here!"

I smiled at his excitement. "Enjoying the pool?"

Nate and Zeke swam to the edge of the pool. Zeke was the mirror image of Nate at that age. "Whatcha up to? Are you coming in?" Nate asked, hanging on the side.

Shaking my head, "No. I'm gonna check out the altar site and make sure it's ready to go."

"Hey! Wait for me, I wanna see!" Zeke said, jumping out of the pool with the agility of a boy. Nate climbed out, too.

"Me too," Nate grabbed a towel off the table and threw one to Zeke.

Both wore cutoff shorts.

"Okay. Follow me. We built a spot in the garden we typically use," I explained as we wove our way through the garden, gathering wild roses, daffodils, and pine needles.

I passed through a narrow opening among the blue spruce trees standing as sentinels. Steps dropped down towards the river. A cedar altar stood in the center, with a dirt ring around it. Long before the white man inhabited the western states, the cedar grew in the ground. I found it on a trek somewhere deep in the Selway Wilderness. The majestic tree had fallen from its long standing perch high on the mountain overlooking the headwaters of the Selway River which flowed into the Clearwater River. I felt the ages, the wildness, animals, climate changes and the few humans passed by. More of my kind, Weres, traversed by than humans, I'm sure, due to the remote location. I convinced Bane, Shay, Jadan, Lance and Tristan into helping me 'port the tree home. It was so heavy it took all of us. Al had been angry when we appeared in the backyard with a humongous tree. But we worked together building the altar. Even Jadan helped. I thought the altar held more magic because of the blood, sweat, tears, and the insane laughter we put in to building it. Tristan and Lance, always hilariously fun, constantly relieved the tension between Jadan and me. The altar was a symbol of the unity and strength of the Nez Perce Coven, our family.

"Wow. OH MY GOD. That is the most amazing altar, EVER!" Zeke ran up to it, halting abruptly a few feet before it. He reached towards it, but stopped short of touching the wood. He looked back at me, asking permission with his eyes.

I laughed, nodding, "Feel free to touch it. My sister, brothers, cousins and I built it, as a magic project." I sprinkled the flowers, walking to the altar.

Nate approached it, as well. He ran his hands along the surface, mov- ing to face me. "It's incredible. Just the magic emanating from it." With awe in his voice, "How did you," hesitating, "do this?"

"We set the altar into the earth. Since we're all earth, either primary or secondary, we bound it, then set a boost spell from the earth to cycle through the cedar and back into the earth. We detoured part of the river to run under it, bringing the raw power of the river to the altar. It's a perpetual boost spell for any magic we work here."

Nate and Zeke looked awestruck. Zeke touched the table with a pointer finger, "Wow! You just thought that up?" Zeke asked surprised.

I bobbed my head, "Yeah, that's kinda what I do." Looking around the ceremony site, I picked up leaves, sticks, debris from the trees and river. Walking over to the river's edge, I cleared the small channel we created to wind through the site. Sticks, leaves, garbage always wash downstream and collect along the bank. I walked out across the rocks, moving them increas- ing water flow through the site. The Kane boys cleaned up along the circle and rock wall.

Lance came through the blue spruces leading Ryan, Dylan, Shay, Finn, Steve, Sarah and a woman I didn't know, with Tristan bringing up the rear. "And here, ladies and gents, is the Nez Perce Coven ceremonial site," Lance swung his arm out as he spoke in his tour guide guise. "This here is the cedar altar carefully con- structed by the angels of the cold mountain over many months of labor and love. As you step through the circle, you may feel a tingle." Smiling and ducking his head, shyly, "It's me. Okay, not all me. We built a channel from the river which flows under the circle, continually feeding raw energy up through the earth. The altar too, is grounded and is part of a perpetual boost spell for any magic conducted on it." He moved to the edge of the circle, away from the river.

Angels of the cold mountain were what we called ourselves. de la Angelino, of the angels and Mendoza, cold mountain. Kid stuff. Everyone fanned out, once in the circle. Sarah walked boldly up to the altar. Ryan and Finn cautiously followed be- hind her. She placed both hands on the altar, grounding her feet. She felt magic course through the altar, and her, back to the earth.

She giggled, gazing at me, "Very well done, Shyenne."

The others walked up and touched the altar. Those capable of earth and water magic felt the power rush through the altar. Those who didn't perform earth or water magic just felt a tingle.

"And of course, for those who haven't met Shyenne yet, this is our coven catalyst. She dreams up great ideas and we all fig- ure out how to make them work," Lance introduced me to his tour group.

Smiling from my perch on the rocks, in the river, "I know ev- eryone, except you." I skipped across and back to the circle. "Shy- enne de la Angelino, member of the Nez Perce Coven," sticking out my hand.

"Kiki Monroe, member of the Orchards Coven," smiling

she accepted my hand. Her short black hair framed her face. Deep brown eyes contrasted with the bright red lipstick she wore on her pale face. As we shook hands, I felt, something. I didn't think I liked her. Usually not one for snap judgments, I filed this away.

"This is a fabulous ceremony site you constructed. Highly impressive," Steve commented, keeping an eye on Sarah. She seemed to enjoy the circle, wandering around, feeling the different magics in the different spots.

"This is my spot," Sarah announced. She stood at the altar, facing the entrance, river to her left side. Finn, Steve, Kiki and Nate began "feeling" for their spots. Kiki immediately stood next to the entrance to the left. Steve stood to the left of Sarah. Nate stood behind his parents, between them.

Tristan headed towards me. Meeting in the middle, we hugged each other. It had been a while since I saw him. "Hey, 'cuz. Long time no see! I hear you took on mass murdering coven leaders! Been busy?" Glad I grew up with Tristan, I was immune to his heart stopping smile. Uncle Al's son, Tristan always felt he couldn't live up to expectations. The only expectations, Tristan placed on himself, and always too much.

I rolled my eyes, "Anything's better than my grandpa's," I replied, kissing his cheek.

Jadan, of course, chose that time to enter the circle. He shot me a nasty look, then ignored me. Bane, Mary, Kayla, and Uncle Al entered the altar site.

"Everyone is finding their spots. As Lance explained, there is a perpetual magic boost coursing up from the earth, through the altar, then back down. Earth and water magic." I moved out of Tristan's arms and moved to the altar. I located my spot on the corner, where the stream also flowed into the altar. "A stream runs under the circle, constantly feeding in new energy. Depending on your magic style there may be spots better suited for you. You should feel when you find it." I placed both hands on the altar and grounded my bare feet into the dirt, feeling the current of the creek flow under the circle, touching the altar.

Shay came and stood at the corner opposite me, where the stream gurgled above ground, then disappeared. Bane stood behind us, between us. Jadan stood behind Bane. Al took the corner opposite me and Lance took the corner opposite Shay. Tristan stood behind and between Lance and Al. Mary found her spot between Lance and me at the altar. Finn stood behind her, back towards the entrance. I noticed Zeke stood behind his brother and parents. He looked to me. I winked and he broke into a huge smile. He found his spot. I laid a crystal amethyst charm on the ground, adjacent to the altar.

Kayla stood between her mother and me at the altar. She placed her hands flat on top and slipped off her shoes, sinking bare feet into the dirt. Her magic met, mix and mingled within the perpetual spell we set within the altar. We were accustomed to the feel of the altar with our magic. Never before had someone outside of us mixed magic. It was liquid. Where the spell resided, colors swirled. The colors grabbed the spell and soaked in, intensifying the power. I let it course through my hands, up into my arms. It slid through my body. Melting into my thighs, slipping down my legs, into my feet, back into the altar and into the stream, intensifying the circle. I let the magic fill me and fed it back into the the altar and the stream. I felt as Shay's magic, Al and Lance added theirs. Sarah's magic jumped in like a wild stallion set free on an open range. Nate grabbed hold of her easing into the meld. It flowed freely, yet controlled. Steve and Mary added theirs, Steve flowing with Sarah, beside her, within her. The magic flowed further, into Bane, Finn and Tristan. As theirs melded into the magic stream, the power extended to Jadan and Kiki. I embraced Jadan's familiar magic as it blended in. Kiki. She had magic. A strong force. But not elemental. Or Wiccan. It was something … else. Her magic ebbed into the flow and began to melt within the colors of Kayla, and Mary's, Sarah's and Steve's. I felt Zeke's eager magic inch in under his brother. Nate allowed it, letting it flow to his mother and just hang on to hers. The two covens intertwined together, until all assimilated into one. As each person filled, Kayla began to slowly withdraw her magic. Mary, Sarah and Steve followed suit, until we returned to the circle, feeling the physical world, once again.

Kayla was the first to find words. "Whew! That was wonderful! I haven't felt this good in years! Thank you!"

"You did it. You bound the two covens." Bane's deep baritone, deeper than I ever heard it. I looked at him. He seemed different. I switched to his aura. He took on some of hers. Huh. I gazed at Kayla. Her aura had changed, taking on Bane's sparkles. That was… interesting.

"Well, that's a very good sign. Our magics blend well together," taking a deep breath, Al stated, "Let's eat dinner and call it a night. Tomorrow is a big day."

The next morning, preparations for the spell started with cleansing Kayla. Her mother, Sarah and Kiki bathed her in infused bathwater, while performing a cleansing spell, then a tea.

Uncle Al, Jadan, Bane, Lance, Tristan, Shay and I did our morning salutation. I couldn't remember the last time we performed the ritual. Together. I felt the power boost as we all conected to the earth, then made it rain. "Today, Mother and Father, allow us the magic and strength to heal one of your children." Uncle Al added to our salutation.

Once we finished, I checked on Kayla. Completed with the cleansing, Mary and Kiki dressed her in navy blue silk kimono robe. I checked her aura, pure as always. I ducked into the astral plane. The impurities from her disease, at least momentarily, removed from her body.

Next, we moved outside through the garden, to the ceremonial circle. Everyone took their spots within the circle. Jadan closed the circle behind us. Bane approached Kayla, gently picked her up and placed her on the altar, lying her down. He placed her head at Lance and Al's end. He moved her arms and legs until positioned correctly, the altar just long enough for her.

Bane placed both his hands on either side of her head. She closed her eyes, as did he. I observed astrally how he healed her. She met him on the astral plane. They stood together. He placed both hands on her head as he did on the physical plane. I stood next to them and moved into Bane. Easier on me, it took less from me to meld with him. Through Bane's eyes, I saw him enter her mind. He touched spots here and there but there wasn't much to heal. Moving through her body, Bane reached her heavily diseased kidneys. With the surgical skills of a witch, Bane healed the ill areas. Entering the blood stream, he fixed the chemical make-up, balancing water and carbon dioxide as they should be. He healed hormones and lymph nodes throughout her body. Once he reached her brain, he focused on the hypothalamus and pituitary gland. He fixed them as best he could. I backed out of his mind as he slowly backed out of hers. On the astral plane, the three of us landed about the same time. As I left the astral plane for the physical plane, I thought I saw Bane press his lips to her forehead. Moments behind me, we re-entered the physical plane and the circle. Kayla opened her eyes with a deep, shaky breath.

"No time like the present. Kayla, feed into the altar," I directed. As Kayla opened her magic to the altar, Sarah immediately jumped in, rampaging mustang, again. Nate caught her and reined her in as the rest of us joined and melded.

Once the magic blended into one, Al, Lance and I entered the astral plane. I brought with me the poultice I created. I went to the spot where I stored my "essence". Picking it up, we entered Kayla's mind. As we moved by her magic area, Al and Lance were awed.

I've never seen anything like it! What? How? Astonished, Al, at a loss for words.

Shrugging my shoulders, *All I know is she is very special. It's this way,* waving my arm down the path. Both followed me. We reached the hypothalamus. I saw Bane's work, but also where the illness started to seep in. I gingerly mixed my essence into the poultice. I rubbed the poultice on the hypothalamus a few times, then moved on. Lance and Al exchanged looks but followed me. We reached the pituitary gland. Here, I rubbed it down with the poultice, then gently pushed it into the "heart" of the gland. *Now.*

Lance and Al began chanting, and I joined them, circling our magic.

We mixed our magic and I fed it into the gland through the poultice. I felt Sarah first, of course, along with Steve, Mary and Shay join us, bring- ing in the circle magic from the physical plane. Our third circle, Bane, Jadan, Tristan, Nate and Finn joined in, their magic harmonizing with us. One was missing. Kiki. There wasn't enough strength! I felt the magic flow into Kayla. The poultice spread, sealing in the healing powers. But the illness raged back. The two covens together, needed just a little more. "Zeke". I whispered.

Immediately, his eager magic jumped into the stream, turning it into a wave. He joyfully grabbed on to his mother and she amplified his wave into a tsunami. Our magic poured from the physical world, into the as- tral world, into the poultice, into Kayla. The magic overwhelmed the disease, transforming the damaged into healthy, replacing chemicals, neu- rotransmitters, fixing the blood, fixing the messages sent from the brain throughout her body. Making Kayla whole again. I don't know

191

how long we continued chanting. One by one, we dropped out of the stream, back to reality. The last ones to leave, Zeke and I let Sarah run free 'til she could run no more. Like a mustang kept in a stall way to long we contained her to the stream, but let her go. Zeke kept pace with her for a little while, then slowed. She kept pace with him and fed him some of her magic. Again, they raced along the waves.

I sank down onto the dirt, utterly exhausted. I don't know how long I laid there 'til I opened my eyes. The crystal and amethyst charm I set there last night. I picked it up, as startled, angry voices argued. It took a moment to comprehend the words.

"Where the fuck did she go? Why didn't she join in? What the fuck was she doing?" Jadan yelled. He stood over top of me. Weakly, I struggled to sit up. I tried turning my head, but became incredibly dizzy and fell back to the ground. I felt someone grab me and pull me back against the rock wall with the altar between us and the entrance. Shay lay next to me. She looked more functional than me. Tristan held us. Jadan jumped back, guarding us three. Bane lay prone next to the river, one arm and leg in.

"I don't know what the fuck is going on!" Finn shook his head, holding it with his hands.

"Alright. Calm down. Everyone is a little out of it," Ryan assumed control. "Let's keep everyone safe, until they come around. The Orchards Coven may know something."

"What the fuck happened?!" Jadan's voice was shaky and pissed.

"I don't know. She grabbed something off the ground by the altar and took off after you all joined," Ryan explained. "When she left, the protection spell dropped. We didn't know what to do. Luckily, Zeke cast the spell before he joined the circle."

I vaguely remembered the circle coming down, then going back up. Beside me, Shay kneeled, then stood. On shaky feet, she walked to Jadan, leaning on him. He put his arm around her, as she laid her head on his shoulder. "What's going on?"

"Kiki grabbed something from under the altar and broke the circle as everyone else joined in. She left! She fucking left!" Jadan exclaimed in angry surprise.

"Holy shit. Is everyone alright?" Steve asked. I raised my head up from Tristan's chest. Steve stood, holding on to the altar.

"Yeah, I think so. I checked everyone and they appear exhausted. Everyone is awake, just not fully conscious yet."Ryan answered as he stood near the entrance. Dylan sat on a step opposite him. Finn made it to his knees. I couldn't see anyone else.

"Kanes?" I whispered into Tristan's chest.

"Shy wants to know if the Kanes are okay," Tristan voiced for me since I couldn't.

Steve nodded. "We're fine. Everyone's coming 'round slowly." Still unsteady on his feet, Steve braced himself on the altar. "Kayla? Kayla, honey?"

I saw Kayla try to raise her left hand but it barely left the table. Like the rest of us, she was out. I don't know how much time passed, but eventually, I sat up. Lance and Al also became cognizant, as did Nate.

Bane, Mary, Sarah, Zeke and Kayla remained incoherent.

Shay checked on them and diagnosed them as okay. "Can Irene bring some tea? It's in the kitchen above the coffee maker, on the second shelf. It'll help a lot." A special proprietary blend, the tea would speed recovery.

"Yes. Can someone put the circle back up if we take it down?" Ryan asked. "My cell is on the other side."

Shay, Tristan and Jadan all said, "I can."

Nodding, Ryan stepped through the circle, grabbed his phone and called the house. "We need the tea on the second shelf to the right as soon as possible in the circle."

The next thing I remember, someone placed a cup of hot tea under my nose. The fumes tickled my nose and invigorated me. I took another deep sniff and drank about half of it. Lance curled up beside me, inhaling the fumes from his tea. Al sat between Bane and me. Looked like someone tried to move Bane a little closer to us, to little avail. Both of them held steaming mugs. Al drank while Bane remained in the sniffing phase. Steve and Nate stood and drank while Sarah and Zeke inhaled, Sarah's arms wrapped around Zeke. Mary sat up drinking, while Kayla laid on her side, breathing in the tea, still on the altar. Shay, Tristan and Jadan finished theirs, standing guard over the rest of us. Finn finished his as well and spoke in undertones with Ryan and Dylan, when his cell rang.

"Hey. What's up?" Finn's face lost all color and he glanced up at Mary. "You have got to be kidding me." His voice lost all emotion. He looked to me, then Shay. "Okay. Let me call you back in a few minutes. I'll see what we can do." He sighed as he ended the call.

He waved Shay and I over to Ryan. Jadan helped me up and kept an arm around my waist, for support. As a rule, I never accept help from Jadan, but I was pretty sure I'd land on my face.

Finn looked at Jadan, then me. "Go ahead," I encouraged, breathless.

He sighed at my breathlessness, quietly. "Scott escaped. Richard is in the hospital, incredibly weak. They think he suffered a heart attack. Swanson wants you to check out the situation determine if magic was involved somehow."

"There's no fucking way. Shy can't even stand yet and she is com- pletely drained," Jadan ordered. "Kiki. She charged a crystal and took it to them." Shaking his head and sighing, he sized up Shay. "Shay and I will go."

Trying to hide my surprise, "I'll boost Shay all I can."

"I will, too," Bane said weakly. "I can't give much, but we're safe here."

"I'll go, too. I'm close to full," Tristan offered.

I thought for a moment, then nodded. "With Tristan full and Shay where she's at, they'll figure out what occurred. Jadan will keep them safe."

Finn looked relieved. "Thanks, I'm just too weak."

Ryan looked around the circle, at all of us. "Dylan can go with you and I'll stay here." The rest of us agreed. Shay and I grasped left hands. I kissed her hand as I transferred all I had. Jadan caught me as I fell to the ground.

The next time I woke, Lance held me, still within the circle. Bane lay curled next to us. Al stood quietly talking with Ryan, Steve and Finn. "Here, drink some of this," Lance held another cup of tea under my nose. I nodded, parched, breathing in the fumes, then gulped down several mouthfuls. Mary sat up, drinking her tea. Someone helped Kayla move off the altar and lay in Mary's lap. She sniffed as she sipped, gingerly. Zeke and Sarah sat up, drinking their tea. Nate stood between Mary and Sarah, protectively.

"How ya feelin'? Lance asked, as I emptied my cup. He handed me another.

Gratefully, I drew in a deep breath of steam before sipping more down, invigorating me. "What's happened since I went out?"

"Bane boosted Shay to about full and he went out. Shay, Jadan, Tristan and Dylan 'ported to the Sheriff's Department. We haven't heard anything yet. Everyone is awake. I boosted Al almost to full so he could..."Lance's thought trailed off.

I nodded, understanding. We needed at least one at full. "Sarah boosted Stephen and Nate both to almost full. She recovered very quickly considering how much magic she gave."

The sky turned from turquoise to midnight blue as stars popped out everywhere while I lay unconscious. It looked like I had been out for a couple hours. Irene entered the circle area carrying a teapot, with steam escaping. Steve took the circle down while Ryan took the teapot from her, then Al put the circle up again. Ryan walked around, filling everyone's cup. After I drank another cup, I felt strong enough to stand. I gingerly made my way to Mary and Kayla. Kayla sat up on her own and drank her tea. "How ya doing?" I asked softly taking her hand.

She gave me a big smile. "Actually, I feel wonderful! I don't think I've felt this good in years! I hope it works."

Nodding, I reached out and placed the charm necklace around her neck. The double crystal and amethyst charm would continue to boost the spell, with her heart chi and the sun constantly re-charging the charm. Meeting her eyes, "I hope it does as well. Time will tell."

I looked to Mary, her eyes filled with tears, happy tears. She quickly wiped them away and took a drink of her tea. I stood up, walking over to Al. I raised my eyebrows. He shook his head.

"We haven't heard anything yet. We don't want to say anything until they return. Until we know what to say."

We stayed in the circle, drinking the healing tea for a couple hours, waiting 'til everyone was at least half full. Shay, Dylan, Tristan and Jadan returned. I walked over to them as they entered the circle. Ryan, Finn, Steve and Al joined them.

Shay took a deep breath, "It looks like Kiki disguised herself as Oscar Grenell. She transferred two crystals to Richard. Richard transferred all his magic into one crystal and then gave both to Scott. The other crystal held a teleport spell. Scott teleported out of jail and is gone. The power transfer occurred too quickly with no safe guards for Richard. He suf- fered a heart attack. Not sure if he'll make it at this point. No sign of Kiki."

I digested the information. Who cast the teleport and power transfer spells into the crystals? Kiki powered the crystals from the altar. I looked to Mary. Did she do it? Kayla?

Steve walked over to Mary and Kayla. He passed on the news. Mary jumped up, crying. "I need to go to the hospital! We need to heal him!"

Bane and I looked at each other. As the only ones who possessed the abilities to heal this type of injury, it wasn't happening. Aside from the fact we were too diminished at this time, no way would we heal someone responsible for murdering Weres. "We can't." I said plainly. I sank back down on the ground, between Lance and Bane.

"I'll take you to the hospital to see him," Tristan offered. He looked to Kayla. "Do you want to go, as well?"

She shook her head. "I'm too weak. I'm staying in the circle."

"Could we get blankets? I'm sleeping in the circle tonight," I asked, laying weakly on the ground.

"While we're at it, let's take a count of who intends to sleep out here and we'll get bedding for all," Ryan stated.

About that time, Dylan's cell phone started playing *Jukebox Hero.* I smiled. "Yo, Bro!" Quiet for a moment, Dylan scanned us. "Would someone mind getting my brother?"

"I'll do it," Jadan volunteered. He walked over, taking Dylan's phone from his hand. "This is Jadan, Shy's brother. If you talk to me, I can prob- ably find you." He was silent for a moment as he made the connection. Jadan handed the phone back to Dylan, then disappeared.

What's up with Jadan being helpful? I 'pathed to Shay.

I haven't had a chance to ask him. Shay responded.

Jadan and Malachi re-appeared and Jadan put the circle up again. Malachi looked around the circle, taking inventory of everyone. When he saw me, he immediately walked over, sank to the ground, picked me up and placed me on his lap. He kissed me, transferring energy to me, bringing me up almost to half. He reached over and grasped hands with Bane, transferring energy to him, also bringing him up almost to half. "So what's happenin' here?"

Ryan filled him in up to date. "Huh. Y'all ever figure out what Rosie was up to?" Malachi asked as he enfolded me in his arms. We all looked at him blankly. "She's up to something. I

196

caught her eavesdropping at the office, twice. There's a reason why she can't get through Shy's protection system."

Irene brought out blankets for those of us sleeping in the circle.

After a few days rest, we returned to normal. Swanson et al headed over to 3-D Investigations to update us. Shay and I sat in the library, drinking tea, reading magic books. "How's Kayla?"

"So far, so good. It appears the ritual worked," I put my book down. "I talk to Kayla daily She says she feels wonderful."

Shay smiled, "Great! What about her dad?"

I raised my eyebrows. "Well, he's still in the hospital. Unresponsive. Scott and Richard didn't perform the transfer like they should have and it's still not clear if he'll survive. He's in a vegetative state."

Ryan stuck his head in the door. "Swanson's here. Let's meet in the conference room."

We grabbed our teas and followed him in. I noticed Rosie's empty desk. She disappeared the morning after Kayla's ritual. No clue where she went or what happened. Ryan and I searched her apartment. We found an orange jail jumpsuit. Scott had been there. And Rosie? She was just… gone.

Swanson, Finn and Karen sat in the conference room. Finn looked totally recovered after the ritual. It had taken a couple days to get everyone back up to par. Bane, Lance, Trystin, Shay and I slept in the circle, with Jadan, Dylan and Malachi staying with us, for several days. Shay and I took our seats around the table.

"Richard and Mindy copped to all the charges and gave a full confession. They admitted to all of the kidnappings and murders of the Weres. Their confessions match the notes kept by Richard, Mindy and Scott. The teenage boys are all being released on supervised probation until age eighteen." Swanson filled in.

"Who was the witch with the boys?" I questioned as I sipped my tea. Finn sighed as Swanson looked to him. "It was Rosie, according to

Mindy." Ryan looked like someone sucker punched him. He shook his head. Malachi was right. She had been up to something. Ryan looked over at me. I just raised an eyebrow.

Huh. There was a reason why she couldn't get through my spell.

"What about Scott?" I asked.

Again another sigh. "We pieced some of it together. Richard appears to be in a vegetative state. Kiki charged he crystal during your ritual. Finn studied the video tapes at the jail. He believes Rosie posed as Grenell to get inside. She passed the two crystals to Richard."

Finn took a sip of his coffee. "The charged crystals held more than enough power to override the prison magic blocks. Richard transferred his magic into the crystal and passed both off to Scott. The detention officers didn't realize what Richard was doing. Scott immediately teleported out. He didn't activate the power transfer in jail."

"What are your thoughts on who cast the spells in the crystals?" Finn directed towards me.

"Mary or Kayla." I said instantly, then thought a moment. "Hold on a sec." I pulled out my phone and called Nate. "Hey. Before the ritual, was Kiki one of the coven members to stay with your mom?"

Hesitantly, Nate replied, "Yeah."

I sighed and dropped my head. "Could she do a teleport spell?"

"It's not a typical spell within her repertoire. Why? What's going on?" Nate asked from the other end of the line.

"We're just wrapping up all the pieces. I'll talk to you soon," I ended the call, then looked around the table. "Nate said it wasn't a spell she typically used." My phone started vibrating. It was Nate.

"Ya know, if someone brought the spell to mom, it's possible she could do it," Nate stated.

"What about placing the spell into a crystal?" I questioned, hesitantly, chewing on my lip.

Sighing deeply, "Yeah. Mom excels at crystal magic. If it was a "good" spell, she could place it in a crystal, then it would only need to be activated. She could set it up to activate any way they wanted." Nate's voice quieted. "If she could control her magic, she'd be the Coven Leader."

"I saw her magic. She is incredible." I hesitated. "Can you tell me who stayed with her the few days prior to the ritual?"

"Aside from family? Kiki." Nate hesitated for a moment. "Mary visited with her, which seemed unusual. Her and mom weren't close."

"Alright. Thanks, Nate." Once again, I ended the call. Looking around the room, "Well, I'd place my money on Mary or Kiki taking the spell to Sarah and she placed the spells in the crystals. If someone got caught with the crystal, Sarah would look like the guilty party."

Everyone sat quietly for a moment. "So, the bottom line is that the scariest person, Scott, is loose in the world, along with Rosie and Kiki," Shaylenne laid out.

"And he's got his father's magic."

www.ingramcontent.com/pod-product-compliance
Lightning Source LLC
Chambersburg PA
CBHW020409150626
46554CB00012B/417